KISS AND TELL

Adam grasped Brandy's hand, pulled her off balance into his arms, and swooped down to claim her smiling mouth in a hard, possessive kiss.

His lips were hungry and searching; his tongue coaxed her mouth open. She swayed, stunned by the force of desire she felt in his arms.

Just as suddenly as it began, the kiss ended. Adam released Brandy and she stumbled back a step. Her fingers longed to touch her lips where they tingled with spirals of electric energy. But she knew too well how that gesture would look.

Instead, Brandy raised her hand and slapped him across the face. His head snapped back, his palm going to his flaming cheek.

"I told you I was not a loose woman, Sheriff. If you try something like that again, I'll...I'll...tell your wife."

Adam threw back his head and laughed. "Well, I'd have to get married before you could do that, and I don't plan on letting you stay around long enough to see that happen."

"We'll just see about that."

Other *Leisure* and *Love Spell* Books by Marti Jones:
TIME'S HEALING HEART

DREAM WEAVER

MARTI JONES

LEISURE BOOKS   **L**   **NEW YORK CITY**

To my family, all of them,
for their love and support.

A LEISURE BOOK®

August 1994

Published by

Dorchester Publishing Co., Inc.
276 Fifth Avenue
New York, NY 10001

Printed in the United States of America.

DREAM WEAVER

Prologue

Oklahoma Territory, 1885

Her dress should have been black.

The problem was Brandy Ashton didn't own a black garment. Her parents' tastes had run to the more flamboyant—orange, purple, yellow. Brandy's tastes followed suit.

At the moment, her skirt of faded but still brilliant lapis lazuli blue was swept up and tucked into her waistband. Because of the unrelenting Oklahoma sun, her flowing cranberry blouse bore half circles of perspiration around the neck and at her armpits. Her sandaled feet disappeared into a hole she'd laboriously bored into the brick-hard prairie ground.

The spade scratched out another inch of stubborn dirt, and Brandy lifted her shoulder in a shrug that swept the trails of sweat from her stinging eyes.

Too soon the droplets reappeared and ran like rivers of tears over her set features. Across from her, the painfully young face of her sister creased with another frown. For hours Dani had held off her grief by scrunching her nose into a tight wad. Brandy wished she'd just bawl and get it over with. It hurt to watch a child of only eight struggle for strength that way.

But Dani would not cry unless her older sister did, and right now Brandy's own suffering went too deep for mere tears.

With more determination than Brandy knew she possessed, she drove the spade into the ground again. Dani appeared at her side and silently offered her a ladle of water. After washing the dust from her throat, Brandy decided it was high time to banish the awful, engulfing silence.

"Pa told me where our next stop was to be. I'm sure I'll be able to find it with no problem." She glanced up at the midmorning sun, amazed it could be so warm in November. Indian summer. She was thankful for it, but knew it couldn't last much longer this late in the year.

"I know it seems early to settle for the winter, but this year I think we'd do well to. We've enough coin for it; there's no question of that. And this next town sounds like just the place to winter."

Dani continued to stare into the hole. She

looked her usual self, except for the fact that she held the hem of her dress in her hands like a security blanket.

Brandy resumed her digging.

Another hour passed. Blisters burned on the pads of her palms, and her nose stung from the sunburn she'd been unable to avoid.

Shick, swish, shick, swish. Methodically, she raked the earth aside. Her head emptied of all thoughts save one—making a cavity in the Oklahoma plain big enough for a man to lie in.

Oh, Pa, her mind cried, *what do I do now?*

Brandy had seen her twentieth birthday seven months earlier. She knew people far younger than herself made it on their own. But Wade Ashton had held their family together for as long as Brandy could remember. How would she ever be able to support herself and Dani without him?

She remembered the day her mother died. After weeks of a lingering illness, it had seemed almost anticlimactic when the time came. There'd been grief and heartache, but not this nearly paralyzing fear.

With a swell of sickening relief, Brandy realized the hole she'd been digging was deep enough. Her hands bled and her shoulders screamed in pain, but now that she'd finished, she wanted to delay the awful moment ahead. For the first time since she'd begun her chore, she looked over to the blanket-wrapped figure lying on the ground. The agonizing loss stole her breath as it surged through her once more.

Dani's eyes grew wide and weepy. The little girl knew the time had come. Silently, they walked to the still figure. Brandy set aside the spade and took the ends of the blanket nearest her. Dani took hold of the other end, and they dragged their burden over to the grave.

"I'm sorry, Dani," Brandy choked out, still struggling to force air past the tight fist of grief pressing her throat closed. Then she gripped the edge of the blanket and pushed, rolling the death-stiffened body of her father into the dry earth.

Dani gasped, a strangled sound that tore viciously at Brandy's already broken heart. Suddenly the tears and sobs that Brandy had thought beyond her began. Her body shook and quivered and she clutched her sister tightly, each drawing what strength and comfort she could from the other. They were all alone now, just the two of them. From this day on, Brandy would have to be mother, father, and sister. She'd never felt so inadequate in all her life.

Too soon the hole was covered, and Brandy couldn't even manage a vocal prayer through her grief. She saw Dani's lips move silently. It would have to be enough. She took her sister's shoulders and turned her toward the wagon.

As they drove away neither looked back. The old wagon creaked and groaned as their horse led them away from the last of their family. Brandy's thoughts were on the future now; the past was something she could do nothing about.

"We're gonna be fine, Dani," she swore, hoping her vehemence would lend truth to her words. "This next town ought to be just the kinda place we're looking for."

Dani's eyes never strayed from the wide open plain stretching endlessly before them. Brandy longed to take her sister's hand, but both hers were firmly gripping the reins. Instead, she nudged Dani's thin, bony shoulder with her own.

"It's called Charming, Dani. Charming, Oklahoma. Now, doesn't that sound like a splendid place to spend the winter?"

Chapter One

Brandy's gaze swept across the small group of people still gathered around the makeshift platform that extended from the back of her wagon. At first she'd been disappointed by the little town. It was a small, farming town with few businesses. However, after a week of peddling her tonic and home remedies for everything from ague to gout, she'd changed her impression.

The deep-sewn pockets on either side of her merchant's apron hung down from the weight of the coins she and Dani had taken in. She looked across to Dani, who was handing out the last of the remedies Brandy had sold that day. Yes, she had to admit there was indeed something charmed, if not charming, about this place. She and Dani had made out quite well.

Brandy straightened, feeling the strain on her tired back. Standing on her feet for hours every day had taken its toll.

The afternoon sun reflected off something across the street and Brandy's attention focused. Suddenly her eyes caught on a sharp glint of metal. A chill feathered across her skin, raising pebbles of awareness on the sun-warmed flesh. A badge. So, he'd returned.

The man lounged beneath a thick, weathered oak, his boots crossed at the ankles and his arms crisscrossed against his middle. He watched Brandy closely as she took his measure. After a long moment, he returned her scrutiny as if to say he could play that game, too.

Sweat pooled at the small of Brandy's back, and she fought the urge to dab her flushed face with the hem of her apron. He was just a man, she told herself. An ordinary man like any other.

She couldn't see the color of his eyes from this distance or the hair beneath his hat. There was no telling his actual height because he continued to lean negligently against the heavy trunk. But still, Brandy's heart thumped madly against her breastbone. For there was one thing she had no doubt of. This man was the sheriff she'd heard the townspeople discuss. He was well liked around town, and it was for sure he was not happy about her being here.

The tilt of his head and the angle of his features told Brandy that he continued to watch her. Was he trying to intimidate her? she wondered.

It wouldn't be the first time she'd had trouble with the law. For some reason, most lawmen saw it as their duty to keep an eye on peddlers. Brandy couldn't help thinking it ironic. After all, if folks didn't like what she was selling, she'd have no choice but to go elsewhere.

Still, she could spot a troublemaking sheriff a mile away, and this one fit the bill. His stance was arrogant, proud. No doubt, he was a man used to getting what he wanted. And what he wanted was her to know he'd be watching her.

The perspiration on her upper lip tingled. In another second, it would trickle into her mouth. She broke the spell that held her and pressed the back of her hand to her lips.

"Brandy?" Dani's small voice cut into Brandy's musing and snapped her attention back to the business at hand.

"What is it?"

"I said who is he?"

Brandy didn't pretend she didn't know whom Dani referred to. She and her sister were close enough to read each other's moods. One had only to fret a moment, and the other smelled it on the wind like a summer storm.

"The sheriff," Brandy said.

Dani must have heard the irritation and apprehension in her sister's voice, because she cut a look at the tall stranger, her eyes settling on his badge. "Do you think he'll give us trouble?" Without waiting for an answer she added, "Geez, I really hate when that happens."

"I don't know," Brandy admitted. "But somethin' tells me we won't have to wait too long to find out."

"That's the last of the customers."

Brandy looked around and saw the townspeople had started to meander away from the platform. She straightened the bottles on the shelves, and together she and Dani jumped down from the platform. Two ropes hung suspended through the roof of the wagon, and by pulling down on them, Brandy and Dani could lift the platform into place across the front of the shelves. Small wooden latches on either side secured it in place.

Her father had devised the makeshift stage/storage area long ago and it served them well. The orange-and-green converted carnival wagon had seen better days, but it, too, would get them through a few more years. After that, Brandy had no idea what they'd do.

Brandy boosted Dani onto the seat of the wagon and then pulled herself up and unwound the reins. She clucked to the old nag they'd traded for remedies several years ago, and she started the wagon moving down the dusty, rutted thoroughfare of the town.

Glancing across the street, she noticed the empty spot next to the tree. A quick scan told her the sheriff had disappeared without approaching her and Dani. Maybe she'd been wrong about him. Maybe he didn't intend to give them any trouble while they were in town.

She said as much to Dani and the thought pleased her sister. Brandy felt a tug at her heart when Dani smiled. One thing the Ashton sisters had inherited from their mother was a penchant for cheerfulness. Despite all their woes, they didn't stay down for long. Brandy had been thankful for it countless times the past few weeks.

How they would have gotten through their father's stroke and death, not to mention the uncertainty of their future, without it, Brandy had no idea.

Outside of town, Brandy turned off the road, and the wagon cut a swath through the thigh-high prairie grass to a massive oak. She pulled the wagon to a halt beneath the tree's far-reaching branches and struggled to set the ancient brake. She and Dani slid from the seats, even more tired and achy after sitting, and systematically went through the routine of unharnessing the old horse, feeding and watering her, and ground-tying her for the night.

A warm breeze caressed Brandy's cheeks, and she could see the faint outline of a full moon even though the sun had not yet disappeared completely from the open Oklahoma sky. It would be a beautiful night, and she couldn't wait until after dinner when Dani went to sleep and she could slip out to enjoy the peace and stillness.

For now though, she had several hours of work ahead of her. Unlike most of the other peddlers she'd come across in her life, Brandy kept detailed accounts of their business. Her mother had always done it, and it was only one of the many jobs Brandy had assumed when she'd died. So after a full day of selling, she still had to cook, clean up, and log the day's work into her ledger. With a weary sigh, she left the fresh air and fall beauty of the field for the dim, cramped interior of the carnival wagon.

Dani had already built a fire in the tiny stove located in one corner of the wagon. With only one eye on top of the stove for cooking, Brandy had made an art of coming up with one-pot dishes that she and Dani enjoyed.

A small larder built into the back wall held their food supplies and the spices and herbs Brandy kept on hand. Against the wall opposite the door, her father had fashioned a table with benchlike seats on either side. He'd also made the small bunks on which Dani and Brandy slept. All in all, it was a cozy, if somewhat congested, home.

While their dinner cooked in a heavy iron Dutch oven, Brandy began the entries in her ledger. Dani straightened the small wagon, sliced bread for dinner, and mended a rip in Brandy's stocking.

Brandy looked on with a winsome smile. Dani was by far the better seamstress of the two, and she never fussed or complained about the amount of work always at hand. Brandy felt a wave of sadness that her mother had not lived to see what a wonderful child Dani had turned out to be.

"What is that?" Brandy asked, seeing the sparkle of some object her sister had drawn from her pocket. Dani flushed and pressed her hands deeply into her pockets.

"N-nothing." Her eyes blinked several times, a sure sign she wasn't telling the whole truth, and Brandy felt a twinge of disappointment and fear ripple through her.

"Oh, Dani, what have you done?" She set aside her pencil and pushed the ledger to one corner of the table. "Come here," she said, sighing with frustration.

"It's n-nothing, really. I promise, Brandy." Dani's face brightened and she flashed an innocent smile. "I found it."

Brandy groaned and raked her fingers through her hair, pulling several strands loose from the ribbon at her nape. For a moment, she felt like crying or, better still, screaming at her sister. *Why, oh, why, did Dani have to do this now?*

"Dani, bring it to me."

Brandy wished she could pretend that she hadn't seen whatever trinket Dani now hid in her pocket. How many times had they played this scene? She'd grown tired of it, and her frustration brought her to the brink of anger.

"I said let me have it, right now!" Brandy's weariness made her tone sharper than she'd intended; her anxiety kept her from apologizing.

Dani's lips trembled at the harsh command, and her wide eyes filled with tears. Her stubborn Ashton chin jutted out, and Brandy saw another confrontation brewing. She longed to forestall the crisis, but it was already too late.

"You're not my ma, Brandy Ashton," Dani wailed. "You're mean and hateful and I don't have to mind what you say."

She threw herself across the lower bunk and cried louder and, Brandy suspected, longer than was truly necessary. There was nothing to do now but wait out her tantrum. In defeat, Brandy fled outside. Her temper would be better served if she didn't stay and listen to her sister's hysterics.

The night was cool, hinting at the approaching end to a mild, pleasant fall. Brandy slid the ribbon from her tousled hair and retied it high on her head to keep the thick mane away from her neck. Two buttons on her blouse surrendered to the call of the breeze, and she parted the fitted bodice to accept the gentle caress of wind on her skin.

She'd discarded her shoes and stockings after entering the wagon, and now her bare feet met the soft, thick grass. Brandy wiggled her toes, enjoying the sensation on her aching soles. How many people got to live their lives under the stars with sweet grass beneath their feet and warm breezes in their hair? No matter how hard life seemed at times, she had to remember the good things and be thankful.

God forbid she should have been a seamstress somewhere, straining her eyes beneath inadequate lighting, or a waitress waiting tables for rude men and snobbish women while she rushed in and out of an overheated kitchen. No, Brandy had a lot to be thankful for. Because of her gift, and her mother's before her, she was able to live in God's backyard. Her roof was the sky, her floor the grass, and her light the bright sun. She took several deep breaths of fragrant air.

Once more she told herself how lucky she'd been in her life. Then she turned back to the dilapidated carnival wagon, feeling better able to face the confrontation ahead.

Inside, Dani had wiped away her tears, and she was checking on the vegetable stew.

"I think it's done, Brandy," she said, no signs of her earlier tantrum remaining. "And it looks really good."

Brandy ruffled her sister's bangs and took the towel from her hands. She lifted the pot to the table, where Dani had laid out bowls, flatware, and two cups filled with lemonade. Brandy decided their discussion could wait until after dinner.

Dani obviously suspected her sister's plan and drew out the simple meal until Brandy could feel her eyelids growing heavy. When Brandy pushed her plate aside, she noticed Dani's shoulders tense. Silently, they cleared the table, then made short work of cleaning up.

Apparently resigned to the forthcoming lecture, Dani sat at the table and laid a shiny pearl hairpin out before her.

Brandy gave a long-suffering sigh as she stared down at the article. "Is this all?" she asked hesitantly. She dreaded asking this particular question. She felt disappointment, but no surprise, when Dani's hand slipped beneath the table to return with a man's tie tack in the shape of a butterfly.

"Very pretty," Brandy admitted ruefully. "Anything else?" She held her breath.

Dani's hand disappeared once more and came up with a wooden button carved in the shape of a flower. Brandy's face twisted in a quirky frown. Apparently there was no accounting for her sister's choices.

"Hell's bells, Dani, what am I gonna do with you?"

"Pa said you weren't to cuss, Brandy. It ain't ladylike."

"Oh, and I suppose stealing is? Don't lecture me about my language. I wouldn't be driven to cursing if you'd stop your collecting."

"I'm sorry."

Brandy raised one eyebrow and stared at her sister's falsely contrite expression. Sure, Brandy thought, wondering if Dani was only sorry about getting caught.

"I don't know what to say to you, Dani. I've said all the same things Pa told you when he caught you lifting, and it hasn't done a bit of good. We may not have much, but we're not thieves. We were raised to be honest." Brandy fingered the three random items and felt another headache coming on.

"Stealing's wrong, Dani. And what's more, you know what will happen if you get caught. And now, with Pa gone, you'd probably end up in some orphanage or with mean folks who want you to do their work while I sit cooling my heels in jail."

Brandy heard the old nag whinny and she looked across to the door of the wagon. Ever since her father's death, the nights had been the hardest. All the sounds that used to soothe her to sleep had become ominous.

Several minutes passed in silence, and finally she turned back to Dani. Her sister was fast asleep, her head resting on the table.

"Poor child," Brandy muttered, scooping Dani from the seat and placing her on her bunk. She considered removing her sister's dress and replacing it with a fresh nightgown, then decided not to disturb Dani. She tucked the light blanket around the girl's shoulders and kissed her forehead.

Brandy knew her mother wouldn't approve. She'd been adamant about the girls washing and changing every night before they went to bed. But Brandy couldn't help it. She wasn't her mother—a sad fact she'd come to terms with years ago. Her mother's energy and vibrancy had seemed almost electric to Brandy. But too soon it had been used up too quickly and burned out.

"Oh, Dani, why do you do it?" she softly whispered.

Her sister knew right from wrong. Their mother had always stressed the value of honesty, especially in their business. But more and more of late, Dani didn't seem to be able to control the urge to take things that didn't belong to her.

A sudden knock on the door startled Brandy, and she whipped around and gasped. Remembering she'd left her father's old shotgun beneath the seat of the wagon, she scanned the small room for a weapon. Darn, how could she have forgotten to bring the gun in with them? Desperate, she grabbed a skillet and eased slowly along the wall to the door. Her breathing seemed overly loud in the tiny area; her heartbeat suddenly pounded a rapid staccato.

Had the thing she'd feared most finally happened? Men had followed her to camp before, but her pa had always been able to send them on their way with a well-placed look and the old shotgun. What would she do if she couldn't handle the men by herself, with only a skillet for protection?

"Wh-who is it?" she croaked, her voice unsteady.

"Sheriff McCullough, ma'am. Open the door."

Brandy felt a second of relief; then her eyes lit on the trinkets still in plain sight on the table. "Oh, no," she mouthed.

"Just—just a minute, Sheriff." She stepped

lightly across the floor, snatched up the trinkets, and looked around for a hiding place. Nothing immediately presented itself.

Another impatient knock sounded, and she whirled around, flashing an angry look at the door. Dani stirred, and in a panic, Brandy stuffed the purloined goods into her own skirt pocket.

"Coming, Sheriff," she called softly.

With her free hand, Brandy unlatched the door and drew it back, meeting the sheriff of Charming, Oklahoma, with a bright smile on her face and her biggest skillet still gripped in her fist.

Chapter Two

Startled by the sight of the peddler hoisting a heavy iron skillet, Adam McCullough took a step backward. Pictures of his head, in the shape of a pancake and imprinted with the words Weston Ironworks, flashed through his mind. The little spitfire was actually wielding the thing at him.

Her slender arm didn't look capable of actually doing him bodily harm with the pan, but he wasn't taking any unnecessary chances. He took another step back and glared up at her.

"Can I assume I took you away from cooking?" he asked dryly.

To her credit she flushed bright scarlet, but she still didn't lower the skillet.

"What can I do for you, Sheriff?"

Adam's ire budded. "If you have a minute, I'd like to have a word with you." He paused, then added, "Without the skillet."

"Social or business, might I ask?"

All right, Adam thought, if she wanted to play games, he would just let her know right off he meant business. The badge on his shirt was no child's toy, as she could well see, and he didn't mind using its presence to express his authority. What the hell did she think he planned to do to her anyway?

Then he remembered the way his gaze had raked her figure in town earlier, and a hint of understanding lit in his eyes. She was a real beauty. No doubt she often had to deal with overzealous customers. For a brief moment, he wondered if she did any extra business on the side. Seeing her up close, he had to admit the thought of bedding her intrigued him. But her less-than-warm welcome and the skillet would seem to discount that idea.

He reminded himself why he'd come. He had nothing against peddlers as a rule; some of them sold things folks out this far couldn't get easily. But medicine peddlers were different. And he especially loathed their kind. They preyed on folks' pain and suffering, and he knew firsthand the damage their dishonesty and false hope could do to people weakened by illness.

Since he could do very little else, he usually handled them all the same way. He'd let them make their pitch and earn a few pennies; then politely, but firmly, he would escort them from town as soon as possible.

"Business," he replied, noticing her slim arm begin to tremble under the weight of the skillet.

She stepped down from the wagon, closed the door behind her, and laid the skillet aside. He caught a glimpse of bare toes and trim ankles and again remembered the way he'd scrutinized her in town.

Her voice, even raised in timbre as it had been when she'd hawked her wares, had put him in mind of warm velvet. Waves of blue-black hair, which rained down over her shoulders like a waterfall, made a man's hands ache to tangle in it. Slowly, his gaze slid down her body. Since she was without the heavy muslin merchant's apron she'd worn in town, he could plainly see her other assets beneath the unconventional clothing she wore. Awareness flared, warming him.

"I may as well save you the trouble and tell you I've heard it all before," she said wearily.

Her voice was less seductive now, Adam noticed. It definitely held a note of anger and resentment. He felt unjust somehow, and the feeling doused his attraction to her and made him defensive.

"Is that right? Such as?" he asked, quirking one pale brown eyebrow.

She brushed the long strands of hair over her shoulders and sighed. He thought she sounded impatient and wondered how she'd turned the tables on him so quickly. He was supposed to be the one performing the tedious task of questioning an undesirable character.

Once more he studied her profile against the full moonlight and quickly rephrased his thoughts. This pretty piece was anything but undesirable.

"I shouldn't plan on staying too long," she said in answer to his question, "and you'll be watching me. If I should step so much as a hair's width outside the law, I'll find my cute little behind behind the bars of your jail. And if you should learn I'm doing any business other than peddling legitimate goods, you'll run me out of town in the blink of an eye. Does that about cover everything?"

Adam did a slow burn. How dare this haughty duffer patronize him and his position? Never mind that she'd hit on his pat phrases and thrown words back at him he hadn't even had a chance to say yet.

"That just about covers it, sister," he said, stepping menacingly toward her. To his surprise, she held her ground, meeting his narrowed eyes with a strength and determination he found intriguing despite his irritation.

"I'm not your sister, Sheriff—"

"McCullough," he supplied.

"And I haven't done anything even remotely out of line," she continued without pause. "So I'll thank you to leave me alone and let me go about my business. I'm merely trying to make a living, and the last I heard, that was not against the law."

Enough of this, Adam thought. There was no way he'd allow her to get the best of him, no matter how comely she looked. He, too, was only doing his job. The people of Charming trusted him to keep out anyone he felt was a threat to the law and order of the town. He'd taken that responsibility very seriously since his election two years earlier.

And this woman—with her innocent-looking face, lithesome body, and seemingly fragile demeanor—had the potential of conning a lot of good folks out of their hard-earned money.

"Maybe not," he admitted. "But trespassing is."

He saw her eyes widen, and a twinge of doubt flashed across their velvet-brown depths.

"Trespassing?" she asked, throwing back her shoulders in a gesture he suspected she used to give the impression of strength.

"Yeah, trespassing. This land you're parked on happens to belong to someone—as does all the land from here to town and for miles in every direction."

"I see," she said, her shoulders drooping slightly. "How many miles?"

"Many." His statement wasn't completely true, but he offered no more information.

She seemed to be deep in thought for a minute. Finally, she looked up and he saw a weariness around her eyes he hadn't noticed before. It made her look smaller, more fragile, and he suddenly felt unreasonably boorish for causing her distress.

"I don't suppose I'd be able to request permission from this person to use the land, would I, Sheriff?"

Adam resisted the urge to put her mind at ease. "It wouldn't do any good," he told her. "I'm afraid you'll have to move on in the morning."

"I see."

For a moment, he considered telling her she could stick around for a few more days at least, but he held back. Beautiful or not, he refused to let her stay and milk the trusting townspeople of their money with her hokey remedies and snake oil.

"If that's all, Sheriff. . . ."

Adam knew a dismissal when he heard one, and he touched the brim of his hat. "Yes, well," he muttered, backing away. "G'night, ma'am."

As the sheriff rode away, Brandy stood beside the wagon, her toes curled in the grass and her hands rubbing her chilled elbows. The sheriff's distrust and obvious prejudice against her and Dani brought back painful memories of past experiences she'd thought long forgotten.

Why did this small-town yokel think he was so much better than Dani and she just because he lived in a community? He acted as though she and her sister were nothing more than common white trash.

A surge of anger rolled within her, replacing the hurt. The man was an absolute clod. He had no right to come out here threatening and insulting her that way. Well, if he thought she'd give up that easily, he was in for a big surprise.

She'd show Sheriff McCullough she was made of sterner stuff than that. She hadn't done anything wrong. And she was certain there was no law against asking the owner of this land for permission to make camp here for a while. If the owner agreed, and Brandy felt sure she could somehow persuade him, there would be nothing the good sheriff of Charming could do about it.

Encouraged by her thoughts, she strolled out into the open to look up at the wide night sky overhead. With her hurt and anger receding, she stuffed her hands into her pockets.

Suddenly a look of chagrin crossed her face, and she was thankful Sheriff McCullough was not around to see it.

Easing the stolen trinkets out of her pocket, she pressed them against her chest and concentrated on slowing her racing heart.

Brandy couldn't believe how well Dani and she were doing. The people of Charming had kept a steady flow of business coming to her platform for most of the morning. Several were return customers.

Some days she just couldn't go wrong, she thought with a smile as she handed another bottle of tonic to a plump matron in rose-sprigged calico.

Brandy looked up and her smile froze in place. Then again, she thought, watching the sheriff's purposeful strides as he crossed the road toward her, some days it didn't pay to get up.

"Sheriff," she said casually, straightening to her full height.

Without appearing obvious, Brandy scanned the street on either side, looking for Dani. Her sister had left earlier to return the articles she'd stolen, and Brandy sent up a silent prayer that the little girl hadn't been caught. Usually Dani was as good at replacing the items with the owners as she was at taking them.

"Ma'am." Adam returned the greeting, touching his hat briefly as he'd done the night before. Brandy thought the way he ducked his head like a shy schoolboy was quaint, but the gesture did little to ease her tension now.

"I assume it isn't illegal to park here for a few hours. If it is, I'll be happy to find another spot."

She had driven her wagon back into town that morning on a dual mission. First, she wanted to talk to whoever owned the land she'd camped on last night and ask permission to stay there through the winter. Second, she wanted at least one more day of sales in town in case the owner refused her.

"I told you last night you'd have to move on. I thought I'd made myself perfectly clear."

Brandy noticed the cords in his neck standing out as he strained to look up at her where she stood on the platform. His discomfort brought her a small measure of satisfaction. She stared down at him from her perch and studied his features in the full light of day.

Wide green eyes held her in their gaze. Beneath the worn Stetson, his strawberry-blond hair just brushed his powerfully broad shoulders. Strong jaw, full lips slightly thinned in irritation, aquiline nose. All in all, a very formidable presence. However, the sprinkle of freckles across his nose ruined the effect and made him look mischievous.

"Perfectly, Sheriff. As a matter of fact, that was my real reason for coming to town today. I was going to speak with the owner about getting permission to camp outside of town beneath the big oak tree. However, as you can see," she said, forcing a grin and nodding to the folks standing near her wagon. "I was detained."

"I'm afraid you've wasted your time. I can assure you the owner will not grant you permission." Adam watched her another long minute, then turned to scrutinize the crowd of eager customers gathering once more around the woman's bizarre wagon.

Several folks had already purchased remedies from Brandy and still more were waiting their turn. Truly, she couldn't imagine why business was so good in such a small town, but she didn't intend to turn her back on it. She'd been in this business too long to ignore a streak of favorable luck when it came her way.

"Why don't we let the owner decide that for himself, Sheriff? As you can see, my goods seem to be in great demand."

A rumble went through the crowd, and Brandy thought she saw the sheriff wince. Good, she silently cheered. Let him throw her out if he thought he could get away with it in front of his whole town.

"I already have."

Adam paused, and Brandy was sure he did so to give his meaning time to soak in. She knew he wasn't disappointed with her reaction. She couldn't stop her mouth from dropping open. Wide-eyed, she stared down at him in dismay. *He* was the owner! Her heart sank, but she immediately regained her determination and assurance.

She'd always said if she wanted to win the battle she had to keep her opponent off guard. So, pasting on her brightest smile, she leaned forward and laid her hands gently on his shoulders.

"If you'd be so kind, Sheriff," she purred, waiting for him to react. This time she was the one rewarded by his look of complete astonishment.

"Help the little gal down, Adam," someone called from the crowd.

Brandy, never one to pass up an opportunity when it presented itself, batted her eyes slowly and whispered in her warmest voice. "Adam, is it? How nice."

Her words seemed to propel him into action,

and he swept her from the platform as though she weighed no more than a babe. He twirled her in a half circle, then set her gently on the ground beside the platform.

Brandy's eyes couldn't seem to leave his. They stared at each other, their breath mingling as the dust settled around their touching toes. His hands continued to grip her waist, their warmth somehow stealing her breath.

"And what are you called?" he asked.

His voice was low, close to her cheek. She swallowed and felt as though the Oklahoma dust had settled in her throat.

"You know my name," he said. "It's only fair I know yours."

"The girlie's named Brandy, Adam," the same voice in the crowd called out. "And we all know how comfortin' brandy can be on a cold winter's night. Or any other night for that matter."

The crowd roared with laughter, and Adam and Brandy spun apart. The sheriff cleared his throat and shot a murderous look into the group of merrymakers.

Brandy recovered quickly. She'd heard all the jokes about her name many times before; they couldn't embarrass her anymore. However, she'd seen the look in those Kelly-green eyes so close to hers. As though the image of Brandy and him together on a cold night had actually played across his mind for a split second. A ripple of shared intimacy passed between them.

What foolishness, Brandy thought. Sheriff Adam McCullough probably had a wife and several children. She'd been through towns like this all her life. Everyone seemed to have someone. Even now, people wandered by in pairs all around her. The West was a lonely place, and folks didn't stay single any longer than it took them to get hitched.

As though Brandy's thoughts conjured the woman from thin air, the crowd parted and a tall, striking blonde stepped up beside Adam. Taking his arm, she pressed her breast invitingly against his side.

"Here you are, darling," she said. "I've been looking all over for you."

Chapter Three

Brandy saw her plan to charm Adam McCullough float away on the warm breeze. Disappointment, mixed with something stronger, closed over her. She'd just have to find some other way to get permission to use his land.

"What can I do for you, Suzanne?" Adam asked the beauty, taking her hand in his.

The woman swept a quick glance over Brandy's canary-yellow, scoop-necked blouse, jade-green skirt, and dusty brown boots. Suzanne's lip tipped up in something resembling a sneer before she turned back to the sheriff, obviously discounting Brandy as beneath regard.

A feeling oddly like shame filled Brandy. For the first time, she noticed the frilly pink confection the woman wore. Yards of lace and ribbon adorned the candy-striped poplin, and she carried a matching parasol in her free hand. Her blonde hair had been swept up in a chignon that reminded Brandy of a spun-sugar treat she'd enjoyed at a fair last summer.

Beside her, Brandy looked bold and gauche. She'd always liked flamboyant clothes, but now she felt tacky in her travel-worn outfit. She had pulled her hair back in a ribbon and let it hang down her back. It was usually hopelessly tangled by this time of day. She touched her cheek, certain that the dust stirred along the road had settled there in streaks. With a grimace, she wondered how she'd ever thought she could charm a man like Adam McCullough.

"Dinner will be a little late tonight, darling. I've been to your aunt's, and she and I spent simply hours poring over the patterns in the new *Godey's Ladies' Book* that just arrived."

"That's fine, Suzanne. I have a bit of business here that's still unresolved."

Suzanne's clear gray eyes darted back to Brandy as though reassessing her. Apparently satisfied once more that the woman on Adam's other side posed no real threat to her territory, she turned back to Adam.

"Good. I'll see you in about an hour then?" She patted his cheek and walked away without even waiting for an answer, obviously secure that he'd follow her instructions.

"Now, Miss—"

"Ashton," Brandy supplied. Her gaze followed Suzanne another few steps, then returned to the sheriff. "Brandy Ashton." She stuck out her hand, determined to get off on the right foot now that she knew where to step.

People were her business, and she prided herself on knowing how to handle them. The first thing she had learned was that she should treat a married man, especially one with a wife like the sugarcoated Suzanne, differently from the way she'd treat a single man.

Adam shook her hand, and once more Brandy felt the warmth of his touch. Lucky lady, that Suzanne. In more ways than one, Brandy thought.

"If you'd care to join me in my office, I'd be happy to continue our discussion there." Adam shot a glance over his shoulder at the encroaching crowd, and Brandy fought back a grin. So, the sheriff didn't like an audience. Well, she could understand that, she supposed. Especially if he planned to run her out of town.

"I'm sorry, Sheriff. I can't leave the wagon unattended. We'll just have to have our discussion here."

Adam frowned and the lines grooved into his face seemed deeper than normal for a man his age. Only thirty-two or -three at the most, Brandy guessed. Yet, it would appear he did more frowning than smiling. A touch of sadness tugged at Brandy's heart.

Her own life had been filled with laughter, despite the occasional difficulties, and she assumed that when the lines began to show on her face they'd tell the tale of a woman who'd enjoyed every moment to the fullest.

Perhaps there was more to Adam McCullough than met the eye. Why would a man with social position, a seemingly comfortable job, a town full of friends, and a wife who appeared devoted spend so much time wearing a frown? It was a mystery indeed.

"And where is your little helper?" he asked, snapping Brandy out of her wanderings.

"My sister stepped away for a few minutes to stretch her legs," Brandy lied, silently hoping Dani hadn't given in to the urge to keep any of the items she was supposed to be returning.

"I'm here, Brandy," Dani called from the other side of the platform. As Dani hurried to her sister's side, Brandy breathed a sigh of relief. Thankfully, her sister had managed to complete her task without incident.

"So, shall we go then?" Adam asked.

Hastily informing Dani where she'd be, Brandy allowed Adam to take her elbow firmly in his hand and turn her away from the crowd. She swiveled her head about and saw Dani climbing onto the platform. Her sister could handle things for a brief time. If a customer had a complaint Dani didn't know the remedy for, she'd simply tell him to come back when Brandy was there. Other than that, all she had to do was read the labels on the jars and collect the money, which she'd done a hundred times.

Brandy surrendered to Adam's will, and together they strolled across the road, down the planked walkway, and into his dusty, dimly lit office.

"Now, then," Brandy said as Adam closed the office door, shutting out the noise from the street and a good portion of the afternoon sunlight. "I thought perhaps a reasonable fee could be agreed upon for the use of your land. I'd be willing to pay say—"

"No."

Her words ground to a halt and she blinked. There was little doubt the sheriff meant to be stubborn. Why, she didn't know. No matter, she'd dealt with stubbornness before.

"I don't need much space; a few feet actually would suffice."

"Maybe you should treat yourself with one of your remedies, Miss Ashton. I believe your hearing is bad. I said no."

He strode to the hat rack, a broken-down, cockeyed piece that had seen many a better day, and whipped off his hat. Thumping it down on a wobbly peg, he raked his hands through his flattened hair and then took a seat behind the battered desk.

"No, you cannot use my land to set up your little Gypsy camp. You cannot park your wagon on my street, and most importantly, you cannot operate your shady business in my town."

Brandy sputtered, appalled at the gall of the man. His sudden animosity took her by surprise, but she recovered quickly. "How dare you?" she cried, smacking her palm on the top of his desk hard enough to raise a puff of dust.

"For your information my sister and I are not Gypsies. We're legitimate businesswomen. And furthermore, what gives you the right to order me about? You act like you own this whole blessed town."

She leaned low over the desk as she spoke, her face inching closer to his with each word until their noses nearly touched. Adam glanced down, raised an eyebrow at the cleavage Brandy's position exposed, and then turned away slowly as though bored with the sight. He reached into a drawer for tobacco and cigarette papers and began to prepare the cigarette with studied movements.

Brandy straightened, refusing to be embarrassed at this man's perusal. She seethed, wishing he would quit acting so blasted superior.

He dug a match out of his pocket and struck it to life. Just before he set the flame to the paper, he met her icy gaze and said simply, "I do."

For a full minute, Brandy watched the smoke drift up to encircle his head. Her shoulders stiffened and she stepped back to glare at him.

"You're serious!" she couldn't stop herself from blurting out.

"Yes, ma'am."

"How is that possible? How can one man own a whole town? I mean, those people—those shops and businesses. You can't mean—"

"That's exactly what I do mean." He drew

deep on the cigarette and Brandy spun away. Even from a distance she could feel the self-confidence emanate from him, and it made him seem virile and dangerous. Crossing to the tiny smudged window, she stared out on the bustle of the small town.

Two main streets ran parallel to each other, and two more parallel streets intersected them, forming a small square in the middle. She'd parked her wagon along one side of the square, but she could see past it now to the rows of clapboard buildings on the other side.

Charming wasn't a large town, she readily admitted. But the very idea that one man possessed so much stunned her.

"My father owned all of the land for miles around. But the nearest town was more than a week away. So, he advertised in some major newspapers for merchants. Each of those who answered the ad were granted a ninety-nine-year lease with low rent and a guaranteed monopoly. You see before you all of those who responded. Each and every one is my tenant, now that my father is dead."

Brandy's mind whirled. She'd never known anyone with so much. Of course, if the merchants and workers held such long-term leases, it wasn't actually as if Adam McCullough controlled the land.

"Why the leases?" she asked, still unable, or unwilling, to face him. "Why not just sell them the land?"

"My father believed that the only limited

commodity of this abundant new world is land. By offering the leases, he guaranteed the land would stay in the family for generations. The way he figured it, land would have to run out sooner or later, and the man in possession of the most at that time would be holding an ace card."

Brandy finally turned, a small smile twisting her full lips. "Smart man. I can see the wisdom of his plan, and it's ingenious." She couldn't help thinking how her own father had never been able to hold on to anything longer than it took him to trade it or sell it to someone for a few coins. Adam's father had been nobody's fool, that was for certain.

Well, if she'd been outdone this time, at least she could take comfort in knowing she'd been bested by a master. Or at least the son of one.

"I'm sure my father would appreciate the compliment. But that's hardly what we're here for, is it?"

Brandy shook her head. "No, it's not. We're here to discuss my setting up my wagon in your town for a while."

"Wrong. We're here to discuss your leaving."

Hands on hips, Brandy stepped back to the front of Adam's desk, looking down at him. "Be reasonable, Sheriff. I've already told you I'm not a Gypsy, a thief, or a prostitute. The people of your town desire my remedies. I could tell by their enthusiasm earlier. And I'm willing to pay whatever fee you think is fair for the use of the land by the square and outside of town."

"Sorry," he said, tapping out the cigarette in a flat metal dish he'd dug out of the rubble on his desk.

Sure you are, Brandy thought with a sneer.

"I couldn't even if I wanted to, Miss Ashton," Adam told her, rising from his chair to prop one hip on the corner of the desk. Once more they were at eye level with one another. The mere touch of his gaze on her face made Brandy aware of the stifling lack of air in the musty office.

"Why is that, Sheriff?" she asked, her tone growing crisper as her aggravation soared.

"We've had ordinances in this town for more than two years now. Every business operating in Charming must have a license and a permit."

"Fine. Where do I get them?"

"Right here."

Her eyes narrowed and she tried to imitate the quelling look she'd seen her father use to intimidate the more ardent of her customers. It didn't work on Adam McCullough, though. He merely continued to watch her, his face totally expressionless.

"Then issue them to me, or sell them to me, or whatever you do." Her voice rose, cracked, and then lowered once more.

"I can't." He shuffled some papers, cleared a small space on the desk, and settled his tightly jeaned bottom more firmly onto the desk's surface.

"This is ridiculous! Don't think I don't know

47

what you're doing, Sheriff."

Still no reaction crossed his face. *Blast, but the man must be without human emotions,* Brandy thought.

"Fine. Tell me who can," she demanded.

"Only the council can issue permits, and I can't sell a license to anyone without a permit."

Finally, she was getting somewhere. For a moment, Brandy had nearly forgotten why she even wanted to stay in Charming, Oklahoma. Then she remembered Dani and winter's inevitable approach. For the first time, they'd have to make it through the rough months alone, and Brandy meant to see that they were safely ensconced somewhere before the weather turned cold.

Besides, her stubborn pride forced her to try to best this arrogant boor.

"Is this council made up of citizens of this town, Sheriff?" She barely caught his brief nod. "Good. I'm sure I'll have no trouble getting a permit, then."

"No, probably not," he conceded.

Brandy's eyes narrowed. She couldn't believe he was giving up. Her suspicions blossomed. What was he up to now? she wondered.

"Is there any problem getting the members together for a decision?" she asked, searching for a fly in the ointment of her plan.

"Nope."

"Then Dani and I will be able to stay in Charming, after all?" Her voice lifted slightly, cautiously optimistic.

"I'm afraid not."

The air whooshed out of Brandy's lungs, and she slumped, tired of the cat-and-mouse game Adam McCullough seemed to be playing with her.

"Why?" She pressed the word out between clenched teeth.

"Because I have to give the final okay for you to set up on a parcel of land."

Ah, the distinctive buzz of the fly. "And you aren't going to do that, are you?"

He shook his head.

"What have you got against me, Sheriff?"

For a moment, Brandy thought he meant to ignore her. Then he heaved a dry sigh and hefted himself from the desk. He walked out into the center of the floor, stuffed his hands into the hip pockets of his denims, and shook his head.

"In a word, Miss Ashton, snake oil."

Anger topped out in Brandy like mercury in a thermometer on a summer day. "I resent that, Sheriff. My remedies are not snake oil or liquor disguised as medicine. I've seen that kind myself and I can't abide them either. But I assure you—"

"And I assure you," he cut in, his voice harsh, "I won't allow it. As sheriff of Charming, it's my job to make sure these people don't get cheated. As a rule, I don't mind peddlers. They're here one day and gone the next. But your kind, I have reason to dislike. You sell false hope to sick folks and tell them your tonic'll make 'em all better. They're desperate and helpless and sometimes beyond hope, and what you do is despicable."

Shock crossed Brandy's face like a hard slap. What had happened in Adam McCullough's life to make him hate her so much? She read pain and anger in his eyes and couldn't stop the desire that rose in her to show him she wasn't like the others. Wouldn't he have a good laugh if she admitted that? He didn't want anything from her, except to see the back of her wagon as she rode out of town.

"Look, Miss Ashton, maybe you really believe in that hokey tonic you peddle. But I don't. And nothing you can say or do will convince me."

Brandy's anger returned full-blown. Gad, the man was stubborn! He refused to even give her a chance.

"I'm not interested in convincing you of anything, Sheriff. Because it's obvious to anyone that your mind is closed tighter than a miser's fist around money. But I'll put my remedies to the test any day."

"And what test is that? Are you gonna make my rheumatism disappear or make my hair thicker?" He scoffed and took a step closer to her. "I don't have rheumatism, and the last time I looked my head was still well covered."

"And thick as hundred-year-old oak, no doubt." Brandy took a step forward. They were close enough to touch now, to feel the feathered breath the other expelled.

Adam's green eyes turned the color of hard,

cold jade. Brandy met his stare easily. "No, Sheriff, I'll not try to prove myself to you. All I have to do is convince the nice folks of your town. Because as my pa used to say before he died, no man stands tall when he stands alone."

"Very nice, little Gypsy," Adam taunted. "But aren't you forgetting one thing?"

Not for every acre of Adam McCullough's precious land would Brandy ask the question he sought. She stood stubbornly, her usually cheerful face pursed into a stern frown.

"You are equally alone."

A hard, cold knot gripped Brandy's stomach. All too well she knew how alone she and Dani were now. Hadn't she shoveled every handful of dirt out of that wretched hole herself? Wasn't she the one who, with Dani's help, had dragged her father's body to the edge, dumped it in, then laboriously replaced that same dirt? She didn't need the likes of Adam McCullough to tell her how alone she felt at this moment.

Oh, how hard it was to face all the difficulties like hard-nosed sheriffs and unobtainable permits without her pa. For a long moment, Brandy wondered if she'd really be able to go on, to support herself and Dani without Wade Ashton. But she'd die trying before she'd give Sheriff Adam McCullough the pleasure of seeing her give up.

With more determination than she felt, and a lot of false confidence she'd managed to muster from somewhere, Brandy smiled. Not a businesslike smile or even a downright friendly smile, but the most seductive, daring, inviting smile she'd ever fashioned her lips into.

Her efforts were not wasted. She saw Adam's eyes widen and then narrow in suspicion. His hands slid slowly from his pockets and inched forward. A quizzical look flashed across his face when she held out her hand.

"Shall we see just whose side the people of Charming are on? Yours, I leave. Mine, I stay. It's as simple as that."

He glanced down at her hand, stretched out in mock cordiality. Again Brandy felt the dizzying current race through her. This time she recognized it for what it was. Desire. The same emotion reflected in Adam's dark gaze. Her heart turned over in response and she knew she'd gone too far.

"Nothing's ever as simple as that, Miss Ashton."

And so saying he grasped her hand, pulled her off balance into his arms, and swooped down to claim her smiling mouth in a hard, possessive kiss.

His lips were hungry and searching, his tongue coaxed her mouth open. She swayed, stunned by the force of desire she felt in his arms.

Just as suddenly as it began, the kiss ended. He released her and she stumbled back a step. Her fingers longed to touch her lips where they tingled with spirals of electric energy. But she knew too well how that gesture would look.

Instead, she raised her hand and slapped him across the face. His head snapped back, his palm going to his flaming cheek.

"I told you I was not a loose woman, Sheriff. If you try something like that again, I'll . . . I'll . . . tell your wife," she sputtered, unable to think of anything more threatening at the moment.

Adam threw back his head and laughed. "Well, I'd have to get married before you could do that, and I don't plan on letting you stay around long enough to see that happen."

Brandy ignored the wash of relief she felt upon learning that the sheriff hadn't added infidelity to his list of faults. She spun on her heel and stalked to the door, then turned back, her hand on the knob.

"We'll just see about that, Sheriff."

Chapter Four

Several people spoke to Adam as he strode briskly down the walkway. But he didn't notice or reply. He could feel the sting of the peddler's palm against his cheek, could still hear her accusing tone as she reminded him again that she *was not* a prostitute.

His boots clumped along the planks as his mind whirled with confusing thoughts. What had made him do it? Why had he kissed her? He told himself he wanted to prove she was a practiced whore. After all, lips like those were made for kissing.

But when he'd kissed her hard and long, he could tell what he'd thought was wrong. She wasn't experienced at anything more serious than a little casual flirting. He'd bet his badge on it. And he suspected even the flirting had been an act to try to get him to give his permission for her to camp on his land. The fear and anger he'd read in her eyes as she slapped him silly seemed to validate that idea, and the thought cut him to the bone.

"'Day, Sheriff," Maggie Bellows said as they passed on the narrow porch outside the general store.

Adam grunted a response without looking up and stalked on. Maggie and her five-year-old twin boys Darrel and David stared after him. They recognized the sheriff's fine temper, and Maggie quickly shepherded the youngsters into the store.

Crossing the pocked dirt street, Adam walked on until he reached the end of Cherry Blossom Street, the main thoroughfare through town. He stopped for a moment outside a white wrought-iron gate and stared up at the conspicuous pillared house.

In a town the size of Charming, it stood out like an apple in a crate of oranges. He considered the wraparound porch and second-story veranda to be ostentatious. And he wondered again why his father, a rugged ex-cowboy, would build such a place.

The gate squealed when he pushed it open, reminding him that he'd let a lot of minor repairs go untended for too long. He'd have to get around to doing them as soon as possible. But first, he told himself, he had a much bigger problem. The peddler could very well ingratiate herself into his town as she'd threatened. He knew the townspeople; they were for the most part a bit softhearted and gullible. It came from living in a place virtually untouched by the wildness of the West.

He'd kept out the saloons—except Nell's Lemonade Parlor, which sold very little lemonade—and the drovers and wranglers. A man could get a drink at Nell's and maybe a sympathetic ear, but that was all. Charming, Oklahoma, was just that—charming. And he planned to see it stayed that way.

He opened the beveled-glass door and kicked off his dusty boots, leaving them on the porch. He'd barely settled his hat on the polished oak hall tree when his aunt spun around the corner.

Adam jumped back to keep the high, thin wheels of her chair from banging his shins, and he bumped the door, causing it to slam behind him. The glass rattled but his aunt didn't seem to notice.

"I was about to get worried about you, boy," she said, rolling the wooden wheels backward until he could step farther into the hall. "That Suzanne stayed near about all day gazing google eyed at the new *Harper's* magazine I got. Like she needs more clothes," she complained with a loud hurrumph.

"Good day to you, too, Aunt Carmel. My trip was fine, thank you, but I am glad to be back." He propped his hands on his hips and smiled sarcastically down at the wrinkled, pink face.

"Of course, you are. What a foolish thing

to say. And don't think I don't recognize a sassy mouth when I hear it. Been out to your place yet?"

"No, ma'am. I thought I'd come here and get cleaned up. I'm having dinner with the doctor's family, and I don't have time to go all the way out to the cabin and back."

"Huh, you're having dinner with Suzanne. She'll get rid of her senile old daddy before coffee's served. I think if the man didn't have to eat to survive she wouldn't even let him in the dining room with the two of you."

"In a foul mood today, Aunt?" Adam guessed, shrugging out of the leather vest he wore, his hands already going to the buttons on his shirt.

"I need to talk to you, right away."

Adam noticed she'd ignored his caustic remark as usual and gone on to whatever was bothering her. This time, however, he knew what it was, and he didn't intend to discuss it right now.

He bent down to kiss her cheek and said, "Later. I'll be late."

When he would have risen and left her, she snatched the front of his shirt in her fist and yanked him back down. "Don't get smart with me, boy. That gal can wait five minutes. This is important."

He could have easily pulled out of her weak grip, but he only smiled at her pluck and mettle. "You always were too bossy for your own good," he told her, straightening.

"Come along then," he said, taking the handles on the back of her chair just to annoy her. "I guess I can spare a minute or two."

"Let go of my chair, you young rascal, or I'll run over your stockinged toes. The day I need help getting this blamed chair around, I'll just lie down and die."

Adam chuckled, but stepped away from the chair. He knew she'd carry out her threats, just as he'd known his actions would spark them. But he couldn't help riling her a bit to keep their relationship in perspective. She'd take advantage of his love and concern for her in a minute and ride roughshod over him, if he let her.

And he couldn't help but love the old biddy. She tried to be disagreeable and, most times, succeeded, but he saw through her. The gray in her once blonde hair couldn't dull its beauty. The lines of age hadn't yet erased the graceful features that had once made her the toast of Boston. And her waspish disposition didn't fool him for a minute.

He went to the sidebar in the parlor and poured himself a glass of whiskey.

"I'll have a sherry, thank you," Carmel said, arching an eyebrow.

Adam shook his head and grinned. He swallowed a sip of the liquor and then set the glass aside. "Before dinner?" he asked, already pouring the red liquid into a cut-crystal goblet.

"Never you mind," she snapped. "Did you get rid of her?"

He stiffened briefly at the direct attack, then relaxed and turned to face her. There was no point in putting off the inevitable. He'd known she'd hear about the peddler; it had only been a matter of time.

"I did." He held the glass out to her, and she narrowed her fiery green eyes.

"No, thank you," she said, turning her nose up a bit.

He clenched the stemware in his hand for a moment, then set it aside. He told himself her ire should come as no surprise.

"You got in late last night. I tried to wait up so we could talk. Then you left this morning before sunup. I wanted—"

"I know what you'd have wanted to do, Aunt Carmel. There's no way I'd have allowed it."

"Don't you tell me what you'll allow," she said, her voice breaking. "I'm still your elder."

He released a heavy sigh and sank into a floral armchair across from the long, narrow window. His eyes swept the scenery outside, but all he could see was the hurt in her eyes.

"How many times, Aunt Carmel? How long are you going to put yourself through this?"

"I heard she was really good. Dorothy said she cured her bunions. And you know how long she's suffered—"

"Dorothy," he grunted. "I should have known. Why does she come here and fill your head with this nonsense? Why doesn't she let it be? Why don't you—"

"Don't you dare tell me to let it go," Carmel

said, her feminine voice rising. "You aren't the one sitting in this chair every day until you get calluses on your behind."

Adam jumped to his feet. He'd anticipated her anger, but he couldn't bear her pain. Plowing his fingers through his hair, he walked to the door.

"I'm going to be late," he told her. "We'll discuss this later."

"She could have been the one," Carmel cried out, stopping him in his tracks.

He turned back to face his aunt and lowered his head. "She was a charlatan, Aunt Carmel. Just like the others. She was barely out of short petticoats," he exaggerated.

"You could have let me seen her or talked to her. Who would that have hurt?"

"You," he whispered, meeting her glassy gaze. "Like all the other times, you would have been the one hurt and disappointed in the end. And I won't allow it. No more, Aunt Carmel."

He spun away, but her words stopped him again. "I can't take being confined to this chair anymore, Adam. I just can't."

He didn't turn back. There was nothing he could say to make her understand. In two years, she'd never accepted her paralysis, and he'd began to wonder if she ever would. The doctor had told them both a week after the carriage accident that her aged hip would not recover. But Carmel refused to accept his diagnosis, insisting he was senile and incompetent.

Granted, the doctor was old and his methods were a bit outdated. But Adam had taken Carmel to Oklahoma City, and the physician there had confirmed the prognosis. Still, she never gave up trying to find a wonder cure. She'd been swindled by every hokey advertisement she read, and she'd put out more than a small fortune on miracle tonics.

The only miracle was that she still wouldn't give up and accept her disability. Every time Adam watched her hopes soar over a new concoction, his heart broke.

He felt the familiar pain now as he walked out of the parlor and up the stairs to the guest room on the second floor. As he stripped off his shirt, he cursed. No one was going to do that to her ever again. Not even a beautiful dark-eyed Gypsy with an innocence he suspected was not feigned.

The cowbell hanging above the door jangled loudly as Brandy stepped into the general store. She'd left Dani straightening the bottles on their shelves while she stopped in for a few things they needed.

Her eyes passed over the barrels of peaches and the table of bolt cloth. Her eyes met those of a woman and she smiled in greeting. The pretty brunette nodded shyly and turned her attention back to the two little boys eyeing the row of glass candy jars on the counter.

"What can I do for you?" the man behind the counter asked, scratching his ear and then wiping his hands on the apron at his waist.

Brandy withdrew her list from her skirt pocket and handed it over. The thin hand reached out and took the paper; the pale blue eyes scanned it. He nodded his head and mumbled, "Be a minute. Mrs. Bellows here is ahead of you."

Disappearing into the back room, the storekeeper left Brandy alone with the woman and boys. She ambled over to a barrel with crackers and cheese laid out on top.

"You're welcome to a bite," the woman said.

Brandy turned around, ashamed to be caught eyeing the food. "No, thank you."

"Ole Bill puts it out there for the customers. If they linger a bit he figures they'll buy more." She shrugged as if to say maybe, maybe not.

Brandy noticed the two little boys each held a soda cracker in their hands. She smiled again and decided she might as well get to know the friendly woman.

"Hi, I'm Brandy Ashton," she said, sticking her hand out.

The woman didn't hesitate. She gripped Brandy's hand and pumped it. "I'm Maggie Bellows. I've heard about you."

"Have you?" Brandy released her hand and her smile faltered a bit. She wondered what the woman had heard. Did everybody know what the sheriff suspected? Had they all heard how she'd disgraced herself in his office that afternoon?

"Yeah, Dorothy said how you cured her bunions. She's talking about it all over town."

Brandy had to chuckle. Her nerves were stretched taut; otherwise she'd have realized that no one knew about the events in the sheriff's office. She certainly hadn't let on what happened, not even to Dani. And she suspected the sheriff wouldn't be advertising the facts where his lady friend could get wind of them.

"I'm glad I could help," Brandy said absently, her mind still replaying the encounter with Adam McCullough. He'd outwitted her in their discussion. But more than that, he'd humiliated her. If he wanted to prove she was a fallen woman, she'd certainly given him the ammunition. Why had she let him kiss her like that?

"Don't touch that," Brandy heard Maggie Bellows admonish one of the boys. She turned her attention back to the store and the business of getting her supplies.

Dani came in, the cowbell announcing her arrival. The noise was overly loud in the silence following Brandy's brief conversation with Maggie Bellows, and she touched her temples, where a headache was starting to form.

"The wagon's all buttoned down tight, Brandy," Dani said, skipping into the store. "That nice Mr. Walker helped me lift the platform."

Brandy noticed her sister's eyes fall on the pearl-handled knife lying on the cheese board nearby. That familiar gleam danced in the doe-brown depths of her gaze, and Brandy stepped quickly between her sister and the appealing object.

After that, everything happened so fast she forgot about her apprehension over Dani's interest in the cheese knife.

The shop owner came out of the back, carrying a crate filled with supplies. A jar of what looked like salt fell off the top of the crate and crashed to the floor.

The smallest little boy had put his hand on one of the jars of candy lining the shelf. As Brandy watched, his back arched and his eyes rolled in his head. Maggie Bellows cried out and Brandy whirled to face the woman. The candy jar that the boy was touching and the one beside it slid off the counter. As the boy fell to the floor convulsing, his mother dropping to her knees beside him, the candy jars shattered, and the sour balls and peppermint sticks splintered into sharp, sugared slivers.

Dani let out an astonished cry. Brandy ran to the second little boy. He stood in the middle of the melee, wild-eyed with fear. Sweeping him up in her arms, she lifted him over the shattered glass and passed him to her sister. Then she knelt beside the thrashing child.

"Call the doctor," Maggie cried, her face stark white. "Hurry!"

The shop owner rushed for the door, and Brandy saw him run into the street, waving his arms frantically at a couple nearby.

"Can I help?" Brandy asked, brushing away the bits of glass and sweets around them. She pulled the handkerchief from her skirt pocket, folded it into a thick square, and cupped the boy's jaw. After prying open the tightened lips, she thrust the cloth between his clenched teeth.

"David," Maggie crooned, lifting the tiny shoulders onto her lap. "David, honey, it's Momma. Can you hear me? It's all right. It's all right."

The fit lasted no more than a minute, but Brandy's already taxed nerves quivered. Her knees shook and her heart raced. It was horrible watching the tiny face twist into a hideous grimace. She looked up at Maggie and watched the woman suffer along with her child.

The doctor ran into the store, causing the obnoxious bell to peal again. He huffed over to the group gathered on the floor and hitched up his pant leg before squatting.

He withdrew a vial from his bag, then removed the handkerchief and shook several drops from the thin jar into the little boy's mouth. Pulling a contraption that looked like a cross between a bear trap and a muzzle from his bag, he attempted to fit it over the small head.

"Stop! What are you doing?" Brandy cried, reaching for the torture device.

"Stand aside, young lady," the doctor ordered. "I'm trying to keep the boy from biting his own tongue off. His kind can do themselves all manner of harm."

"No," she said, reaching for his hand again. "You don't have to do that. The handkerchief works as well, or a wooden spoon will do."

Brandy turned to the boy's mother, but Maggie's burst of adrenaline had deserted her with the doctor's arrival. The woman sat on the floor, slumped in her skirts.

The doctor fitted the metal device over the boy's head, placing the leather-covered brace between his teeth despite the fact the seizure had already passed.

The little eyes focused and then closed. The small body went limp.

"I've told you before, Maggie, the boy needs to be put away. You can't restrain him now. What are you going to do when he gets bigger? He'll hurt someone or himself."

The woman sat weeping, the evidence of the boy's destruction around her. She didn't respond, only brushed the baby-fine hair off his forehead through the grill of the mask.

The doctor grunted and pushed to his feet. "Take him home, then. Tie him to the bed the way I showed you."

Brandy gasped in horror, her eyes going from the angelic face so peaceful in repose to the doctor's grim expression.

"Who owns that wagon out in the square?" the doctor asked, glancing around the store.

Brandy looked up in alarm. "I do."

He frowned and studied her a moment.

"Sorry, thought it was someone else." He shook his head at her. Brandy saw his eyes glaze over, and he suddenly looked confused. His gaze darted around the store, searchingly, then lit on the couple by the door and immediately cleared.

For the first time, Brandy noticed the sheriff and Suzanne standing together in the doorway beside the shop owner. Her gaze met the Kelly-green eyes frowning at her with displeasure, and her concern over the doctor's strange behavior fled.

"Go on home, Suzanne," Adam said, passing the soft white hand he held to the doctor as he passed. The woman opened her mouth to reply, but the doctor clasped her fingers, as though grateful for the support, and quickly drew her from the building.

Adam McCullough walked across to where the three still sat on the floor. He held out his hand to Brandy.

"Come along. I'll help Maggie get the boy home."

"Now, wait a minute, Sheriff," the store-keeper spoke up, setting the forgotten crate on the counter. "I got a mess here. And damaged merchandise. Who's gonna pay for this?"

Brandy stiffened. The sheriff's fingers clenched hers and she saw his lips thin.

"Put it on my account, Mr. Owens," Maggie whispered, scooping the boy into her arms. She drew her feet beneath her to rise, and Adam stepped forward, taking the child and offering the mother a hand up.

"That's three times already, Miz Bellows," the man called as she started for the door, her other purchases forgotten. "You ought not bring him in here. I can't keep replacing everything he breaks. And you cain't afford to keep paying me for it."

Brandy watched the sheriff lead Maggie out to the street. Her eyes followed them to Maggie Bellows's wagon, where Dani stood with the other child. Her sister waved good-bye to her new little friend and came into the store. Once more the bell jangled, and Brandy longed to snatch it down and throw it as far as she could.

"I'll have your order in just a minute, miss," the storekeeper said, collecting a broom from the corner. "As soon as I clean up this mess."

Brandy cut the man a hard glare and shook her head. "Never mind," she said coldly. "I've changed my mind."

She took Dani's elbow and half dragged the girl from the shop. Once outside, she stopped and took several deep breaths to calm down.

"What happened, Brandy? You said we needed a few things."

"We don't need anything from that man," Brandy said, struggling to hold onto her temper. She ruffled Dani's bangs and threaded her fingers through her sister's. "Come on. Let's go."

"Where are we going? I thought the sheriff said we couldn't stay."

Brandy lifted Dani into the wagon and climbed up beside her. "I know what he said. But I've got a few things to do before we leave."

"The little boy?" Dani asked. "Are you gonna help him?"

"If I can," Brandy whispered, turning the wagon in the direction of the oak they'd parked under for the last week. "Him and some of the others. That doctor is living in ignorance, Dani. He'd put that beautiful little boy in an asylum where God knows what they'd do to him."

"You're not gonna let that happen are you, Brandy?" her sister said with confidence.

Brandy shook her head and snapped the reins. "No, Dani, I'm surely not."

The dust left by Maggie Bellows's wagon directed their way out of town. Brandy's heart guided her actions.

Chapter Five

So, the pretty little peddler had taken his advice and left town.

Adam surveyed the empty spot across the square with mixed feelings. His aunt would not be happy to know the girl was gone for good. Carmel hadn't spoken a word to him since their argument the previous day. But he'd done the right thing, the only thing he could have done in all good conscience, he told himself again as he opened the door to his office and went in.

He dropped a few small logs into the belly of the tiny cookstove in the corner and stoked it to life. After putting coffee on to boil, he sat in his chair, put his boots on the edge of his desk, and rifled through some old wanted posters.

But his mind, and his eyes, kept straying to the empty spot by the square. He'd been tough on the girl. Maybe too tough?

She was young, beautiful, and he suspected, not as self-assured as she pretended to be. Of course, her innocence and sincerity could have been a calculated disguise to convince him she wasn't the charlatan he'd accused her of being. With a stab of unexpected guilt he feared her ruse might have worked. After all, he hadn't been able to stop thinking about her, out there alone with a little sister to look after.

His thoughts brought a grim frown to his lips. He knew all about taking on responsibility at a young age. Some would say he knew too much. His sisters Jenny and Beth would agree. So would Aunt Carmel. How many times had they told him he'd grown too old for his years? How many times had they pleaded with him to forget all the responsibilities he'd once been charged with?

But he couldn't. Jenny and Beth, both happily married now and living in nearby towns, had needed him after their parents were killed in a fire while staying at a hotel in Oklahoma City. He'd been left behind to watch the girls, and after the tragedy, they'd depended on Adam to be both mother and father. At sixteen, he'd been responsible for two lonely, scared little girls and a whole town of his father's tenants. Even after Aunt Carmel had learned of their parent's deaths and come to help out, he'd been the one his sisters counted on for guidance.

The coffee boiled over, snatching him from his thoughts of the past. He grabbed the tail of his shirt, jerked it from his denims, and used it to remove the hot pot. He poured an earthenware cup full of the strong brew and settled at his desk.

Again his mind went back to Brandy Ashton. He forced aside his compassion and hardened his heart. After all, he told himself, he'd handled all the heavy burdens his parents' deaths had placed on him. The Gypsy could handle one little girl and herself.

She was very good at her vocation. His whole town had been evidence of that. Look how quickly she'd ingratiated herself into their good graces. Besides, he reminded himself, Suzanne would certainly be glad to hear he'd gotten rid of her.

He sipped his scalded coffee and grimaced, his ears burning all over again when he remembered Suzanne's tantrum the night before.

After he'd returned from helping Maggie Bellows home, he'd stopped by the doctor's place to apologize to Suzanne for their ruined dinner. But she'd been too irritated to reason with. Most of the time she was sweet and amiable around him; that was why he continued to see her. But occasionally, she'd shown him another side of herself, like last night. And that was one reason he procrastinated, despite her pleas to make a commitment, when it came to furthering their relationship.

Suzanne refused to understand why he felt it his duty as sheriff to help not only Maggie, but the rest of the people in town. And she'd all but ordered him to get rid of the peddler and her sister—a fact that set his teeth on edge whenever he remembered her harping. Brandy Ashton and her remedies were cutting into Doc's business, and that cut into Suzanne's purse.

He pushed thoughts of Suzanne from his mind and focused on Maggie. Thinking of her made him decide to ride out to check on her and the boys again. Since her husband had run off a couple of years ago, she'd had a rough time of it. And that afflicted child only added misery to heartache.

Adam scooped his hat off the edge of the desk and worked it down onto his head. He might as well check on his own place while he was at it. He hadn't been to the cabin since his return, and there was no sense going back to Aunt Carmel's with her in a snit.

Brandy pulled the wagon to a stop and looked at her sister.

"Not much of a place, is it?" Dani said, frowning with chagrin.

Both glanced back at the cockeyed little shack surrounded by tall prairie grass. Brandy had decided after seeing the sheriff leave with Maggie yesterday that it might be better to wait until this morning to carry out her plan. She didn't want to run into the sheriff at Maggie's home so soon after their confrontation.

"It's got to be the right place," Brandy said. "The man at the harness shop said you couldn't miss the cabin if you stayed on the road until the second turn off. Besides, see that?"

The yard held an assortment of rusted, broken farm implements and the old flatbed wagon Brandy had seen Maggie and her sons leave town in yesterday. A line of laundry hung on a rope strung between two porch posts on the back of the house.

"Let's go," she said, taking up the reins and snapping them lightly.

They rolled into the yard, and two little faces peered out of a tall patch of dried cornstalks. Dirty and smudged, with patches on their trousers and their feet bare, the boys watched the orange-and-green wagon closely as it approached them.

Dani smiled and waved, calling to the little boy Darrel, whom she'd briefly spent time with the day before. On cue, the twin boys darted from behind the corn and ran to the wagon.

"Heya, Dani," Darrel said, scampering up the spokes of one of the wheels before it came to a complete stop. The smaller boy, David, held back but Brandy could see his eyes widen with wonder.

"Heya, Darrel," Dani mocked, grabbing his arm and hauling him onto the seat beside her.

"This is so neat. Do you really live in this wagon. Does it get cold? I bet it's crowded. Does it have a bed or do you sleep underneath it?"

Brandy chuckled and set the brake. She jumped down as Dani patiently answered

Darrel's questions one by one. On the other side of the wagon, David hung back. Brandy smiled down at him.

"Is your mama home?"

He nodded.

"Do you think she'd mind company?"

Instead of answering, he turned and ran onto the porch. The door was open and she heard him shout for his mother as he sailed into the shack.

Maggie Bellows came out as Dani and Darrel were climbing down from the wagon. She wiped her hands on a much-mended apron. Her dress, obviously old, showed signs of wear. Her hair was pulled back with a man's handkerchief and wound into a knot.

Brandy wondered if the woman couldn't even afford hairpins. She must have been wearing her best dress when she'd gone to town, Brandy thought.

Brandy's eyes strayed to the pitiful garden growing beside the porch. "I hope we're not disturbing you," she said, stepping closer.

"No, that's all right," Maggie said, her hands sweeping down over the mends and threadbare spots on her cotton gown, as if trying to take stock of her appearance without being obvious.

"I'm Brandy Ashton. We met in the general store yesterday."

"Yes, I remember," Maggie Bellows said, glancing nervously over her shoulder. "Would you, um, like to come in?"

"If we're not bothering you."

The woman smiled, finally, and Brandy relaxed a little.

"I'm gonna stay out here with Darrel and David, okay, Brandy?" Dani asked.

"Sure, why don't you show David and Darrel around the wagon?"

The boys squealed with delight as Dani led them grandly to the side door and opened it with an exaggerated flourish.

"Now, just you don't mess with anything in there," Maggie called to the boys as the three children disappeared inside.

Brandy followed the woman into the one-room house and suddenly she understood Maggie's hesitation. The room was dark, the floor nothing but dirt. Not even one window had been added to draw light.

In the center of the room was a big, rough wood table and four unmatched chairs. The legs on one of the chairs had been replaced with sticks that hadn't even been smoothed out. In one corner was a large mattress covered with brown homespun fabric with several ragged blankets for cover. In the other corner was a metal drum with a rack on top, substituting for a stove.

Brandy had never felt so rich as she did in that moment. She carefully hid her dismay and smiled at Maggie.

"Have a seat. Would you like some coffee?" the woman asked.

"That would be nice," Brandy said, thankful to have something to say.

Maggie took two dented tin cups from a shelf over the barrel and poured coffee from a pan on the rack.

"I'm sorry I don't have sugar or milk to offer."

"That's all right. I usually take mine just plain," Brandy lied.

She sipped the coffee and forced another awkward smile. It was so weak she could see the bottom of the cup through it. She hated accepting what must have been the last of Maggie's coffee, but she'd have felt even worse wasting it.

"Umm, this is good," she said, nodding at Maggie's anxious expression. "I do hate when coffee tastes like it's been boiled twice."

"Oh, yes," Maggie gushed, sitting at the table, her eyes bright once more. "So do I."

Brandy was glad she'd put the woman at ease.

Maggie leaned in and touched Brandy's arm. "I'm so glad you came by. I wanted to thank you for what you did yesterday in the store. Most folks won't come near David when he's having a fit, but you just rushed right in and helped. You weren't scared at all."

"Scared? Why he's a precious little boy. What on earth would I be scared of?"

Maggie glanced out the door and bit her lip. "Most folks act like they think they might catch what he has. The rest don't know whether he's crazy or possessed by the devil."

"What silliness. I don't know a lot about

epilepsia, but I know it has nothing to do with demons."

"Dorothy Walker said you was real good. You know Doc's been trying to get her to let him cut on her bunions for years, but she wouldn't do it. She says she felt better after only two days of using the salve you gave her."

"Well, I'm sure the bunions aren't gone, but the oils and garlic will soften them up and they'll eventually dissolve. I told her she's gonna have to stop wearing tight shoes, though."

"She had on a pair of Henry's old boots when I saw her, with two pairs of socks," Maggie laughed.

"Good, that's the best thing for her."

Brandy sipped the coffee and slowly got around to the real reason she'd come to see Maggie Bellows.

"I was thinking—"

"I was wondering—"

Both women spoke at the same time and then laughed and fell quiet again.

"Go ahead," Brandy encouraged.

Maggie stared into her cup for a moment and then looked into Brandy's eyes. Her own were bright with unshed tears.

"I was wondering if you have any miracle in that funny wagon of yours that'd help my Davey."

"I don't perform miracles—"

"Of course, I wouldn't have no money to pay you even if you did. But I'm real strong and able-bodied and I sew real good." She glanced down at the ragged dress she wore and added softly, "If you was to buy some proper fabric, that is."

"I don't know if I can help Davey or not. I've never treated anyone with his problem."

Brandy saw Maggie's face dissolve into a mask of despair, and she reached for the woman's hand.

"But my mother did one time, and I still have all her notes and remedies written down. Plus I heard about something when we passed through Wichita that I added on my own. I'd like to try, if you don't mind—and if you understand it might not do any good at all."

"I'd try near about anything right now. Doc says I ought to send him to Oklahoma City, to the asylum there. But I just can't do it. I'd miss him, and Darrel would, too. They're twins you know. Oh, they don't look much alike, but that's cause Davey's been poorly all his life. It'd just kill us both to send him away."

"Then we don't have anything to lose, do we? I've got what I need in the wagon. Would you like to come out and help me get it together? I'll bring it in and show you everything you'll need to know."

Maggie took her arm when she rose. "About the money—"

"You let me worry about that. I might take you up on your offer to sew me a new dress." She fingered the fabric of her olive-green skirt and grimaced. "I don't think I exactly fit in around here like this."

She didn't add that, compared to the sheriff's lady friend, she felt like a cheap trinket next to a pearl. But the encounter had shaken her confidence. She hadn't realized how much until that morning when she'd found herself wishing for a looking glass so she could check her appearance.

They found the boys lying on Dani's bed in the wagon, eyeing an assortment of treasures the little girl kept in an old cigar box. When they entered, Brandy saw Dani snatch something off the bed and thrust it into her skirt pocket. Another wave of apprehension swept over Brandy as her eyes met Dani's guilt-filled gaze.

Fearing her sister had purloined yet another trinket, Brandy vowed to have a stern talk with Dani as soon as possible. But with Maggie and the boys nearby, she knew the discussion would have to wait until they were alone in the wagon once more.

"We'll be in the house for a while, Dani," Brandy said, hiding her displeasure. "Why don't you let Sal out of the harness?"

"All right, Brandy," her sister said, scooting past the women and out the door like a shot. Dani's eagerness to be away from her told Brandy all she needed to know about the item her sister had hidden on their arrival.

"Now, then." Brandy took several jars and bottles down from various shelves inside the wagon and handed them to Maggie. Next, she went outside and, with Dani's help, lowered the platform. She climbed up and collected the rest of what she needed.

Back in the house, she instructed Maggie how to prepare the first treatment out of gotu kola, skullcap, pony root, and calamus root powder. Dani kept the boys entertained with the horse, the wagon, and whatever pilfered treasure she hid in her pocket. The sounds of their laughter had both Maggie and Brandy smiling in maternal affection.

Brandy opened a small flour sack and measured several scoops of the yellowish-brown powder into a wooden container. "This is something new I heard about in Wichita. It's called brewer's yeast. You mix two tablespoons into Davey's milk twice a day."

Brandy saw the embarrassed flush cover Maggie's face and remembered too late that the woman had said they had no milk.

"Don't worry," she said, trying to cover the awkward moment. "We'll think of something."

Next they brewed a syrup of mashed garlic cloves and honey. And, finally, they made a mixture of garlic and olive oil combined with black and blue cohosh, skullcap, and vervain. This they put into a wide-mouth canning jar and covered with a pint of vodka. Brandy explained that this last would have to stand for two weeks, then be strained and bottled for use as drops to be inserted into the boy's ears each night.

It was the empty pint bottle of vodka that

Adam spotted first as he stepped up to the door of Maggie's shack.

"Hello, Sheriff," Maggie said, noticing him standing in the narrow doorway. "Won't you come in?"

Brandy's hand shook and several drops of garlic oil splattered onto the tabletop. She recapped the bottle slowly and turned to face the man who'd humiliated her and robbed her of a good deal of her confidence in the last two days.

"Sheriff," she said coolly.

"I was surprised to see your wagon outside," he told her, cutting through the niceties. "I thought I made it clear I wanted you gone."

Brandy stared back at the angry gaze pinning her down. For a long minute, she couldn't think of a thing to say.

"Brandy's offered to help Davey," Maggie cut in, sensing the friction between the two. "Isn't that wonderful?"

Adam's eyes swept over the bottles and containers sitting in various disarray on the table. A grim line tightened his mouth.

"How is Davey?" he asked.

"Oh, he's fine today. A little tired and confused, but that's normal after a bad fit like he had yesterday."

Adam nodded and turned back to Brandy. "May I see you outside, Miss Ashton?"

"We're kind of busy right now. You'll have to wait—"

"Now."

Maggie touched Brandy's arm. "I'll finish up here."

Brandy disliked taking orders from the arrogant sheriff, but she didn't want to cause a scene in front of her new friend. After a few brief instructions to Maggie, she wiped her hands on a piece of cotton cloth and smoothed down her skirt.

"All right, Sheriff."

He stepped aside and she brushed past him as she went out onto the porch. She stopped by one of the posts, but when she would have turned to face him, he took her arm and led her around the corner of the house.

"Just what the hell do you think you're doing, you lying little cheat?" he snarled, gripping her elbow in his strong grasp.

Chapter Six

"Take your hands off me," Brandy said, pulling her elbow from the sheriff's grasp.

"I warned you that I won't stand for you swindling these people. God, you make me sick, taking advantage of that poor woman."

Brandy didn't know why the sheriff was so upset. She hadn't done anything but try to help Maggie. Still, she could understand his assumptions based on his earlier accusations and the empty liquor bottle, so she tried to explain.

"It's not what you think. I'm not selling Maggie liquor disguised as medicine. I know you believe I'm just peddling snake oil, but I would never give any child liquor. The vodka is for—"

"I know what vodka's for. And you can find some other town to sell your trumped-up booze in. Charming is my town, lady, and it's off limits to you and your kind. Take your sister and your painted wagon and get out. This is my final warning."

"Now just a minute, Sheriff," Brandy started.

"Sheriff."

Maggie's voice reached the pair and Adam quickly stepped back, finally releasing Brandy's arm.

She rubbed the red spot where his hand had held her captive, and she felt the tingling warmth of his skin still present there. With a frown, she looked up at him, wondering why her flesh should be pebbled with excitement instead of throbbing with pain.

"I think you misunderstood, Sheriff," Maggie said, coming around the side of the house to where Brandy and Adam stood. "I was the one who asked Brandy to help Davey. She came to my aid in the general store yesterday before you and the doctor arrived."

"Maggie, I know how you feel about Davey. If there was any way to help the boy I'd be the first to say do it. But everybody," he said, shooting a cold look at Brandy, "knows there's no cure for epilepsia."

"I'm not claiming to have a cure for the child," Brandy defended herself. "I'm only offering—"

"False hope." Adam cut her off again, his green eyes hard and angry. "No doubt at an exorbitant price. I know the way your kind works."

"Sheriff, you're wrong," Maggie told him. She smiled reassuringly at Brandy and took another step, putting herself between the sheriff and her friend.

"She hasn't asked me for a penny, Sheriff. Everything she's done today was out of the goodness of her heart, not for pay."

Adam stared down at Maggie, sadness softening his eyes. "Then tell me why she came here in the first place. Did you send for her, or did she just show up conveniently offering her assistance?"

"It wasn't like that," Maggie said, but he could see he'd hit on the truth.

"Don't you know what she's doing, Maggie? She'll probably give you the first batch free and make you think she's only concerned with helping Davey. It's when you come back for more that she'll have you right where she wants you. And then you can bet she'll want a great deal in return. Her kind always do."

Brandy realized something in that moment about the arrogant sheriff of Charming. He'd been hurt. Someone had made him distrust people. No, not people in general, she corrected, watching the way his eyes softened when he spoke to Maggie. Peddlers. People like her and Dani. Oddly, she realized she wanted to assure him he had nothing to fear from her.

"Sheriff McCullough."

He spun back to face her, and the tender expression was once more replaced with the dark mask of animosity she'd come to expect from him since her arrival.

"I'm not here to cheat anyone. I truly want to help, if I can. And I would never take money for something I didn't believe in, not from Maggie or anyone. If the people of your town aren't happy with my remedies and treatments, I'll leave."

"You'll leave, all right. But before you sell one more bottle of tonic."

"Sheriff, please, listen to her. The doctor hasn't offered me any hope. If she can help—"

"Doc didn't offer you hope because there isn't any, Maggie." Adam took the woman's shoulders gently in his hands and shook his head sympathetically. "Don't you know if I thought for a minute she could help Davey, I'd pay her myself."

The sound of a piercing animal scream rent the air, shattering the tender moment Adam's concern had bred.

Brandy froze, staring at the two combatants facing off in front of her. Before she could collect her scattered wits, Adam and Maggie both fell silent and then suddenly began running toward the back of the house. Brandy followed. Dani and the boys sprang out of the corn patch, where they'd been playing a game of hide and find, and fell in behind the adults.

Several yards from the meager vegetable garden, Brandy could see the top of her horse's head bobbing up and down in a clump of the tall, dry grass. She stopped, still unsure for a moment what had happened to cause the cry of pain from the animal.

"Oh, lordy," Maggie cried, hitching her skirt up and running forward. "Your poor horse must have fallen in the burn pit."

"What?" Brandy flattened her hand against her pounding heart and turned to the sheriff, hoping for some kind of an explanation.

"The pit where they burn the garbage," he replied grimly.

She watched, stunned, as Adam raced up behind Maggie, stopping at the edge of the hole. The thick prairie grass had grown so tall it hid the crater in the ground. The horse must have wandered off the edge, unaware the ground fell away suddenly.

Sal screamed again and Brandy snapped out of her confusion. Instantly she went into action.

"Help me get her out," she cried, passing Adam and Maggie. She slid down the side of the steep-edged pit, her clothes catching on the stiff stalks of grass, her scuffed boots sinking into the small amount of garbage that had been thrown in, but not yet burned.

"It's been so dry I was afraid to burn," Maggie babbled anxiously, watching Brandy's descent as she stood wringing her hands on her apron.

Adam slid into the hole beside Brandy, their heads disappearing beneath the tall yellow grass. The garbage pit wasn't deep, maybe two feet, but the grass grew tall from within it, making it seem deeper.

Brandy swiped earnestly at the dry brush, desperate to get closer to Sal.

Adam circled around and came up on the other side of the frightened nag. The terrified horse rolled her eyes and bucked, emitting another high-pitched roar.

"She's hurt," Brandy cried, her head disappearing beneath the tall grass as she dropped down to examine the horse's legs. "I can't see anything down here. We have to get her out."

"Stay here. I'll be right back."

Adam pulled himself out of the hole and scrambled to his knees. His hat fell off and landed in the patch of dirt edging the garden.

Maggie, Dani, and the twins all stood staring, their faces lined with worry.

"We'll need a blanket and some rope," Adam shouted. "And some heavy nails and a hammer."

He scanned the yard and cursed. The only tree in sight was a scraggly oak trying to spring up next to the corn patch.

"I have the blanket and the nails, but I don't have a rope or a hammer, Sheriff," Maggie wailed.

"We have some," Dani said, grabbing Darrel's hand. "Come on."

They darted off—Maggie to the house, Dani and the boys to the wagon, each trying to find the items the sheriff had ordered.

Adam turned back to the hole and saw the horse rear up once more. "Get out of there,

Miss Ashton," he called. "She might just trample you."

"She's frightened," Brandy shouted, grasping the bridle to hold the animal down. "I can't leave her alone."

"You're not going to do her any good if she kicks your head in," he warned, a note of alarm rising in his voice as the horse reared once more.

Maggie came running, clutching two old blankets and a handful of nails. Dani and the boys slid to a stop by her side.

Taking the rope and the blanket, Adam disappeared into the hole again.

"Hold this," he said, tossing the rope to Brandy. She caught it with one hand, the other still frantically holding the bridle.

Adam folded the blanket and wrapped it over the horse's back, the ends dangling down her rounded belly. He reached over her and took one end of the rope. Within minutes he'd fashioned it into a sling with two loops, one behind her front legs and the other in front of her hind legs. The blanket padded the rope and kept it from chafing the tender flesh of her belly.

"Climb out," he shouted to Brandy, crawling up the incline with the rope in his hands.

"No, I'll stay with Sal. I don't want her getting any more frightened than she already is and hurting herself worse."

"I need you up here to help me pull," he told her, his tone harsh enough to forestall further argument. "I can't do it by myself."

Without waiting for Brandy's reply, Adam jogged to the tree. Maggie appeared beside him and handed him the nails, which he hammered into the tree's scrawny trunk. He wrapped the rope around the tree and threaded it between the two nails.

Brandy gave Sal one final pat and hastened up the steep incline. She dashed up to the tree, breathing heavily, her face lined with worry.

"You better hope this tree holds, or she'll be worse off than she is now," he told her.

He positioned Maggie and Dani on the end of the rope. He took hold of the taut side, motioning Brandy in place behind him. Together they tugged, digging their heels into the hard earth.

"Pull!" he yelled, his face already red with exertion.

Brandy was startled by the feel of his hips and buttocks pressing into her lap, but she recovered quickly and did as he said. As he strained his arms on the rope, his bottom pushed harder against her. The feeling unsettled her, again drawing her mind from the urgency of the situation, but she couldn't step back without losing her footing.

"Take up the slack, Maggie," he shouted. "And wrap the rope around the nails so it can't slip back."

The first pull only succeeded in gaining them a few inches. Brandy dug in harder and reached her hands closer to Adam's on the rope.

"Pull!"

Sal tried to jerk back, but the nails held the rope and wouldn't allow her to undo the small amount of progress they'd managed to make.

Together Brandy and Adam pulled until Brandy's arms felt wrenched from the strain. Her hands burned as the hemp dug into her palms. Still, the rope only moved a few inches. Maggie and Dani quickly did their part, and the horse's head was at long last visible through the towering grass around the hole's rim.

Finally, Sal's front hooves got a hold on the top edge of the hole, and she sprang eagerly from the pit, throwing Adam back suddenly and toppling him in a heap on top of Brandy.

Maggie laughed out loud, all the while wrapping the slack around the bending tree in case the horse should try to go back again.

Adam hurriedly scampered off Brandy's legs and jumped guiltily to his feet. Without glancing backward, he started forward, slowing his steps as he eased up to the frantic horse.

One of Sal's back legs was bent, her right hoof barely resting on the ground. Brandy released the rope and went to the animal.

"Oh, poor Sal," she crooned. "Let me have a look, girl."

She examined the knee and the joint, relief rushing through her. "It's not broken," she said, releasing a sigh. "She's going to be all right." She smiled and turned to Adam with a happy laugh. "She's going to be just fine. Thank you, Sheriff."

Spontaneously, she threw her arms around his neck and hugged him. She missed the startled look of desire and dismay that swept across Adam's face.

Damn, in a minute she'd have him celebrating their success with a hearty dose of her vodka-laced tonic. With a harsh reprimand, Adam reminded himself whom he was dealing with here. His love of animals had demanded he help the horse, but he told himself again he felt nothing but loathing for the scheming peddler.

Brandy turned back with a smile, but it died on her face as she met the sheriff's stern countenance. Once more his face was filled with anger and distrust.

"This doesn't change anything," he said coldly. "I still want you out of town by tomorrow."

Maggie had come up behind them and she gasped at Adam's harsh words. "Sheriff, you can't mean that. Why, anyone can see this horse ain't fit to go nowhere."

"She'll have to get another one," he said, facing both of the women. "Joe at the livery has a couple I'm sure he'd be glad to sell."

"But, Sheriff—" Maggie said.

"I don't have enough money to buy another horse, Sheriff," Brandy told him frankly. "My sister and I have to settle for the winter. We barely have enough to get us through as it is."

"I thought business was particularly good

for you while I was gone?" he reminded her shrewdly.

Brandy met his gaze and forced herself to remain pleasant. Nothing was ever gained by throwing oil on a flaming fire. And the sheriff's temper had been a raging inferno waiting to explode ever since he'd seen her in town.

"Your town has been generous, Sheriff. They appreciate my remedies. But I still have to find a place to stay before the weather turns bad and travel is impossible."

"Then I suggest you get going. Because you won't be staying here."

"Adam," Maggie said, touching his arm. "She can stay here. She and her sister are welcome to park their wagon on my land."

"That's kind of you, Maggie," he told her, obviously disgusted that the woman he saw as naive and kindhearted had been taken in so quickly by Brandy. "But you know I can't allow that."

"You can't allow or disallow it. This is my land. Or have you forgotten my father was one of the few settlers already here before your father built up the town?"

Brandy could see the pair readying themselves for a standoff and she stepped in. "Can I speak with you, Sheriff?" she said.

Adam looked from Maggie to Brandy and back again.

"I'll take the children inside," Maggie said, herding the three wide-eyed youngsters away from the confrontation brewing.

"I can't stay here," Brandy said as soon as they were out of hearing. "Maggie barely has enough to get by on now. If Dani and I stayed, she'd only put herself out for us. You saw her face; she feels responsible for Sal's injury."

"So, leave."

"I can't do that either. I meant what I said. I don't have enough money to buy a horse and still get me and Dani through the winter months. Let me stay in town until Sal's leg heals, and I'll move on."

"No. I won't let you peddle that worthless elixir in town."

Brandy blew a loud breath out and clamped her teeth on a harsh retort. She counted slowly to ten and regained her temper before answering.

"All right, I'm willing to accept that. I'll park my wagon under the big oak outside of town. I won't approach any of the people in town."

He quirked an eyebrow and narrowed his eyes in doubt.

"But," she added, holding her hand up, "you agree that I can do business with anyone who comes looking for me, requesting my remedies."

Already he was shaking his head. "No, that isn't any kind of solution."

"I can always stay right here and conduct my business, and there isn't a thing you can do about it. Maggie said she owns her land. This isn't part of your father's property, is it?"

He grudgingly shook his head.

"Let me try to help Maggie and Davey. I swear to you I won't accept a penny from her, now or in the future. But I have to support myself and my sister, Sheriff. I have to take care of Dani."

That hit a nerve and Adam winced. How many times had he made a similar statement about his sisters? No one thought he'd be able to keep his family together, but he had. Through sheer guts and determination. If he lost something of himself along the way, it had been a small price to pay. Could he deny this young woman's request?

The question was whether he had any choice. She had him penned. If he refused her request, she could easily stay on Maggie's land for the entire winter, conducting all the business she liked. At least, if the woman were camped under the oak, Maggie wouldn't be put out and Adam could keep his eye on her better. With a disgusted shrug, he had to admit she held the ace card this time.

"I'll pull your wagon to the oak," he finally said, hitching his thumbs in the hip pockets of his denims. "But don't let me catch you drumming up business in town, or I'll be just as happy to pull your wagon to the county line and leave you there."

Brandy nodded. "As long as you know I won't turn away anyone who comes to me for help."

"Just promise me you'll leave Maggie and her boys alone. They've had a hard time of it the last couple of years since Jim ran off."

"I will promise you one thing. I'll keep my word and not take a penny from her. But you've got to let me try to help Davey. In fact," she added quickly, before he could protest, "you can help, too."

"What do you mean?"

"I gave Maggie something called brewer's yeast. A man in Wichita claims the nourishment can help children like Davey. But those boys need milk, and Maggie doesn't have the money for it. And that's one thing I can't do anything about."

He eyed her with trepidation and suspicion. Was she up to something? he wondered. He didn't trust her, probably never would. But she was right about one thing. Anyone could see Davey's frailty. It was obvious, even to Adam, that the boy needed nourishment above all.

"I think I can do something about the milk. But I'm warning you, Miss Ashton, if I find out you've stepped one hair outside of our agreement, you won't have to worry about where you'll spend the winter."

"How's that, Sheriff?" she asked, certain she knew what his answer would be.

He bent down and picked up his hat from the ground, slapping it against his thigh to rid it of the dust it had collected in the fall. "You'll have a nice warm room behind the bars of my jail, ma'am."

He set the hat atop his head and went to hitch his horse to the converted carnival wagon.

Chapter Seven

"For crying out loud, Dani, do you know what you almost did?"

Brandy's sister hung her head and lowered her eyes. "I'm sorry, Brandy. There was all that commotion when Davey had his fit. The pretty knife was just sitting there, and no one was looking. I couldn't help it."

"You've got to learn to help it! If you'd heard Sheriff McCullough, you'd know why I'm so worked up. He doesn't like us, Dani. And he's sure we're up to no good. If he knew about this—"

"I'll take it back," Dani said, her voice rife with regret.

"That isn't going to work this time. He forbade us to go back into town. How can we show up the very first day without a good reason for being there?"

She pressed her fingernail to her lip and tried to think of a way out of this predicament. The sheriff meant what he'd said, she was certain of that. He'd driven the wagon to the oak tree for them, using his strong gray gelding. Brandy had walked behind, to keep from sitting so close to him on the wagon seat and to keep her eye on Sal, tied behind the wagon.

But he'd repeated his warning before going on his way last night. And Brandy didn't doubt he'd carry out the threat.

"We have to go into town for supplies some time since we didn't get any the other day," Dani said. "I can put Mr. Owens's knife back on the cheese barrel then."

"Don't you think he's already missed it by now? If it mysteriously shows up on the barrel, and you were in the store when it went missing and when it reappeared, he'd get suspicious."

Brandy plopped down at the table and breathed a ragged sigh. Dani's bottom lip trembled and she brushed a tear off her cheek.

"I suppose I should punish you," Brandy ruefully told her sister. "But Papa never was much on discipline, and I'm not even sure what one does in a case like this. But I know you have to stop stealing, Dani." She scanned the small room, searching for guidance and a possible solution. Her eyes lit on the Bible on the shelf. She stood and collected the book, bringing it back to the table.

"Here," she said, thrusting it into Dani's startled hands. "Memorize five Bible verses that talk about stealing. Maybe that'll curb your wrongdoing. And keep me out of jail."

Dani thumbed the thin pages of the Bible and then cast a tearful gaze at Brandy. "I don't mean to get you in trouble, Brandy."

"I know. It'll be all right," Brandy told her, holding her hand out to her sister. They clasped hands for a moment; then Brandy brushed Dani's bangs back from her forehead and placed a kiss on the crown of her head.

"Go on now. Look in there. Maybe you'll find something that'll help. But please, Dani, don't take anything else. I surely don't relish the idea of spending a cold Oklahoma winter in a jail cell."

"So, she's still here."

Adam looked up from his desk at Suzanne, her figure outlined in the sunshine coming through the open door. She stepped into his office and shut the door behind her with a sharp slam.

"Hello, Suzanne," he said, wincing. His mouth turned down in an annoyed frown.

"Don't you hello me, Adam McCullough. You told me that dirty little duffer would be gone yesterday. Imagine my surprise when Dorothy Walker, of all people, told me she was camped out on your property at the edge of town." Suzanne wrinkled her nose, as though smelling something foul, and took another step toward him.

"Her horse is lame." He shuffled papers on his desk, trying to ignore the sharp stab of irritation Suzanne's presence seemed to bring with it more and more lately.

"I want you to get rid of her, Adam," she announced, straightening the bodice of her lime-green-and-rose-chintz day dress.

"I can't exactly run her out of town if she has no way to get out. Be reasonable, Suzanne." He tried to forestall another tantrum, sensing it was a useless effort considering the snit Suzanne appeared to be in today.

She huffed and stared down at the buttons on her gloves, fiddling with them as she waited for him to give in to her demand. In a moment, she looked up through her golden lashes, gauging his reaction to her annoyance.

He stared back, refusing to give in to her tantrum. He'd been subjected to one too many of her outbursts lately, and he'd begun to wonder what he'd ever seen in her in the first place.

"Oh, pooh," she said, crossing to his desk and waiting for him to rise and offer his chair. He hesitated a minute, irritated with her proprietary attitude. But his manners soon got the better of him and he stood up.

Suzanne sank into the squeaky wooden seat and adjusted the skirts of her dress across her lap. Reaching up with one hand, she removed a long, porcelain hatpin from the crown of her straw bonnet and set the hat aside.

Each move she made was smooth and practiced, calculated to make Adam notice the line of her jaw and the fullness of her breasts as she lifted her arms. And she didn't fail.

Arousal stung his loins. Exasperation quickly chased it away. He'd grown tired of Suzanne's teasing flirtations some time ago. He had to admit the only reason he'd continued to see her was because of the lack of female company in town. Sometimes he liked to share a meal with a woman, listen to her soft voice as she talked, or just enjoy her feminine scent. But lately his pleasure with Suzanne dimmed beneath her demands and broad hints. She wanted him to propose. But when he thought of a life with her, he backed off like a smart trout from a hook.

He liked living in the cabin he'd built after his sister's marriage. Jenny and her husband had lived in the big house while they'd saved enough money to buy some land in the next county. With both girls grown and Aunt Carmel to see to the house, he'd decided to take the opportunity to breathe a little. He found he enjoyed the cabin more than the grandiose structure his father had built, and he had no intention of moving back to town. But he knew Suzanne wanted to live in the pillared house when, and if, they ever married.

"Darling," she said, drawing his attention back to her. She'd removed her gloves and was running them through her hand slowly. "Daddy hasn't had two patients since that dreary peddler and her little sister came to town. You've got to do something." She tipped her head to one side and smiled up at him.

As much as he wanted Brandy Ashton out of Charming, Adam didn't like Suzanne's wheedling. He could tell she expected him to do her bidding, and the fact grated on his already taxed nerves.

"She'll move on as soon as her horse is able to pull the wagon, and not before," he said, realizing he enjoyed vexing the blonde, even if it meant putting up with Brandy Ashton for a little longer. "Besides, if I tried to throw her out into the middle of the prairie without a means of transportation, the folks around here would run me out of office."

"So what?" she said, snatching her hat off the desk and flouncing to her feet. "It isn't as though you need this job. Really, Adam, it's ridiculous anyway. You have more money than you could ever spend."

But not more than she could, he knew. If he married Suzanne, she'd bleed his accounts dry in no time. And even if he managed to control her spending by keeping a tight rein on her, he knew he'd pay the price everytime he refused her something she felt she had to have. Thinking of a life spent that way nearly made him shudder. He'd been considering breaking it off with her for good lately. It would be for the best to do it soon, he knew.

"I have work to do," he told her, taking her elbow and escorting her to the door. "We'll finish this discussion later."

He pulled the door open and stopped short as Brandy, still holding the knob in her hand, was jerked forward into his chest. Releasing the knob, she stumbled back.

"Excuse me," she stammered.

Adam reached to steady her, felt Suzanne's elbow stab into his ribs, and exhaled painfully.

"Miss Ashton. I'm surprised to see you here."

Brandy looked from Adam to Suzanne and back again. "I wanted to let you know my sister and I had come into town for a few supplies. We walked. The wagon's still outside of town. We won't be long."

He nodded and Brandy saw white lines of anger appear at the sides of the other woman's mouth. She didn't know why the blonde should dislike her so much or why she should care. Her only purpose for coming to the sheriff's office was to notify him that they were in town so he wouldn't come into the store to question them while Dani was trying to return the cheese knife.

"Fine, Miss Ashton," the sheriff said, drawing her attention back to the sheriff and her reason for being in town. Brandy realized the sheriff and the woman had been on their way out and she was blocking the door.

"Good day," she whispered, turning and hurrying back down the walkway.

The bell rang as she entered the general store. Dani stood by the counter, a small pile of staples in front of her and a peppermint stick in her mouth. Mr. Owens wasn't around.

Brandy hustled up to her sister. "Did you give the shopkeeper our order?"

"Yep, he's in the back getting it together now."

"I wish we didn't have to trade with him at all after the way he treated Maggie. But I suppose we have no choice in the matter now. Hurry and get it over with while I keep watch."

Brandy twisted her hip against the counter so she could see both the curtained doorway leading to the back and the barrel her sister was approaching. Her nerves stretched and tightened until she felt an ache begin at the base of her neck. She restlessly drummed her fingernails on the wooden counter, the tapping keeping sync with her accelerated heartbeat.

She saw Dani kneel beside the barrel and ease the knife halfway behind it. Mr. Owens would eventually see it there and, Brandy hoped, think it had fallen.

She heard the storekeeper's footsteps and tensed. His hand reached for the curtain; then she heard him mumble and turn back toward the storeroom. Her heart leaped to her throat, and she swallowed hard, feeling it drop back into place.

"All done," Dani assured Brandy, scurrying back to her side. She popped the sticky candy back into her mouth. The shopkeeper came out of the back room and smiled at Brandy. "Howdy, ma'am."

"Mr. Owens. How much do I owe you?"

He told her the amount and she counted

change from her pocket. Then she and Dani gathered up the supplies, placing them in a wicker basket they'd brought along, and hurried out into the bright sunshine. The air was crisp, a reminder that, despite the warmth, summer had given way to fall.

"That was close," Brandy whispered, hating the feeling that she'd unwittingly become her sister's coconspirator in crime.

"It was a cinch," Dani told her, smacking the peppermint.

Brandy frowned down at her. "I swear, Dani, sometimes I don't think you realize how serious this is, despite the Bible verses."

Dani rolled her eyes and groaned. "I told you I'd learned my lesson. And I put it back without any trouble, so stop worrying."

"Stop worrying? Dani, the sheriff was not happy to see me just now," she said, remembering the blonde. Why had she thought he'd be distracted by her with a woman like that around? She clutched her crocheted shawl around her shoulders and felt every bit as dowdy as she knew she must look.

"If his lady friend had had a mind to go in that store," Brandy said, "we'd have been caught."

"No, we wouldn't have. I ain't never been caught taking nothing before, nor putting it back neither. Now, smile," Dani coaxed, skipping along beside Brandy's long strides. "Remember what Ma always said. Nothing's ever so bad you can't find some good."

Brandy tried to recall her mother's words, but it was difficult to drum up any cheer. Always before, she and Dani had been able to find something to be happy about. But with their father's death, Brandy had inherited the burden of supporting herself and a little girl. Would it be more than she could handle?

"There's always a first time," she murmured, remembering her fear when Mr. Owens had nearly come out of the storeroom.

"Brandy?"

"Hum?"

"At least we met Maggie and Darrel and Davey. I've never had a best friend before. Now I have two."

Brandy smiled. "You're right, Dani. As long as you have friends, there's always something to be happy about."

She took her sister's hand and felt the tacky sugar. A grin covered Brandy's face. Maggie really was nice. And because of her, Brandy and Dani had a place to stay for a while. Maybe even the whole winter, if she could convince the sheriff she meant his town no harm.

Seeing Brandy's expression, Dani smiled, obviously assuming all was forgiven.

As they approached the edge of town, Dani's gaze was drawn to the big pillared house. She slowed her steps and stared up at the second-story veranda.

"Look at that," she said. "I noticed it first thing when we arrived in town. Who do you suppose lives in such a fine place?"

Brandy, too, had noticed the house. She shrugged, her eyes taking in the bright windows and shiny black shutters. She'd never seen anything so grand, and she wondered what it would be like to wake every morning in a fire-warmed room with ruffled curtains and rugs on the floors.

Knowing those kind of thoughts were useless, she tugged her sister's hand. "Come on, Dani," she said. "We'd better get going."

As they turned to walk away, Brandy heard the door open behind them. A strange sound, like wagon wheels on wood, made her stop and look back.

"Wait, please," a feminine voice called.

Brandy stepped closer, her eyes straining to see the shadowed area of the porch beneath the veranda.

"Yes?" she said, not certain whether the woman had spoken to her or someone else. She glanced around. Several townspeople hurried along the main street of town, but she and Dani were the only people anywhere near the house.

"I'd like to talk to you."

Dani clutched Brandy's hand, and she looked down into her sister's wary brown eyes.

"Who is it, Brandy?"

Shaking her head, Brandy said, "I don't know."

They took another tentative step toward the gate, and Brandy could see the shadow of a person in a chair.

"Are you talking to me, ma'am?" she asked, squinting.

"Yes. Please come closer."

Brandy reached for the gate latch, but Dani's fingers held hers in an unsteady grip. She smiled to reassure her little sister and released the latch. The gate swung open with a long, low cry of aged metal, and the two stepped into the yard.

"You're the herbwoman, aren't you?"

Dani's grasp loosened as she felt her sister relax. "Yes, yes, I am. Is there something I can do for you?"

Confident now that the woman had summoned her for business purposes, and not to scold them for gawking at her home, Brandy walked briskly up onto the porch. Her steps faltered a moment as she noticed the cane-backed wheelchair the woman sat in.

"Hi," Dani said, her usual vivaciousness getting the better of her hesitancy.

"Hello," the woman answered, motioning them forward. "I thought you'd gone. I'm happy to see you're still here."

"My horse went lame," Brandy explained, taking one of the white wicker chairs the older woman offered. "We'll be staying on a little longer."

"Oh, that's fine," the woman said. "I'm sorry about your horse, but I'm afraid your misfortune is my good luck. I wanted to see you. I wonder if you'd join me for tea?"

Brandy and Dani exchanged startled glances.

They'd never been invited to tea before. It sounded so glamorous to Brandy that she had to fight the urge to giggle. Dani's bright eyes suggested she felt the same. But Brandy remembered the sheriff's warning and shot a worried look down the street.

"I'm not supposed to do business in town," she said, noticing Dani's expression droop. She knew her sister was excited at the prospect of seeing inside the grand house, and she admitted to herself that she would like nothing more than to accept the invitation. But she couldn't risk the sheriff's wrath.

"Well, then, you're in luck. Technically my property is on the edge of town. So, you're not breaking any laws by being here. Besides, you don't seem to have any tonics or restoratives with you, and there's no ordinance against socializing."

Brandy smiled, already taking a liking to the woman. "Then we accept, ma'am."

"Just call me Carmel," she said, turning the wheeled chair around and leading them to the beveled door.

Dani's eyes widened as they entered the foyer. Her head swiveled from side to side, taking in the gleaming furnishings and the porcelain and brass figurines in the corner curio cabinet.

Seeing her sister's interest in the knick-knacks, Brandy cringed. Would Dani's urges get the better of her? Could her little sister resist such pretties? She'd have to keep her eye on Dani every moment.

111

A porcelain bird seemed to hold Dani's attention an unusually long time, drawing Carmel's notice. Brandy tried to distract her sister by taking her hand and tugging, but the girl continued to stare at the object.

"Pretty little thing, isn't it?"

Dani nodded. "I think it's about the most beautiful thing I've ever seen," she whispered.

Brandy's apprehension blossomed into outright alarm. Her fingers tightened on Dani's hand, and finally the girl looked away from the bird. But her eyes were confused as they read the fear on Brandy's face. Had she been thinking of taking the bird?

"It's not a very expensive piece," Carmel was saying, opening the door of the cherrywood cabinet. "In fact, you can buy them rather cheaply in a shop in Oklahoma City." She lifted the bird and fingered the feathered wing. "But this one seemed special somehow."

"It's the eyes," Dani said, surprising both Brandy and their host. The woman arched an eyebrow and looked back at the bird.

"Why, I believe you're right."

Dani stood next to the wheelchair and touched the bird's cornflower-blue head. "You see," she said, pointing her stubby finger at the beady eye. "You can see his free spirit in there. Like he just loves being a bird and flying across the sky."

A long silence followed Dani's childish observation. Then, Carmel looked up at Brandy and a trace of the spirit her sister had recognized in the figurine crossed the older woman's eyes. Brandy swallowed hard, feeling Carmel's pain. She'd been a free spirit once, too, Brandy felt certain. Her gaze fell to the chair.

"Take it, child," Carmel said, pressing the bird into Dani's hand.

Brandy's heart slammed against her ribs. What would her sister do? To have the object of her desires offered up to her might be too much for her to resist. She stepped forward to offer a protest, only to be startled by Dani's reply.

"No, thank you, ma'am. You keep it. Me and Brandy, we get to live in God's backyard. That's what my mama always called it. But you have to live in here, like that," she added, motioning to the wheelchair in childish innocence. "You need him more than I do."

Her short fingers gently set the bird back in the cabinet, and Brandy's breath rushed out in a whoosh. Pride rushed to her eyes in the form of tears and she smiled at Dani.

"You're a sweet child," Carmel said, taking Dani's hand. "Come on. I bet we can find you a treat."

They went into the parlor, where a cart held an ivory-and-gold teapot and a matching cup. A plate of cookies and tiny cakes caught Dani's eye, and her tongue darted out one side of her mouth.

Carmel rolled to the door and called for someone named Jean to bring two more cups. A young woman in a cotton dress and white apron hustled in and smiled at Brandy and

Dani as she set the extra cups and saucers down. Brandy noticed the terrible case of acne the otherwise pretty girl had, and immediately her mind began thinking of remedies to help her. But the maid left and Brandy's attention turned once more to her host.

"Now, then," Carmel said, pouring both Brandy and Dani a cup of tea and offering milk and sugar. "Tell me how it is you know so much about healing."

Brandy poured a generous amount of milk into her sister's cup and then a smaller amount in her own. Dani eyed the treats and Carmel pushed the plate toward her.

"My mother was an herbwoman. She taught me a lot before she died. Afterward, Dani, Pa, and I traveled around selling remedies. I picked up a few things of my own along the way and added them to what Mama showed me."

"Brandy has a real gift," Dani said, around a mouthful of iced cookie. She dusted crumbs from the corner of her lips with her tongue and added, "Pa always said so."

"I've heard good things about you from my neighbors," Carmel told Brandy. "I hope what I've heard is the truth."

"I've helped a few folks."

Carmel nodded and set her cup aside. "Would you be willing to help me?"

Brandy knew what was coming. She'd wondered about the woman's injury from the moment she saw her on the porch. Immediately assessing a person's needs and ailments was a habit of hers—as it most likely was for anyone in her business.

"If I can."

Brandy sipped her tea nervously, feeling oddly out of place in the fine surroundings. The walls were covered in a floral-print wall covering, with a contrasting border around the ceiling. The doorway held a pair of rose velvet draperies on a brass rod. A round table in the corner was covered with an embroidered lace shawl and held a porcelain lamp.

"My nephew's been giving you a hard time, I understand," Carmel said, drawing Brandy from her study of the room.

Brandy sipped the tea once more and raised her eyebrows. "Your nephew?"

"Adam McCullough."

Brandy's cup slid from the saucer in her hand and crashed to the floor. Beside her, she heard Dani choke on her tea cake.

Chapter Eight

Brandy swatted Dani between her shoulder blades, startling her sister into another fit of coughing. Reassured that Dani was all right, she grabbed a napkin from the tray and dropped to her knees to clean up the mess.

"Here, here," Carmel said. "Leave that. Jean'll clean it up."

Brandy sat back on her heels and surveyed the damage, cringing at sight of the fine china lying broken on the floor. Her stomach quaked and a momentary panic coursed through her. Gripping the smooth, wooden arms of her chair, she pulled herself limply into the seat, her hands tensing in her lap.

"Your nephew is Sheriff McCullough?"

Carmel nodded. "That's right. My sister Josephine's boy. Adam's a good fellow, but sometimes he gets wound up real easy. I keep telling him he needs to learn how to relax."

Dani sent her sister an anxious glance through eyes filled with tears from her coughing jag. Another short hack escaped and cookie crumbs shot from Dani's mouth. Brandy wished the chair would come alive and swallow her. If she had needed further proof how little she and Dani fit in with the people of Charming, she'd just been given a large dose.

"Yes, he was a bit intense," Brandy agreed.

Carmel laughed and handed Dani an embroidery-edged napkin.

"Intense. Yep, that's Adam all right. Of course, most times I just call him dull or boring. He wouldn't know how to have fun if the devil came up and gave him lessons personally."

Brandy forced a stiff smile, all the while wondering how fast she could get her sister and herself out of Carmel's parlor. If the sheriff should catch her having tea with his aunt, he'd run her out of town so fast her cheeks would have windburn.

Carmel offered Brandy another pink-iced cake, which she graciously declined. Nothing would get past the mountain of dread rising up in her throat.

"Not that it's his fault," their hostess continued. "You see, he lost his parents when he was only sixteen. And he had two overindulged little sisters looking to him for their every need. When I learned of my sister's death,

I came right away. But by then, they'd been on their own for nearly a year. Adam always took his responsibility so seriously. Even after I came, he wouldn't relinquish it. When the girls married and moved off, he took to mothering the whole town. Somewhere along the way, he forgot how to loosen up."

Nodding sympathetically, Brandy scanned the room for the quickest possible escape. She scooted to the edge of her seat and wriggled nervously.

"I bet you know how to have a good time," Carmel observed with a brisk nod of her graying head. "Why, you look like a girl with a real zest for life. You'd be good for my nephew."

Brandy jumped from her chair as if she'd been stabbed in the bottom with a hatpin. "I really should be going," she said, waving her hand at Dani, whose eyes bulged with surprise. "Thank you for the tea."

"Wait," Carmel said, grasping Brandy's fidgeting hand. "You haven't told me if you can help me."

Brandy glanced longingly at the curtained doorway. She wanted nothing more than to haul Dani out of the house and back to the wagon as fast as possible. The sheriff was going to kill her when he found out about this meeting. And his aunt was getting ideas. Brandy had seen that gleam of mischief flash in her sharp eyes.

But then, her gaze fell to the wheelchair and

Carmel's anxious expression. After one last, frantic glance at the doorway, Brandy slowly sat back down.

"Tell me what happened."

Carmel smiled. "Almost two years ago I was going to Oklahoma City. The stage lost a wheel right on the crest of a hill. We tumbled over and I was thrown out. Broke my hip. I was bedfast for three months. When I tried to get up after that, my joints had quit working. I haven't been able to take a step since."

"What did the doctor say?" Brandy asked.

Carmel hurrumphed. "That quack. He told me these things sometimes happen at my age. Can you imagine? I'm only fifty-two." She looked slightly abashed and added, "Well, maybe fifty-five. But that old beetle brain is ten years my senior if he's a day. I wanted to smash him over the head with my chamber pot. Adam's been advertising for another doctor for near about a year now, but we don't have a lot to offer the younger ones fresh out of university. They would rather practice in some city where they'll get paid in cash, not livestock."

"Have you tried to walk?"

Carmel glanced down and nodded. "I tried all the time at first." She met Brandy's gaze once more. "I couldn't do it then. But I know if I had some help for the pain and stiffness, I could now."

"You have feeling then?"

"Yes, yes, I can feel. Oh, some times I ache so I can't stand it. But I tell myself that's good.

To feel the pain, I mean. It is, isn't it?"

Brandy stared into the emerald eyes pleading with her for hope and couldn't speak. What if she offered the woman false encouragement? Fifty-five wasn't old, nor was it young. Complications could arise from a broken hip. Brandy had seen such cases before. Of course, she'd also seen women older than Carmel recover without difficulty. But this was the sheriff's aunt! What would he have to say about Brandy getting involved?

Dani leaned in, her expression expectant and uneasy. Brandy longed to tell them both she'd do it. But still she hesitated. Adam McCullough had made himself very specific on this point. Her responsibility to take care of her sister closed in on her. She had to think of Dani. The chill in the air was nothing compared with a bitter winter snow. Or worse, a jail cell.

"Brandy can do it, Miss Carmel, I know she can," Dani spouted, shooting her sister an anxious glance. "She can do anything."

"Dani!" Brandy's dismay filled her. What had her sister done?

"It's all right, Miss Ashton," Carmel said, seeming to sink farther into the chair. "I appreciate your sister's confidence and enthusiasm, but it's your help I need. I can pay you. Whatever you ask. Money is no problem, I assure you."

"It isn't that," Brandy said quickly, worried again what the sheriff would think of all this. She met two pairs of hopeful eyes, two equally staunch supporters. How could she refuse to help this sweet woman if there was anything she could do? The answer was obvious. She couldn't, even if it meant risking the sheriff's ire. Her better judgment took flight like a startled bird, and she felt her resolve topple.

"All right," Brandy finally agreed, certain she'd just made the biggest mistake of her life. "I'll do whatever I can. But I can't promise you anything, and I warn you your nephew isn't going to like this a bit."

Dani leaped to her feet and hugged her sister. Carmel's hands covered Brandy's and squeezed gratefully.

"Let me handle my nephew," Carmel said with a sly grin.

Still apprehensive despite Carmel's assurances, Brandy wondered how long it would be before she felt the full wrath of Adam McCullough.

As it turned out, she didn't have long to wait. That evening, just a few hours after she and Dani returned from town, the sheriff's heavy-handed pounding shook the walls of the wagon.

"Open up, Miss Ashton." He knocked again, harder this time. "I know you're in there."

Dani dropped the wooden spoon she'd been using to stir the potato soup she and Brandy had made for dinner. Her dark eyes flew open and her little rosebud mouth formed a surprised O.

122

Brandy forced a stiff smile and brushed back her sister's bangs. "Well, that didn't take long," she said, feigning a calm she didn't feel. "Stay here."

She opened the door, apprehensive but still mildly amused to see that her sister had retrieved the spoon and stood beside her brandishing it like a club.

"Good evening, Sheriff."

"The hell it is," he snapped. "I told you to stay away from my town. I warned you—"

"I have to have supplies, Sheriff. I went to your office to tell you we were there."

"I'm not talking about this morning and you know it. We had a deal. You said you wouldn't peddle your swill in town."

Brandy stepped down from the wagon, her bare feet carefully feeling the way as she continued to meet Adam's angry stare. "I don't sell swill, and I didn't break our agreement."

"Damned if you didn't. I just came from my aunt's house. She tells me you're going to make her walk again," he drawled sarcastically. His hands made fists at his sides, and she backed away, truly frightened by the force of his rage. He shook with it, trembled with the effort it took to keep his hands off her.

"I can explain."

"No!" he shouted, grabbing her shoulders. Dani cried out and Brandy's face paled. "Let me explain something to you. I'll drag your wagon to the county line and burn it if you go near my aunt again. I don't give a tinker's damn about you or your sister. I want you to stay out of my town and away from the people I care about." He shook her once and released her with a little push. "Do you understand me, Miss Ashton?"

Brandy grasped her upper arms where they continued to throb with the feel of his heated fingers. She drew a ragged breath and let it out with a huge sigh. "I understand, Sheriff."

He turned away, digging his hands through his thick hair. His chest rose and fell rapidly with each harsh breath he expelled. His steps as he started to walk away were stiff and measured.

"But I can't do it," Brandy said, knowing her words would unleash the fury he'd barely managed to control. He whipped around, and she forced herself not to cringe at the black look he wore.

"What did you say?"

"I said that I can't stay away from your aunt."

"Oh, yes, you can. And you will," he told her, his long legs quickly bringing him back to stand in front of her.

When her little sister's pudgy fingers twisted in her skirt, Brandy slipped an arm around Dani's shoulders. "I made a promise," she said firmly.

"Yes, you did. To me. And broke it in less than twenty-four hours. You're lucky I don't lock both of you in jail."

Dani trembled and Brandy felt her temper

rise. This man was frightening her sister. No matter that her own knees shook or that her heart slammed against her ribs until she felt bruised and breathless. She couldn't stand there and let him terrify a little girl.

"I haven't done anything wrong, Sheriff McCullough. And you have a lot of nerve coming here and threatening me. Your aunt asked for my help, and our bargain stated plainly that I could help anyone who came to me."

"Not my family," he ground out through clenched teeth. "Do you hear me? No one is going to hurt my aunt like that again. Carmel might not seem vulnerable most times, but in this situation, she can be very trusting. Especially with people she has no business believing." He shook his finger in front of her face. "I won't allow you to come through here weaving your dreams of miracles and then leave me to pick up the pieces."

Adam strode to where he'd tied the big gray horse. Brandy watched him swing into the saddle and take off across the field at a dangerous pace. Slowly, her pulse returned to normal.

"That wasn't so bad," she told Dani, drawing her sister close to her side.

Dani looked up at her with shock and doubt written across her young features. Brandy laughed nervously and Dani joined in.

"All right, so maybe it was," she admitted ruefully. At least she now knew the reason he disliked her. And despite her anger, she could even understand it.

"But he didn't order us to leave." Brandy saw his profile in the distance as he rode in the direction away from town, and she shook her head. "Not yet anyway. But I'm sure he will when he learns I've ignored his warning and continued to see his aunt."

Dani smiled broadly and hugged her sister, and Brandy knew she'd won the girl's respect. Maybe, just maybe, she'd do all right in her new role as surrogate parent, she thought.

Adam rode hard all the way to his cabin. He slid from his horse before it came to a full stop; then he tossed the reins over the post in the yard.

God, he wished he could just go into the little house and sleep in his own bed. He wanted peace, away from town and Aunt Carmel. But tonight was Jean's night off, and he always stayed in the house with Carmel so she wouldn't be alone in case anything happened.

He tossed a few things into a saddlebag and took a moment to fix himself a glass of whiskey. The amber liquid burned his throat and warmed his gut. Dropping into an old overstuffed chair, he propped his booted feet on the stone hearth.

The day had gone from bad to worse. And all of it could be traced back to the peddler with the Gypsy looks. Why had she chosen his town?

Between Suzanne's disdain and Carmel's illusions were his own confused thoughts. Brandy Ashton stirred him with her beauty and vibrance. He'd never known anyone who seemed so full of life. At the same time, he didn't trust her for a minute. No matter that half the town seemed to love her.

He knew her for the cheat she was, and he wouldn't be taken in by her looks and aura of virtue. No doubt it was a practiced trait she conveyed to persuade her customers and further her shady business.

He refused to let her get close to Carmel. He'd meant every word he'd said to Brandy Ashton earlier. He didn't wish the girl harm, but he would not allow her to beguile his aunt.

No, his mind was made up. It nettled him that in getting rid of the pair he'd be giving Suzanne just what she wanted. She'd obviously think he'd done her bidding yet again. But it couldn't be helped.

The peddler and her sister would have to go. The sooner the better.

The sun shone brightly the next morning, but the air held a threat of approaching winter. A nip bit into Adam's cheeks as he rode toward Maggie's cabin. He'd have liked to have gone faster, but as he turned to check the brown-and-white milk cow he led by a rope attached to his saddle, he slowed his pace even more.

The ramshackle house dismayed him every time he saw it. How could Jim have gone off like that and left Maggie and the boys alone? Adam knew the man sent money occasionally, no doubt to ease his conscience, but still his family had to struggle for every meal. He had to admit Brandy Ashton had been right about one thing. Maggie and the boys needed better nourishment.

He stopped in front of the house and tied his horse's reins to a termite-infested post. A chunk of the crumbling wood broke off and fell to the ground, turning into a pile of dust at his feet.

He shook his head and stepped gingerly onto the rotting porch.

"Maggie," he called, raising his hand to knock on the door.

She opened the door immediately, running her hands over her loosened bun in an effort to restore it to some order. She wore the same frayed cotton dress and apron she'd had on the day he and Brandy had pulled the horse from the garbage pit.

"Hello," he greeted, glancing past her to where the boys sat at the table eating breakfast. He could see their plates, and all they had on them were a short stack of flat cakes made of flour and water. His stomach tightened, and he swallowed the pity that welled up inside him. "I hope I'm not interrupting."

"Of course not, Sheriff. Won't you come in?"

Adam stepped into the cabin, sliding his hat from his head as he ducked through the low entrance. A chill permeated the room even though he could see the barrel in the corner releasing a thin stream of smoke.

"Can I get you something to eat, Sheriff? I'm afraid I don't have any coffee," she said, lowering her head in shame. "I haven't been to town for supplies since Davey's fit the last time."

Adam knew she had no money for things like coffee. Owens had told him her bill at the general store continued to grow, and she hadn't received any money from Jim in a while. Again he wished he could get his hands on her worthless husband.

"That's all right," he told her, setting his hat on the table and ruffling both boys' hair as he passed. "I've already eaten."

"What can I do for you?"

He watched her eye the boys as they finished off the last of the flat cakes, and he wondered if she'd had any or if she'd given it all to her children.

"Well, I hope you can do something for Earl Hawkins. I was talking to him the other day, and he told me how his favorite milk cow Tilly had gotten real mean lately. She won't let his other cow in the same pasture with her or in the barn either. Darnedest thing, but that's what he told me. So, I was thinking, you have all this land and I was wondering if maybe you'd mind keeping the other cow here for a while. Earl said you were welcome to all the milk she gave if you'd oblige him by letting her stay until Tilly gets this bee out of her bonnet."

"A cow? I don't have any place for a cow, Sheriff."

"Well, I could build a little lean-to out by the side of the house. That'd do her for a while. And a little fencing alongside would keep her penned. You'd get some good butter and cheese out of the deal, too. Maybe enough to last through winter."

Maggie's eyes narrowed suspiciously as Adam shuffled his feet and cleared his throat. He saw her back stiffen and felt certain she'd figured out what he was up to. Then her gaze fell to the two little boys wolfing down the dry flat cakes and her expression softened.

"I'd be glad to help Mr. Hawkins, Sheriff. You tell him it'd be my pleasure to keep his cow. And, Sheriff," she added, staring at him with wide, bright eyes. "Thank you."

Adam nodded, embarrassed. She'd seen through his ploy. But she loved those boys more than she valued her pride, and so she'd accepted. He'd paid Hawkins a fair price for the cow and sworn him to secrecy, not knowing if Maggie would even take the animal. Now, he was glad he'd done it. If anyone asked, they'd be told the story he himself had just told Maggie. But the cow was hers.

Earl Hawkins, a widow these last three years, had been only too glad to help Maggie and her boys. Adam suspected he had a soft spot for her. But as long as she was married to Jim, Earl could only be her friend.

"I'll start on that lean-to and fence right

away. We can't have the cow wandering back to Hawkins's place. No telling what old Tilly would do."

He retrieved his hat from the table and went outside. The morning was clear and cool, and he went to work immediately. Soon, the boys came out and joined him, and together they worked until late that evening. When he left, Maggie pressed his hand and again thanked him. The boys stared up with worshipful gazes and he felt ten feet tall—until he remembered whose idea it had been to get the cow for Maggie. He had to admit he owed Brandy Ashton a debt of thanks, if only for this one thing.

Chapter Nine

Adam passed the carnival wagon on his way back to town. He considered stopping long enough to inform Brandy about the cow. After all, it was her idea. She deserved to know that Maggie and the boys were enjoying milk with their breakfast for the first time in a long time.

But he remembered how they'd parted, and he tipped his hat over his forehead and rode on. She might be happy to learn about the cow, but she certainly wouldn't be happy to see him at her door again.

Again, he felt bad because of the way he'd spoken to Brandy. But on this one point, he would not be swayed. She would have to leave his aunt alone.

He went on to Carmel's house, his thoughts

still on the beautiful peddler. When he stepped through the curtained doorway into his aunt's parlor, he thought his mind had conjured Brandy up. But when she glanced at him and he saw her eyes widen with alarm, his anger topped out.

"What are you doing here?" he demanded, striding into the room.

Brandy set her teacup on the low table and shifted in her seat. Adam saw her sister scoot closer to Brandy on the forest-green velvet settee, and he felt a twinge of remorse, but he refused to let it deflect his ire.

His aunt wheeled her chair closer to where he stood. "I invited Brandy and Dani for tea, and they were gracious enough to accept."

Adam's gaze fell to the cluster of brown corked bottles on the table, and his mouth thinned into a grim line. "Tea, huh? What is all that, condiments?"

Carmel flushed and Brandy took her sister's hand. "I also asked Brandy to help me. Again, she was kind enough to agree."

"Get out," he ordered, facing Brandy coldly.

"Adam!" Carmel shouted, wheeling up next to him. "Stop it right now. You're being rude."

"That's the least of what I'm going to be if that cheat and her sister don't leave right now."

"I said stop it. I invited them here. They're my guests."

"And this is still my house. I want both of you out of here this minute, Miss Ashton. And don't ever let me hear you've come back."

Carmel reached out and clutched his forearm, her bony fingers digging into the rigid muscle there. "Stop it, I said. You have no right to do this."

Brandy leaped to her feet and dragged Dani along with her. She circled the small sofa and skirted the sheriff.

"I promised your aunt I'd help her, Sheriff. I gave her my word."

"Your word!" He snorted derisively and took a step toward her. "What good is that? A promise made by a charlatan?"

"I'm not a charlatan. I've told you before—"

"And I told you, stay away from my family. If the rest of this town has nothing better to do with their money than throw it away on your snake oil, there's very little I can do about it. But I forbid you to swindle my aunt."

"Adam, please," Carmel pleaded, clutching his taut arm. "Let her help. I know she can."

The desperate pleas cut through Adam's anger, and he faced his aunt, his eyes softening. He knelt before the wheelchair and grasped her hand. "Don't you think I'd do anything if I thought it would make you walk again? Don't you know I'd give every penny I have? But this woman is a fraud. She can't heal people. Aunt Carmel, we've been through this before. How much money have we spent on potions and tonics? How many advertisements have you sent away for out of those magazines? Nothing worked. The doctor told you there was no cure. Please don't do this to yourself again. Don't do it to me."

"She can help. I know she can. She helped Dorothy, and she's even offered to help Maggie's little boy."

Adam sprang to his feet and dropped his aunt's hand. "How much?" He looked at Brandy, his features lined with bitter resentment. "How much did she tell you it would cost for this cure?"

"I wanted to talk to you about that, Sheriff—" Brandy began.

"Nothing," Carmel cut in sharply. She faced her nephew proudly, her wrinkled chin tilted up. "She isn't charging me a single cent."

"What kind of trick is this?" he asked, looking from Brandy to his aunt and back again.

"It isn't a trick," Brandy said. "Can we talk somewhere?"

"Yeah, right here. I want my aunt to hear everything you have to say. What are you going to tell me? That you know there's no cure? That's why you aren't going to charge her? Answer me, Miss Ashton."

"I didn't promise your aunt a cure, Sheriff. I offered to help her. And I thought you and I could work out another deal."

"Oh, you did, huh? Like what? I pay you some exorbitant amount and you leave my aunt alone? Is that what this is all about?"

"No. I try to help your aunt, no promises. If I do any good at all, you let me and Dani stay here for the winter. If I can't help her, we'll leave before the first snow."

Already he was shaking his head. "No. I don't want you anywhere near my aunt. For that matter I don't want you in my town. It was a mistake to let you stay. I should have known you wouldn't keep your end of the bargain."

"I did keep it. I didn't bring my wagon back to town. I've only helped the people who've come to me."

"Are you telling me my aunt came to you for help?" He lifted one eyebrow sardonically. "You'll understand if I find that difficult to believe."

"I'll go out there if I have to, Adam," Carmel told him. "I told her I would and I meant it. But Brandy offered to come here to make it easier for me."

"I'm sorry, Aunt Carmel," he said, turning back to face Brandy. "I can't allow her to do this."

"You can't stop me, Adam. If you force Brandy to go, I'll follow her. I can do it, too. I have some money of my own, you know. And I'll pay her whatever she asks. You can't prevent me from seeking her help. You can only make it more difficult for me. Or you can make it easier. I'm determined to do this, Adam. I just have a feeling about it this time."

"I want to help if I can, Sheriff," Brandy added. "And if I can't, I'll admit it. Then my sister and I will leave Charming, for good. You have my word. No matter what you think, I always keep my word. Give me half a chance. I'll prove it to you."

Adam shoved his hands into the pockets of his denims and stared at Brandy Ashton. Her little sister watched him with enormous brown eyes full of fear and hope. He turned to Carmel. She smiled at him, her lined mouth reminding him of his mother's smile.

"I don't see that I have a choice in the matter," he said, shaking his head grimly. "I've never seen you so resolute before." He turned to Brandy and the compassion fled from his eyes. "But know this, Miss Ashton. I won't change my mind. If I don't see some improvement in my aunt soon, you and your sister will leave my town. And I don't ever want to see you here again."

Brandy nodded, her hand clutching Dani's in the fold of her skirt. She suppressed her joy, knowing there was a possibility it was premature. But as she watched the sheriff storm from the room, then heard the front door slam behind him, she couldn't stop the smile that spread across her face.

Adam loved his aunt very much. Underneath his gruff exterior, he really did have a soft heart. No matter how he might bark and growl, someone with a tender soul would always be kind and fair in the end. She should have realized it sooner, but his hostility toward her and Dani had cloaked his true nature.

"He really is a good fellow, when you get to know him," Carmel said, her pink cheeks lined with a frown. She offered an apologetic look to Brandy and Dani.

"I can see that," Brandy told her, surprising the older woman. "What I don't understand is why he acts so boorish."

"I told you before. He forgot how to have fun. He hasn't smiled or laughed in so long I'm afraid his face would crack if he tried to."

Dani went to sit on the settee next to Carmel's chair, and the woman took her small hand and patted it reassuringly. Brandy continued to face the doorway, her mind following the sheriff. Could she help him? He wouldn't appreciate it if she tried. If he knew what she was up to.

With the first germ of an idea niggling her mind, she forced her attention back to Carmel.

"This is wintergreen oil," she said, picking up one of the brown bottles. "I want you to rub it into the hip joints at least twice a day. Now, let's talk about your diet."

Adam pushed aside his annoyance and resigned himself to staying in the big house in town for a while. At least until the peddler and her sister left town and his aunt was safe from their machinations. He couldn't very well keep his eye on what schemes Brandy might be cooking up if he weren't nearby.

He'd have liked to have stayed earlier to see just what concoctions Brandy had foisted off on his aunt, but he still had work to do, a town to run.

"How long are you gonna keep me in here," an irritated voice called from the far cell. The husk of intoxication still sounded in his voice.

"Until you learn your lesson," Adam told his prisoner, Rib Burnett. "This is the third time I've had to haul your carcass out of Nell's for unruly behavior."

"I done tole you that little blonde gal she's got working there has had her eye on me."

"It looked more like the heel of her shoe to me, when I arrived."

"She acts all sweet faced whenever Nell's lookin', but she wants me all right."

"Well, Nell doesn't. I told you the last time to stay out of her place. This time you're going to have to cool off here with me for a while."

"It ain't fair, I tell you," his prisoner complained.

"Fair or not, I'll let you go in the morning—if you pipe down and let me get back to work."

The man grumbled a rude comment and settled back down on his cot. Adam spent the rest of the day doing paperwork and considering the odd turns his life had taken since he'd returned from Oklahoma City.

He was no longer attracted to Suzanne, an eventuality that had been coming on for some time. There was a woman he had to admit he found extremely desirable in Charming now, but Brandy Ashton's questionable character definitely took her out of the running as a possible companion.

He told himself he really should spend time

with her, just to ascertain her motives and methods of operation. But he knew his urge to see her again had more to do with the way she looked at him out of her strange dark eyes.

He felt those eyes had seen a lot in the course of her short life, but her travels hadn't hardened her. In fact, she seemed incredibly innocent and sincere at times. Which was, no doubt, why she fared so well at her business. Folks just took to her natural exuberance and wanted to purchase a piece of the vivacity she possessed. He had to admit he'd felt himself drawn to it more than once.

When the shadows shifted and Adam's office darkened, he looked toward the window, surprised to see the sun setting. He'd burned daylight thinking of the peddler; Carmel would be expecting him for supper soon.

Rachel from the hotel restaurant came in with a plate for Rib. The man groused some more, but finally ate his dinner.

Adam shuffled the unfinished paperwork aside for another day and collected his hat from the rack. After saying good night to Rib, he locked his office and strolled down the street, checking on the bank, the general store, and the harness shop. All the doors were locked, the lights inside extinguished. The only places still open were the hotel restaurant and Nell's Lemonade Parlor.

He went into the latter and ordered a whiskey before going home. He felt certain he'd need it to withstand the lecture Carmel was sure to give him over dinner. His behavior today had been inexcusable, but necessary.

"Trouble, Sheriff?" The buxom redhead asked, leaning over the polished bar.

Adam downed the drink and she poured another. "Nothing I can't handle, Nell. How are you?"

"Good, real good. Better now."

"How's that?" he asked absently, savoring the second whiskey. He sipped it slowly.

"Since Brandy took care of my bursitis."

Adam choked and the whiskey burned a fiery trail down his throat to his gut. His stomach clenched in reaction to the sudden heat, and he pressed his hand against the buckle of his belt.

"You all right, Sheriff?"

He nodded, wiping the back of his hand across his mouth. He pushed the half-empty glass of whiskey aside.

"That girl's a wonder, ain't she?" Nell continued, unaware of Adam's discomfort. She lifted her arm and made a big circle in the air with her elbow. "You see that? I can't tell you the last time I could move my shoulder so good."

"Nell, I didn't even know you had bursitis. Why haven't you seen Doc about it?"

"I went to see the doc," she said, pursing her red lips. "Suzanne told me I had to have cash money before I could get seen. Well, I didn't have no cash, business being down and all. This ain't no boomtown, you know, in the best of times."

"I didn't know Doc was turning away patients."

"Not patients, Sheriff. Saloon owners. And it ain't the doc doing it. It's Suzanne."

Three furrows appeared between Adam's golden brows as he digested this new bit of information. "So, how'd you get our little peddler to help you. You're not telling me she did it for free?"

"Nah, but as it happens I had plenty of what she needed."

"Which was?" The furrow disappeared as he arched one brow.

"A pint of vodka. Said she needed it for Maggie's kid. The one with the fits. If you ask me I got the best end of that bargain."

She nodded her head once, the feather over her left ear bobbing. She grinned and shifted her shoulder again to emphasize her point.

Adam absently finished off his drink and said good night. He didn't know what to make of this latest development. If Brandy had gone to Nell for the vodka, then that meant she didn't keep her own stock of liquor on hand. Did that mean she didn't use it often? Somehow, that thought made his steps lighter as he walked home.

Of course, it could just mean she'd run out. That made more sense, and it substantiated his impression of her as nothing but a swill-selling charlatan.

He opened the gate, wincing when it shrieked even more loudly than usual. Tomorrow, he'd stick around and catch up on the needed repairs he'd been neglecting.

Laughter greeted him when he entered the house. For a moment, he stood frozen in the foyer. The sounds sent warmth flooding through him, reminding him of school days when he'd rush in and hear his parents chatting and laughing together. Time rolled back, to before the fire. He could smell the grass and the rain in the air. He could see his sisters, Jenny and Beth, bounding down the stairs, their ruffled dresses swaying and their pigtails bobbing against their shoulders. For an instant, he felt the corners of his mouth begin to turn up.

Just then, Dani darted through the parlor doorway and skidded to a stop in front of him. Her dress was made of coarse, faded malachite fabric and had several spots worn thin. Her dark hair shone, but it was untidy and tied with a frayed pink ribbon.

"Hiya," she said, throwing her hand up in greeting as she took off across the parquet floor and disappeared into his dining room.

A hot wave of resentment coursed through him. Instead of being the welcoming abode he'd expected, his house had turned into the enemy camp.

He followed the little termagant into the dining room and felt surprise wash over him anew. Brandy was dishing up several steaming bowls of vegetables and instructing his aunt on avoiding something called nightshade plants.

"Adam," Carmel called, a bright smile of welcome crossing her face. "Come in. Brandy made supper, and I tell you, it looks delicious."

His resentment blossomed into anger. "Actually, I was thinking of going to the hotel for supper," he lied.

He knew his feelings were childish and petty, but he couldn't help it. Why had Carmel insisted on letting the woman stay?

"Nonsense. Brandy's made more than enough to go around. She's instructing me in the proper diet I need to follow for her treatment to work."

He belatedly remembered his hat and removed it, hanging it on the corner of his chair. He took a seat at the table and eyed the delicious-smelling food. His mouth watered and he remembered he'd skipped dinner after finding Brandy with his aunt.

"Help yourself, Sheriff," Brandy said, passing him a bowl of bright orange carrots.

"They look funny," he observed.

"Adam!" Carmel admonished.

Brandy grinned nervously at Adam. She told herself it shouldn't matter, but she secretly wanted him to be pleased with her efforts.

"They're steamed, Sheriff," she informed him without rancor. "It's healthier than boiling."

She passed several bowls around, filling her own plate as well as Dani's. She watched Adam's face anxiously as he took his first bite and breathed a satisfied sigh when he nodded his approval.

"Very good," he reluctantly admitted. Actually they were the best vegetables he'd eaten in a long time, but he refrained from mentioning that fact. Instead, he forked another carrot into his mouth.

"Thank you," Brandy said, feeling a flush color her cheeks. When she looked up at him, he seemed to notice the blush she couldn't hide. His eyes widened in surprise, and a bewildered expression filled his Kelly-green eyes.

Carmel grinned, apparently pleased with their shaky truce, and shoveled a spoonful of greens into her mouth. Dani ignored the adults, intent on eating all the food laid out before her and experimenting with the heavy sterling flatwear, crystal goblets, and china dishes.

The rest of the meal passed pleasantly, and Adam was glad he hadn't gone to the hotel after all. And not just because the food was better. Brandy and her sister entertained them with stories of all the places they'd been. Too soon Dani's head began to nod, and Brandy declared they'd stayed way too long.

"Adam, why don't you walk the girls home?" Carmel suggested, touching Dani's hair lightly. She stared longingly at the little girl, missing the alarmed look Adam and Brandy exchanged.

"Really, that isn't necessary. It's not far."

Adam saw the flush cover Brandy's cheeks again and thought how strange it was for a woman of her experiences to still blush so easily.

"I'd be glad to," he heard himself saying.

Brandy and Dani said their good nights to Carmel, who thanked Brandy for all her help and impulsively hugged Dani. The little girl hugged her back and patted Carmel's wrinkled cheek affectionately.

Outside the air nipped their cheeks, and Brandy removed her shawl and draped it across Dani's small shoulders. Adam saw the gesture and wondered if the thin brown shawl was all the two had to get them through the winter. It wouldn't be enough when the snow came and the temperature dropped below freezing.

Again he wondered why he should even care. Their welfare was no concern of his. He had enough on his plate just worrying about his Aunt Carmel and the people of his town.

They walked along silently until the oak tree came into sight. Dani's feet dragged and her head drooped as she made her way to the wagon.

"Go on and get ready for bed," Brandy told her. "I'll be right in."

For once, Dani didn't argue. The combination of the abundant supper and the walk home had drained the last of her youthful energy.

"Good night, Sheriff," Dani whispered.

Her squeaky voice reminded him of his sisters at that age, and Adam felt a lump rise in his throat. "Good night," he said.

As the door closed behind Dani, Brandy

realized she and the Sheriff were all alone. It seemed intimate somehow, standing beneath the overhanging branches of the huge tree, starlight glistening above them, the moon's bright yellow glow illuminating the golden grass around them. She cleared her throat nervously.

"Thank you for seeing us home, Sheriff."

Adam's gaze swept over the carnival wagon and he grimaced. How could anyone refer to the thing as home? Yet the two seemed happier than he'd ever felt in his father's house.

"Well, I guess you've noticed I'm no match for my aunt when she gets an idea in her head. I've never been able to refuse her much of anything."

Brandy had indeed noticed, and she thought it said a great deal about his character. "She's a wonderful lady. I like her a lot. And Dani seemed taken with her from the first moment."

"Carmel's had a lot of experience with little girls. She helped me raise my sisters after my parent's death."

"She told me about the fire. I'm sorry. It must have been a difficult time for you."

He shrugged. "I did all right."

Brandy wondered if that were entirely true. She suspected the tragedy had taken its toll on him in a lot of ways.

"I better go in to see about Dani," she said, realizing she didn't want to leave him yet. The relief she'd felt when she learned he wasn't married to Suzanne swept over her again. She remembered their kiss and looked up into his eyes. Was he remembering it as well? Was he thinking of kissing her again?

He reached out and laid his hand on her arm. "I want to apologize for my behavior earlier. I had no right to say some of the things I said to you."

Brandy's face registered her surprise, but she quickly recovered and said, "You were just looking out for your aunt. I can't fault you for that."

"I meant what I said. I don't want her hurt again. But that was no excuse for my rudeness. I know my aunt better than anyone. If she wanted to see you bad enough, she'd have found a way."

"I swear I didn't make her any promises save one. That I would do all I could to help her."

He nodded and Brandy could feel the tense silence engulf them. He leaned in as if he meant to press his lips to hers once more, and she felt her breath solidify in her throat.

Then, he stepped back and dipped his head. "Good night," he murmured, turning and disappearing into the shadows of the night.

Chapter Ten

"Mornin', Sheriff," Dorothy Walker called as she strolled by the gate the next morning on her way to town. The large pair of men's boots she'd donned clumped along like paddles, but she wore a broad smile.

Adam lifted the oilcan he'd been using to lubricate the gate hinges and called back, "Mornin', Miz Walker."

She walked on, and Adam swung the gate back and forth, testing it. Satisfied, he stood up.

"Mornin', Sheriff," Hershall Putner greeted him.

Adam leaned against the low fence and tipped his hat back. "Mornin', Hershall. How's things at the harness shop?"

The young man stopped, scratching his chest

absentmindedly. "Good, good. I just passed that peddler's wagon back a ways. I'm glad to see you changed your mind about lettin' her stay on."

"Her horse went lame. What could I do?"

"Yep, that's the way I heard it," Hershall said, nodding his approval. "Still, I can't say I'm too broke up over her bad luck. She tell you she fixed up my ulcer?"

Adam sighed and shook his head. "Nope, she didn't mention it," he said.

"Sure enough. Said I had everything I needed growing wild right in my own yard. Showed me how to brew myself a batch when the one she give me runs out."

"Well, I hope it helps," Adam grudgingly offered.

"Oh, it's done helped," Hershall told him, patting his slightly rounded belly where it puffed over the waistband of his trousers. "I've been eatin' like a hoss these last four, five days."

Adam felt his irritation growing. Was he the only one who didn't think of Brandy Ashton as some kind of miracle worker? His fingers tightened on the handle of the oilcan, but his face remained impassive.

"She's not at all hard on the old peepers, either. Eh, Sheriff?"

Adam wasn't about to admit to Hershall that he'd noticed that fact right away. The man's flapping lips would have the news spread through town before dinner. Adam clenched his teeth and remained silent.

"Well, I better get along. See ya round."

"Good-bye, Hershall," Adam said brusquely, slamming the gate closed so hard the latch fell into place and wedged tightly.

He stooped down to inspect the latch, noticed the latch pin was rusted, and applied some of the oil to it. He set the can aside and tried the latch again, but it still didn't move.

"Mornin', Sheriff," another voice sang out.

Adam grunted and kept tugging on the stubborn piece of metal. Finally the voice registered. His gaze focused through the rails of the fence and his eyes widened. He looked up, past the full purple skirt to the yellow blouse swooping low on the smooth pale skin of Brandy Ashton's throat and, finally, to her deep black eyes.

"Miss Ashton." He pushed to his feet, knocking the oilcan over and spilling the thick liquid onto the ground. With a curse, he set the can right, then realized his fingers were coated with oil.

"We're here to see your aunt," she told him, glancing down at the closed gate.

He brushed his hands down the front of his denims and grimaced at the stains they left behind.

"I'm having a little, um, trouble with the latch. It seems to be stuck." He tried once more to force the metal back, but it refused to budge. "Here, let me give you a hand."

Reaching across the waist-high fence, he

grasped Dani under her arms and hefted her over to his side. He turned to Brandy.

"Uh, that's all right, Sheriff. Maybe I can just—"

"Come on. It'll only take a second."

Color flooded her face and she glanced help-lessly to Dani. But her sister had already trotted up the steps and disappeared into the house.

"Miss Ashton?"

"I don't think—"

"Just come closer and I'll lift you over."

Again she hesitated. Thoughts of the first time he lifted her from the wagon flooded her mind. Something warm and fluttery swept through her middle. She remembered the way he'd kissed her in his office, like a man dying of thirst dipping cold water from a well.

"I do have other things to do," he said, snap-ping her out of her fanciful thoughts. Brandy realized she was being silly. He'd only offered because there was no other way into the yard. Nervously she took a step forward, easing up to the fence.

His strong arms reached over the rail. One went behind her back. He bent at the waist and tucked the other below her knees. In a steady, fluid motion, he swept her off her feet and against his chest. Swinging about, he lifted her over the rail. But the wide swath of her skirt caught on one of the spires.

"Ooops," he said, juggling her higher in his embrace. "You're caught."

"Oh, don't tear my skirt. It's one of my best."

Brandy winced. Why had she blurted that out? She hadn't wanted Adam to know she'd taken care with her appearance this morning in case he should show up at Carmel's again. She was thankful he didn't seem to notice her slip. His attention focused on their predicament; he furrowed his brows and bent to loosen the material.

Again he juggled her, and this time her breasts came into contact with the solid wall of his chest. He cursed and attempted to set her on her feet, but that only succeeded in lifting her skirt up and exposing her pantalets. With a flush covering his cheeks, he bounced her up into his arms again.

"Here, let me try," she said, reaching behind her. He turned with her so she could maneuver the fabric free. Her fingers were steadier than his had been, and she accomplished the task in a few seconds. She thought she heard him breathe a ragged sigh as he let her slide to her feet.

"Thank you," she whispered, smoothing the skirt back into place.

He cleared his throat and turned his attention back to the gate. With a swift jerk, he pulled back on the latch. This time it slid up easily.

"Would you look at that?" he said, disgustedly. He plopped his hands on his hips, one leg bent at the knee, and frowned at the cantankerous fence.

Brandy bit back a smile. "Well, I better get

155

inside." She turned away, snapped her fingers, and looked back. "I almost forgot. I told your aunt she'd have to give up things like eggs and milk and cheese for a while. They aggravate the swollen joints in her hips. She told me about the cow you took to Maggie. That was a real sweet thing to do." She smiled, but he only continued to look at her with his usual stern countenance and she felt the grin die. "Anyway," she said. "We thought maybe you could ask Maggie to look after Carmel's chickens for a while. Your aunt thought it would be a good idea."

"I'm very busy, Miss Ashton. I don't have time to deliver livestock all over the county."

Brandy noticed his jaw twitch as though he'd clenched his teeth. A spark of fire lit his eyes, turning them to emerald flames.

"I'm sorry, Sheriff, but my horse is still lame. And those little boys could sure use some fresh eggs."

Adam nodded sharply. "I'll gather the chickens and take them out to Maggie and the boys."

He didn't meet her eyes, and Brandy wondered what she'd done wrong this time. When he'd walked her home last night, she'd thought they'd come to some understanding. He'd even apologized. And his offer to lift her and Dani over the fence had seemed chivalrous to her. Now, however, he was back to his usual rude self. She frowned and looked away.

"Thank you, again," she mumbled, gaining

the porch steps and leaving him standing in the yard.

She knocked and the door was answered by Jean, Carmel's young maid. The girl stepped back with a wide grin.

"Howdy, Miss Ashton," she said, looking back over her shoulder. "I was hopin' you'd come today."

"Hello, Jean. Is everything all right?" Brandy couldn't help noticing the girl's excitement.

"I wanted to talk to you, if you've got a minute."

"Sure. What can I do for you?"

The girl pushed the door closed and glanced behind her once more. "I've been saving some money for a new dress to wear to the fall festival. But I was wondering—that is, if you have something that'd make a man set up and take notice, I'd surely appreciate it."

Brandy felt a tug at her heart. She saw the girl's expressive hazel eyes flicker with expectation. "I'm sorry, Jean. I don't make love potions."

The animation left Jean's face. She slumped slightly, clasping her hands in front of her and staring down at them. "Well, thank you anyway," she said, looking more than a little embarrassed.

"Jean, wait," Brandy said, stopping the girl when she would have walked away. "Why would you need a love potion? You're a real sweet girl."

"Well, I've been hankering after Hershall

Putner, the harness maker, for a long time. He's so handsome and kind. And he's always real nice to me. But Hershall, he likes a pretty face, if you know what I mean."

She flushed and the shade only emphasized the clusters of bumps on her cheeks. Without the acne, Jean would have been very pretty. Her eyes danced brightly when she spoke; her features were attractive. Her figure lacked nothing. Brandy took her hand and smiled up at her.

"Well, don't you worry," Brandy told the girl. "I may not have a love potion, but I do have something that'll help. Come on."

She led Jean into the kitchen and showed her how to make an oatmeal mask for her face. Then she found a bottle of witch hazel in her basket and instructed Jean to use it at least twice a day until the problem showed signs of improving.

"Then use it once every day, the oatmeal at least once a week."

Jean nodded and clasped Brandy to her for a hug. "I will, I promise. The festival is only two weeks away, though. Do you think it'll work by then?"

"Maybe not completely," Brandy admitted, refusing to give the girl false hope. "But you, and Hershall, will certainly see a difference by then."

"Thank you, Miss Ashton," the girl said, drawing a handful of coins from her pocket. "Here."

She held all the money out to Brandy, but Brandy pushed her hands back. "Just call me Brandy. And you keep that. Take it and get yourself a new dress, Jean. Hershall won't be able to take his eyes off you. Now, I better get in there to see how Carmel and Dani are doing."

Adam tossed his hat on the rack and slammed the door of his office behind him. He sneezed and fished a fluffy feather out of his shirt pocket. How had he been reduced to hauling hysterical chickens around the countryside?

He sank into his chair and clasped his hands behind his head. He knew how. Brandy Ashton. She'd thrown a stake into the spoke of his wheels ever since she arrived in Charming. Of course, he had to admit he was glad she'd thought of taking the chickens to Maggie. The woman still hadn't heard from Jim, and he could tell things were getting desperate. She'd all but cried over the fowl, which hadn't been pleased with their capture and caging. They'd tried to peck Adam to pieces before he could get them turned loose, and he'd been picking feathers off his person ever since.

But Maggie and those boys needed them, and once more, Brandy had come to the aid of someone in his town. For that, he had to be grateful to her, even if he didn't like her. He quickly amended that thought, realizing he *did* like her. He'd admitted some time ago that he admired her courage and strength. She'd taken over the raising of her sister without muttering a word of complaint. In fact, she seemed pleased to have done it, though he knew from experience it wasn't an easy task. The problem, the insurmountable conflict between them, was that he didn't trust her. Not for a minute.

The biggest mistake he'd ever made was agreeing to let her stay in the first place. Half the town thought she was heaven-sent; the other half probably soon would. She had a gift for making folks believe her spiel, whether she had any talent for healing or not. And he suspected, the longer she stayed, the harder it would be to get rid of her.

Already he found it impossible to stop thinking of her. He'd lain awake most of the night wondering how to protect the townsfolk without actually tossing the two peddlers out. He couldn't do that now, not with Carmel so attached to the girls. His aunt was just foolish or desperate enough to follow them. So he'd made the bargain, against his better judgment, to prove to his aunt and the other people in this town that Brandy Ashton was just what he'd said she was. A fraud.

However, he realized that proving his point wouldn't give him the pleasure he'd once thought it would. Brandy had had a hard time of it, losing both parents and being forced to provide for her sister. But she hadn't let it affect her jovial personality.

And when he thought about the situation in

those terms, he couldn't blame her for earning a living any way she could. He admitted he'd have probably done the same thing in her position.

Suddenly another thought occurred to him, and he leaned forward, propping his elbows on the desk and his chin in his hands. Maybe she would be happier staying in town with a respectable job and a real home. He wouldn't mind at all if Brandy stayed in Charming, as long as she'd give up the hokey medicine selling.

Maybe that was the solution. He felt certain he could come up with an occupation that would enable her to stay in town and take care of her sister.

If he approached her with the suggestion, she might be willing to admit her business was a hoax. She'd probably be glad for the chance to do something legitimate.

The door opened and a shaft of sunlight threw a wedge of yellow across the floor. Adam looked up.

Fatigue settled over his shoulders, and his head lolled forward, then back up. He stared at Suzanne, her perfectly piled hair, her stylish dress. He shook off his disappointment, realizing that, for a brief moment, he'd wished it were Brandy.

"Hello, darling," she said, sweeping into the office and closing her matching parasol of striped chintz. She patted her hair into place and dampened her lips with her tongue. Her actions were clearly designed to capture

Adam's attention. Her ploys had worked in the past, but now they irritated him somehow. Had he been that blind to her manipulation? Or had seeing Brandy Ashton, with her natural grace and guilelessness, opened his eyes?

Whatever the cause of his cooling ardor, he knew his feelings for Suzanne no longer existed beyond that of a concerned sheriff for one of his townspeople.

"Suzanne."

"I was over to the general store," she said, turning the parasol on its tip and leaning against it. "And Bill's got two new bolts of cloth just perfect for a dress for the fall festival. I just couldn't decide. So I thought I'd come and collect you and get you to help me choose."

"I don't have time for that right now, Suzanne," he said, disgusted with her shallow vanity. "Besides, you have more clothes than you could ever wear."

He'd seen true poverty that morning, in Maggie's little shack and worn cotton dress. Yet, Maggie had those two little boys she adored, and she loved them so much she didn't mind doing without. And Brandy and her sister lived out of a wagon, but they had shown more caring and concern in one morning than Suzanne had in the whole time he'd known her.

"Why, I wouldn't think of going in a dress I've already worn. How would that look? My father is a prominent member of this community, like you, and we have a standing to uphold."

Adam had never thought of himself as anything but another citizen. That Suzanne put him, and herself, above the people he'd grown up loving and caring for only made him realize anew how foolish he'd been to be interested in her at all.

"The citizens of this town couldn't care less what you wear, Suzanne. Most of them are concerned with putting food on their tables and scraping a living out of the hard, dry plains."

"Well, what has put a burr in your saddle? I just wanted you to walk over and have a look." She sidled up to him and smiled crookedly, displaying the single dimple in her left cheek, which she was very proud of. "You don't have to act like an old bear. I'll go alone and let you get back to work. Just tell me if you're partial to gold and brown, which really show up my hair, or the blue-and-green plaid that sets off my eyes."

Adam knew in that moment that he had to end it with Suzanne once and for all. She obviously took it for granted that he'd be taking her to the festival. He bristled at her proprietary attitude.

"It's up to you, Suzanne. And whoever escorts you," he couldn't help adding a bit spitefully.

"Hah!" she laughed sharply. "What is that suppose to mean?" She lifted the parasol and tapped it against her palm. "You're my escort, darling. Same as always."

Adam rose and walked around the corner of his desk. He tucked his fingers in the front pockets of his trousers and rolled his tongue to one side of his jaw, trying to find a way to say what had to be said without throwing Suzanne into a tantrum.

One look at her gray eyes, snapping with irritation at what she considered his quarrelsome mood, told him there was no hope of that.

"I mean, Suzanne, I hope you weren't counting on me to take you to the festival. I've made other plans. After all, I don't believe I mentioned taking you."

"You can't be serious," she said, the parasol dropping to her side to hang forgotten. "Of course you're taking me. Available men aren't exactly a premium around here."

"That's not the point. I've made other plans, and you'll have to also."

"I will not! Adam McCullough, you will be my escort to the festival. I don't have time to find another at this late date."

"Go with Hershall Putner. He's always had his eye on you."

Again she laughed, and this time Adam noticed the sound grated on his nerves like nails on slate. "The harness maker? I hope you're joshing me."

"Hershall's a nice man, and he's got a good business."

"He is a bumpkin. I wouldn't be caught dead with him at a dance; his feet are the size of small boats."

"Find your own escort, Suzanne." Adam collected his hat from the rack, screwed it down on his head, and walked to the door. "I have work to do."

"You can't do this to me, Adam," she shrieked, slamming the point of her parasol against the rough wood floor hard enough to bend the tip. "You're just being hateful. And don't think I don't know who's behind this. It's that little peddler, isn't it? What's she doing, selling more than remedies now?"

He stopped, his hand on the knob, and turned back. "Don't say another word, Suzanne. You're upset, and I can understand that. But this has nothing to do with Brandy. I'm simply not taking you."

"Are you taking her?" she demanded, her face twisted with ugly scorn.

Until that minute, Adam hadn't considered asking Brandy. She'd probably refuse him anyway, after the way he'd treated her. Then again, maybe she wouldn't. And it would give him the opportunity to speak with her about his idea.

Besides, even suspecting her the way he did couldn't keep him from noticing how she made the most of whatever situation she found herself in. Maybe, for once, he'd actually enjoy this shindig.

"Yeah, I think I will. Thanks for the suggestion, Suzanne."

He chuckled dryly at the unladylike curse she threw at his back as he closed the door behind him.

Chapter Eleven

"I told you not to try walking until I said so," Brandy admonished Carmel as she helped her back into the wheelchair. They struggled together until the older woman slumped in the seat, panting and exhausted. "You could have hurt yourself."

"Well, I didn't. Unless you're talking about my pride. That's sure takin' a beating."

"Whatever made you think you could walk so soon? My goodness, it's only been a week. You've been in this chair for two years, the bed for six months before that. It's going to take time."

"There was a coldness in the air this mornin'," Carmel said, taking Brandy's hand. "Time is somethin' you don't have much of."

"Don't worry about me and Dani. We'll be

fine. Why, we've made so much money since we arrived, we can make it through the winter with no worries. And that's a blessing we can't lay claim to very often."

"Still, I'm worried about you girls, especially Dani. It just isn't good for a young girl to live a transient life like that. Oh, not that you're not doin' a good job with her," Carmel added quickly, patting Brandy's hand in reassurance. "But I sense that child needs some stability right now."

Brandy thought of the cigar clippers she'd found in Dani's pocket that morning. She hadn't had a chance to question Dani yet, but she feared this meant her sister was advancing her crimes to include picking pockets. She'd never seen Dani perform that task, but her stealing had taken odd turns before, usually when times were tough.

However, Dani knew they'd done well in Charming. They could continue to do well if the sheriff didn't find out about Dani's habits. Why had her sister jeopardized them by continuing to steal? Brandy had thought she'd finally gotten through to her with the Bible verses. Obviously she was wrong. So maybe Carmel was right. Maybe Dani needed something more, something Brandy couldn't provide.

Jean came in to deliver tea, and Brandy noticed her eyes were red and puffy. The blemishes on her face had shown improvement, though they weren't completely gone.

She wondered what could have upset the girl.

"Has she been crying?" she asked Carmel after Jean had deposited the tray and gone.

"Yes, poor child." Carmel poured tea, her hands still shaking from her earlier exertion. "That old beetle brain, Hershall Putner, is the cause, I'd wager."

"I don't understand. Didn't she want to go to the dance with him?"

"Yep, and that's just the problem. I heard he's taking Suzanne."

"Suzanne! The doctor's daughter? But I thought—"

Carmel met her eyes over her china cup and lifted one brow. "That she'd be going with Adam? I imagine she did, too. Sure makes you wonder, doesn't it?"

Brandy hid her face behind her cup, unwilling to admit just how much Carmel's revelation affected her. Her heart sped up. She felt a flutter in her stomach.

She'd thought Adam and Suzanne were married when she'd first seen them. Then she'd assumed they were a couple. But this new information had her reconsidering her earlier assumptions. Heat suffused her cheeks, and she could feel the warmth on her lips. It reminded her of the kiss Adam and she had shared in his office.

She'd been appalled at the time, thinking he was married. When she realized he wasn't, she'd relived the moment in his arms and discovered the feeling not unpleasant. In fact, just the memory could bring back all the whirling sensations she'd felt while pressed against his chest, enfolded in his embrace.

"Brandy?"

She snapped her attention back to Carmel and felt another flush cover her face. "Yes?"

"I asked whether you'd like to stay for supper. Jean's been cookin' all day, no doubt to get her mind off that harness maker. She'll be disappointed if we don't put a dent in the spread."

"Thank you, that would be nice," Brandy murmured, her thoughts still on Adam and Suzanne.

Several times Brandy wished she'd been paying closer attention to Carmel's invitation. As they passed around the huge dishes of pork roast, sweet potatoes, peas, fried hoe cakes, and fresh peach cobbler, she worried about the coming encounter with Adam. He hadn't made any comment when he'd learned they'd be sharing a meal again, but Brandy had seen the flash of irritation in his eyes and she thought she understood. Carmel would no doubt ask him to see Brandy and Dani home once more.

Why hadn't she considered that sooner? She didn't relish being alone with him again, and she was certain he felt the same. But he'd do his duty as he saw it, and she'd be obliged to accept his company.

And that was something she'd dreaded ever

since her wild thoughts of him earlier. Every time she glanced his way and caught his gaze on her, she felt a crimson stain spread up her neck to her cheeks, and she remembered the hot waves of attraction she'd experienced just thinking about the kiss they'd shared.

Brandy tried to tell herself it hadn't been an act of desire or passion on Adam's part; his kiss had been designed to insult and humiliate her. All the same, her body warmed each time the image slipped across her mind—as it seemed to do more and more each time they were together.

As expected, Carmel suggested Adam accompany Brandy and Dani to their wagon. Brandy opened her mouth to protest, but Adam cut her off.

"I'd be happy to," he said, jumping up and collecting his hat and coat from the rack.

Brandy stared, stunned, for a moment. When Adam motioned her toward the door she wondered if he were that eager to be rid of them.

"I'll see you tomorrow, Carmel. Tell Jean the supper was delicious."

"I surely will. Now, take care out there. And bundle up. I feel the nip in the air."

Carmel glanced toward Adam and nodded mysteriously. He ducked his head and clamped his hat down tight, ignoring the signal she sent him.

Again, Adam noticed that Brandy and Dani only had one shawl. As she'd done previously, Brandy draped it around her sister. He'd worn his leather jacket with the fringe across the chest and down the sleeves. Without considering his actions, he slid out of it and settled it on Brandy's shoulders.

She looked up, startled, as her fingers closed around the supple leather.

"It's chilly out tonight," he said, looking up at the cloudy night sky. He could feel her gaze on his face, but he didn't want to meet her dark, deep eyes beneath the moonlight. Already he'd experienced disturbing thoughts just being in her presence. She stirred him in a way Suzanne never had. Her vibrance was like a flame, and he felt like a moth who couldn't resist the allure even though he recognized the danger.

"Thank you," she whispered, starting forward again.

They walked on in companionable silence the rest of the way to the oak tree. Dani slipped inside, after saying good night, and Adam and Brandy found themselves alone once more.

"Nice night," he said.

Brandy started and looked up at the puffy white clouds drifting slowly across the ink-black sky. She thought it looked like rain, but said simply, "Yes."

Another pregnant silence fell between them, and Brandy shifted her feet in the thick grass. She needed to get inside before Dani fell asleep so she could question her sister about the cigar clippers. But Adam stood between her and the door, and he didn't seem to be in any hurry to move. As the wind blew and the grass swayed around her, Brandy shivered.

"You're cold," Adam said. "I should go."

"No, I'm fine. Thank you for lending me your jacket." She reached up to remove it, but his hands stilled hers. He clasped her fingers where they rested on her shoulders and gazed down at her.

"I wanted to talk to you," he said, holding her that way for a long minute. "I've been trying to talk to you for a week."

"Oh, well, I've been here and there," she told him, misunderstanding his hesitance.

"I, um, I've been talking with some of the folks around town. They think I've been too hard on you. They think—well, they implied I haven't been fair to you and your sister."

"I can understand—"

"I don't know—maybe I have been stubborn. I thought I was doing what was right for the town, but the town doesn't seem to want my interference. They like you." His gaze dropped from her eyes to her shoulders, where their hands were still joined. "I've found myself liking you, too, despite how I feel about what you do. I thought maybe, if you'd like to that is, you and Dani might join Carmel and me at the festival."

"Me? I mean us? You want to take Dani and me?"

"Yes, that is, if you'd like to go."

"I don't know. That might not be a good idea. Folks might think—"

"What?"

They both stopped, staring into each other's eyes for a long minute. His closeness disturbed her, but she couldn't look away. Even in the dim light, she could see his bold stare assessing her. His head came closer, and she thought wildly that he meant to kiss her.

But he adjusted the collar of his jacket and stepped back, removing his hands and the warmth they'd provided. Brandy shivered again, this time from unfulfilled anticipation, disappointment.

"So, what d'you think?" Adam asked.

Brandy realized she hadn't answered his original question, and she cleared her throat nervously. She really couldn't refuse him, she told herself. He was offering a gesture of friendship; it was up to her to accept it. She tried to ignore the tiny thrill of excitement that coursed through her at the thought of being Adam's companion for the evening. After all, it wasn't as though he'd asked to court her.

"We'd be glad to accompany you and Carmel to the festival," she said breathlessly, quickly removing the jacket and handing it back to him. Their hands brushed, but she released the leather and stepped back. "Thank you for the invitation." She smiled and ducked into the wagon before he could see her silly grin and sparkling eyes. She was afraid of what her expression would reveal to him.

Adam slid his arms into the leather sleeves and felt a shock as Brandy's warmth greeted him. He pulled the jacket closed and noticed her scent—lilacs and spice—clung to the leather. He breathed deeply and hoped he hadn't made a mistake by inviting her to the festival. She could disrupt his well-ordered life. Already her closeness affected him in ways he hadn't known he could be affected by a woman. He felt drawn to her; he longed to touch her, to kiss her. At the same time, he knew he couldn't trust her. He couldn't let his guard down, though he felt his wariness fade beneath his pleasure whenever she was around.

Brandy studied the bolt of plain powder-blue cotton fabric. She'd never owned anything pastel, but she'd decided she couldn't go with Adam and Carmel in the clothes she usually wore. Compared with the other women in town, she knew her clothes seemed odd. Adam might even be embarrassed by her appearance, and she didn't want him to have any reason to regret inviting her.

"I don't know," Dani said, eyeing the cloth with her button nose wrinkled in distaste. "I think it's kinda plain."

"Plain is what we want," Brandy said, deciding to go with the blue cotton. "Let's pick some ribbon and thread, and we'll need needles, pins, everything. I don't think Maggie has much and what she has is old."

They selected their purchases and paid Mr. Owens. When he'd asked her how much yardage she'd be needing, she'd impulsively taken the whole bolt. She felt certain he thought her crazy, but she had a plan.

"I didn't know how much it would take for the dress," Brandy said. "So I bought the whole bolt."

"Mr. Owens could have measured you a dress length. I think he took advantage of you, Brandy." Maggie poured her a cup of strong, rich coffee.

Bill Owens had told Brandy that Maggie had been in with butter and cheese she'd made from the milk cow Earl Hawkins had sent over. He'd bought the extra from her so that she could replenish her meager supplies. The boys looked better already, and they'd taken to the cow and chickens like pets. Even now, they had Dani out in the yard, chasing the chickens around the yard.

"I know it's short notice, but when the sheriff asked me I couldn't say no."

Maggie smiled. "Who would? Adam's a wonderful man. And it's no hardship lookin' at him, either."

"That's probably true, but that isn't the reason I'm going. You know I need his permission to stay the winter in Charming. And Dani and I are doing so well I'd hate to leave now."

It wasn't the entire truth, Brandy admitted to herself. But it was as much as she was willing to concede at this time. Maggie didn't look convinced, but she let the subject go.

"It's good fabric. And the simple pattern you

picked out will be easy to finish in time. Are you sure you don't want something a little more becoming?"

"Plain. I want plain."

"Then you've got enough for a couple of dresses here," Maggie said, unfurling the cloth along the table and measuring it off in her mind.

Brandy laughed. "No thanks, one like that is enough. You take the extra and make yourself and the boys something new."

"Oh, no, I couldn't—"

"Of course you can. I don't want it. I'm only doing this for the festival to gain Adam's approval and assure Dani and myself a place for the winter. I don't plan to change my tastes to suit him. Besides, Dani refuses to wear anything made out of it. She said it looks like mattress ticking."

They laughed together, but Brandy could see Maggie sizing up the cloth. She knew it would be enough for at least two dresses with some left over to make the boys new shirts. She'd had to spend some of her precious savings, but her expenditure would be worthwhile if it helped Maggie and pleased Adam.

As Brandy sipped her coffee, she assured herself her only interest in pleasing Adam was the one she'd stated to Maggie. But deep down, in the part of her no man had ever reached, she knew she lied.

Chapter Twelve

The day of the dance arrived brisk and overcast. Brandy dug into the trunk of her mother's clothes and found a paisley shawl that wasn't too worn. She threw it over a low-hanging branch on the oak tree to air.

She'd been dreading the day when the weather turned cold since she had only her father's ragged brown coat to wear. For tonight, she wanted something prettier. But after splurging on the whole bolt of cloth, she didn't dare spend any more money on extras. Adam could still make Dani and her leave, and they might not do as well in the next town. She knew the shawl wouldn't offer much warmth, but her vanity won out over her comfort.

Maggie had delivered the dress that morning as she headed into town. Brandy eyed it now with uncertainty. Never had she worn anything so—sedate. Dani had stuck her tongue out and made a face, pronouncing her thoughts of the dress loud and clear.

But if the dress pleased Adam, it would be worth wearing the drab thing. After all, she told herself, this could mean the difference between Dani and her staying the winter or having to move on. And her bare toes on the cold ground told her winter wasn't far off.

The afternoon wore on slowly. Carmel had told Brandy not to come today for their exercises and rubs, so she had very little to keep her busy. She washed a few things that really could have waited. She fixed several loaves of carrot and raisin bread to add to the bounty at the festival. And she washed her hair with rosewater.

Brandy also decided to speak to her sister once more about her illegal tendencies, worried tonight might offer temptations too great for Dani to bear.

"You've promised," Brandy reminded her sister, as she sat on a chair in the sun drying her hair. She'd washed Dani's as well and was combing it free of tangles. Dani shifted where she sat between Brandy's knees and looked back over her shoulder.

"I already told you I wouldn't take nothin'. Pinky swear," Dani added, holding her hand back for Brandy to grab her smallest finger. Brandy playfully swatted her hand aside and continued working with her comb.

"That's what you said before the clippers."

"How long are you gonna go on about that? I told you I took 'em back."

"You made the man think he'd dropped them, Dani. And then you accepted a nickel from him for returning them. That was wrong."

"I done told you it would'a looked funny if I had refused his nickel. I had to take it."

"You did not; you wanted it. And then you bought candy with it."

"But I gave the candy to Darrel and Davey," Dani defended herself staunchly.

Brandy stilled her comb, her shoulders slumping in defeat. "Yes, you did. And while that was a nice thing to do, it doesn't make up for the fact that you took that man's property."

"But Darrel and Davey don't get many extras, like candy. You said so yourself. And that way it wasn't like I kept the money for myself."

Brandy grasped her sister's shoulders tightly and bent her head down level with her sister's. "Just promise me you won't take anything else, Dani. I can't stress enough how serious this is."

Dani stared up at her with knowledge in her brown eyes that surpassed her age. "I know it, Brandy. I promise I'll try harder."

"And you'll do five more Bible verses."

"Oh, Brandy," Dani whined, puckering her lips in pique.

"No arguments, Dani. You've got to be disciplined, and that's the only punishment I can think of to get my point across."

"All right," her sister finally relented.

Brandy smiled. "Good girl," she whispered, hugging Dani to her.

Wagons and carriages began rolling past Brandy and Dani's wagon by early evening. The festival attracted people from the far reaches of the county, and some came early and stayed late. Some even stayed overnight, sleeping beneath their wagons.

Adam had told Brandy that he would come by for Dani and her at sundown. They'd walk, since the festivities were set up in the town square, and collect Carmel on the way.

Brandy had pulled her hair back and tied it with a piece of blue ribbon at the nape. But somehow her usual style lacked the sophistication she'd hoped for.

Dani came out of the wagon and Brandy glanced over at her. The little girl had pulled the top layer of her hair back with a ribbon at the crown of her head, and she wore a daffodil cotton dress with a chestnut-bibbed apron over it.

Brandy couldn't help envying Dani her colorful clothes. She felt drab in her plain blue dress. The bodice was tight, and she was unaccustomed to being hemmed in that way. Her usual loose blouses and skirts gave her room to move and breathe. The full skirt hung all the way to the ground and covered her scuffed brown boots, and for that she was glad. But the longer length hampered her steps and made her feel ungainly.

Already she felt an ache pressing against her temples. She'd pinned all her hopes on making a good impression on Adam tonight. Carmel felt better, but she'd shown no signs of regaining the strength in her legs. The nip in the air threatened an early winter. Soon, Sal would be fit to travel again. Adam would expect to see some improvement in Carmel's condition, or he'd have every right to claim victory in their bargain and ask Brandy to leave.

As she stood outside the wagon and waved to the townsfolk passing by, she fought off waves of apprehension. Finally the sun began to set, casting rose and apricot hues across the sky. The colors swirled with the puffy white of the clouds reminding Brandy of warm taffy being pulled at a fair.

Dani darted around the wagon, edgy now that the time had come to go. She fell once, staining the knee of her stockings. Brandy snapped at her, and then felt remorse when she saw the little girl's bottom lip tremble.

"I'm sorry, Dani," she said, dabbing at the brownish-green smears with a damp handkerchief. "I guess I'm a little on edge tonight, too."

Dani smiled and hugged her neck. "Everythin's gonna be fine, Brandy. You look just like a proper lady."

Brandy laughed at the lie, knowing her sister disliked the dress she wore. But she couldn't help the softening in her heart when she realized that Dani cared enough to try to make her feel better.

"I second that," a familiar voice came from behind them.

Brandy gasped and jumped to her feet. Dani scampered up next to her.

"Adam, I didn't hear you come up."

For the first time he seemed to notice Brandy's plain attire and he frowned, then covered it with a friendly smile. "All ready?" he asked, eyeing the two.

Seeing his frown, Brandy wished she'd allowed Maggie to add just a few frills and trims to the dress.

"All ready," Dani chimed in.

"Yes, just let me get my things," Brandy said.

Brandy hurriedly fetched her reticule and shawl from the wagon. Adam took the paisley shawl from her and draped it across her shoulders, and she was thankful for the pretty accessory.

"Thank you," she said, lowering her head shyly. Dani looked back at the pair and rolled her eyes heavenward. Brandy felt a fiery blush creep over her cheeks, but Adam just laughed.

"Come on, scamp," he said, taking Dani's hand in his. "Maggie said the boys are busting to show you the spun-sugar booth."

They stopped to collect Carmel, and Adam wheeled her chair along the planked sidewalk. When they reached the square, she ordered him to park her on the edge of the platform that had been set up for dancing.

Maggie and the boys came up, and Brandy saw that Darrel and Davey both wore fresh new shirts made out of the blue fabric. Their trousers were the same worn, patched ones she'd seen them wear before, but they were washed and pressed and their shoes were polished.

Carmel dug into the pink-beaded reticule she carried and took out three nickels. "Here you go," she said, handing one each to Dani, Darrel, and Davey. "Go along and get yourself one of those spun-sugar balls." She dug out another nickel. "And bring me one back."

"Thanks," they chorused, running off into the crowd.

Adam, Brandy, and Maggie laughed, but Carmel paid them no attention. The fiddler had started warming up, and already she was tapping her toe to the music.

"I better go make my announcement," Adam said, tipping his hat to the three ladies, "before the music gets so loud no one can hear me."

"You go on and do your bit. We'll wait right here," Carmel told him, her ear turned to the tune.

Adam strode across the square, greeting folks as he went. Brandy watched him all the way to the covered pavilion in the center. As he climbed the steps, she saw Suzanne step forward and take his arm. She leaned forward, but whether she whispered in his ear or kissed his cheek, Brandy couldn't tell from her position.

She heard Maggie's quickly indrawn breath and Carmel's hurrumph.

"Ladies and gentlemen," Adam shouted, holding his hands up to quiet the group. "Can I have your attention for a minute?"

The crowd settled down, but Brandy's gaze was focused on Suzanne. The woman had stepped up to the top step of the pavilion and was smiling at the gathered group as though she were the one about to address them. Brandy realized she meant to present herself in connection with Adam, despite the fact that he hadn't escorted her to the festival.

"The nerve," Maggie whispered behind her.

Brandy wanted to pretend Suzanne's actions didn't bother her, but she couldn't tear her eyes from the pair on the raised dais. A sharp stab of jealousy ripped through her. She clasped her hands in front of her to hide their trembling as a raw ache settled in her chest.

Suzanne had gone all out on her appearance. She wore a golden dress with braided trim along the neck and sleeves. The overskirt was scalloped along the bottom and fastened with pretty yellow bows, showing the yellow silk underskirt beneath. Her silver-blonde hair swept to one side and fell in an array of cascading curls over her left shoulder. She was beautiful, and Brandy felt like a moth beside a butterfly.

"You all know this festival is to raise money for the new church roof, the steeple, and the bell tower. Now, if we want a bell to put in that tower, everybody's going to have to dig deep into his pockets. That shouldn't be too difficult with all the booths we have set up here tonight. There's the spun-sugar balls. All the sugar was donated by Bill Owens," Adam added, never one to forget gratitude. "And Nell and her gang have the lemonade booth, which is only serving lemonade tonight, gentlemen."

The men in the crowd groaned, and the women chuckled and a few clapped. Adam continued, "And of course, there's plenty food for everyone. The ladies were generous enough to bake up some extra goodies, but if you want to take these home you'll have to pay for them."

Again the men groaned, but their complaints were halfhearted at best. Everyone meant to do his part to raise the roof on the church.

"So, come on and have a good time, dance and eat, and spend your money. It's for a good cause."

As Adam walked away from the pavilion, Suzanne captured his arm once more, gazing up at him and flashing a flirtatious smile. Brandy saw him stop and whisper something into Suzanne's ear, making the blonde go off in peals of laughter. Brandy turned away.

Several men had gathered on the makeshift dance area, and they picked up their instruments and began a rendition of Turkey in the Straw.

Someone tapped Brandy's shoulder, and she turned, hoping Adam had returned. Her smile drooped slightly as she faced Hershall Putner.

"Howdy, ma'am," he said, lifting his hat and then setting it back on his head. "May I have this dance?"

Brandy scanned the crowd and spotted Jean in her new pink dress. Her eyes were locked on Hershall, and a grim white line appeared around her mouth. Brandy glanced around, looking for Adam, but she couldn't see him in the crush of people crowding the platform.

"I, um," she stammered, not wanting to hurt the man's feelings, but not wanting to accept his invitation, either. She couldn't hurt Jean that way, and besides, she wanted to dance with Adam.

"The lady's spoken for this dance, Hershall," she heard Adam say from behind her. Brandy whirled, a smile breaking easily across her face. "Why don't you dance with your own date?"

Hershall's lips thinned and he adjusted the string tie he wore. "Suzanne said she isn't interested in dancing tonight," he told Adam with a sneer. "Not with me anyhow," he added.

Adam started to reply, but Brandy stepped forward. "Hershall, Jean's over there by herself. I bet she'd like to dance. And doesn't she look pretty in that pink dress?"

Hershall turned to follow her direction, and Jean straightened in response to his perusal. He frowned, rubbed his jaw, and faced Brandy.

"That she does," he said. "And there's something different about her, too. I can't put my finger on it, though."

"It's the dress," Brandy said, pushing him gently in the back. "I think pink brings out the russet in her hair."

Hershall sauntered off in Jean's direction and Brandy bit her lip nervously. She hoped she'd done the right thing.

Suzanne stomped away from the festivities, her rage making an ugly grimace on her face. Damn Adam McCullough. And damn that Gypsy. She'd tried one last time to recapture the sheriff's interest, but to no avail. Wearing her finest dress and coiffed to perfection, she'd approached him. But he'd made a flip comment about Hershall and her, and she'd had to laugh his words off as though they didn't matter. But they did.

She'd never settle for Hershall Putner. Adam McCullough was the only decent catch in this two-horse town, and she'd decided long ago she'd have him or nobody.

"Father," she cried, slamming into the house moments later. She aimed her bonnet and gloves at the hall tree and didn't bother to pick them up when they slid to the floor.

"Suzanne? What are you doing home so early?" her father asked, running his hands over his gray hair. "I thought the festival would go on for hours." He removed his tiny oval spectacles and rubbed the lenses with his handkerchief, then replaced them on his nose. His vest hung open over a rumpled white shirt, and his brown trousers were creased at the crotch.

189

"Hah, it probably will. But it so happens I'm not that desperate for entertainment. Really, I've never seen anything so provincial. It was a big bore."

"I'm sorry to hear that. I planned to go over as soon as I finished up here."

"Don't bother. Besides," she said, taking his arm, "I want to discuss something with you."

"What's that?"

"Leaving Charming," she announced, flouncing into a wing-backed chair, one of a matching set flanking the fireplace.

"Leaving? You can't be serious."

"I'm dead serious. I'll never find a proper husband in this hayseed place. I want to go on an extended trip. Somewhere expensive and elegant, like San Francisco, where men appreciate a woman with my attributes."

Her father cleared his throat and turned away from her. When he turned back, she stopped straightening her skirts and eyed him warily. "What is it?" she asked, seeing the strained look on his face.

"I thought you'd eventually marry Adam," he said softly, not meeting her eyes. "He seemed interested, even though he recognized your faults."

"Faults! That's good, coming from my own father," she declared.

"It's because I'm your father and I care about you that I'm going to tell you this now. I haven't made a lot of money doctoring, Suzanne. Most folks around here couldn't afford to pay in cash.

And what I have made, you've more than spent over the years on gowns and baubles."

She sat straighter, her ice-blue eyes narrowed. "What are you saying?"

"I'm telling you that you'd better make up with Adam, whatever it takes. There's no money for trips, or much else anymore. And I won't be able to work much longer."

"Why not? That peddler has to leave sooner or later and then you'll—"

"I'm sick, Suzanne. On good days, I'm aware enough to know I've got a degenerative disease of the nervous system. My mind is going. Before long, I'll be little more than a shell of the man I am now."

Her expression darkened with real fear. Slowly, she shook her head. "Father, you're just getting old. Everybody does. It's nothing to worry about."

"This is more than age, daughter. And you need to know now how things are going to be. I should have told you sooner, but I kept putting it off. I'm getting worse, though. So I knew I couldn't wait any longer to speak with you."

"If you are sick, then that's all the more reason to go to the city. We'll find a place where you can stay and be taken care of."

"You're not listening to me, Suzanne. There's no money. No money for trips, no money for hospitals or private nurses. You'll have to take care of me, as much as I hate the thought of burdening you that way. There isn't any other way."

Suzanne's mind whirled with thoughts of the aseptic examination room, the metal chamber pots her mother used to have to empty after some of the patients. A wave of revulsion swept her and she curled her lip.

Jumping from her seat, she slammed her hands onto her hips and glared at the wizened little man before her. "You'd better just start remembering something about that peddler that'll get rid of her for good, father," she warned. "Because I'll not be cleaning drool off your chin and washing your filthy sheets. Adam McCullough and his money are the only shot we have now, and it isn't going to be easy to get him back in rein with Brandy Ashton in town."

Thrill to the most sensual, adventure-filled Historical Romances on the market today...

FROM ⊾ LEISURE BOOKS

As a home subscriber to the Leisure Romance Book Club, you'll enjoy the best in today's BRAND-NEW Historical Romance fiction. For over twenty years, Leisure Books has brought you the award-winning, high-quality authors you know and love to read. Each Leisure Historical Romance will sweep you away to a world of high adventure...and intimate romance. Discover for yourself all the passion and excitement millions of readers thrill to each and every month.

Save $5.⁰⁰ Each Time You Buy!

Six times a year, the Leisure Romance Book Club brings you four brand-new titles from Leisure Books, America's foremost publisher of Historical Romances. EACH PACKAGE WILL SAVE YOU $5.00 FROM THE BOOKSTORE PRICE! And you'll never miss a new title with our convenient home delivery service.

Here's how we do it. Each package will carry a FREE 10-DAY EXAMINATION privilege. At the end of that time, if you decide to keep your books, simply pay the low invoice price of $14.96, no shipping or handling charges added. HOME DELIVERY IS ALWAYS FREE. With today's top Historical Romance novels selling for $4.99 and higher, our price SAVES YOU $5.00 with each shipment.

AND YOUR FIRST FOUR-BOOK SHIPMENT IS TOTALLY FREE!

IT'S A BARGAIN YOU CAN'T BEAT! A Super $19.96 Value!

⊾ **LEISURE BOOKS** A Division of Dorchester Publishing Co., Inc.

GET YOUR 4 FREE BOOKS NOW—A $19.96 Value!

Mail the Free Book Certificate Today!

Get Four Books Totally
FREE— A $19.96 Value

PLEASE RUSH
MY FOUR FREE
BOOKS TO ME
RIGHT AWAY!

Leisure Romance Book Club
65 Commerce Road
Stamford CT 06902-4563

AFFIX
STAMP
HERE

Chapter Thirteen

"Always helping someone," Adam said as he took Brandy's hand and led her to the platform. The lively tune gave way to a slow ballad, and he positioned her in his arms.

Brandy's blood heated, speeding through her veins as his hands touched her. Her knees shook; her legs turned watery. Adam held her close, leading her around the wooden floor in graceful swirls and turns.

"I noticed you have a new dress," he said.

"Yes. Do you like it?"

He studied her a moment, then frowned. "It's very nice."

"Something's wrong?"

He spun her about, and his hand slipped from her back to the dip of her waist. "No, nothing. It's just that I kind of got used to your colorful clothes. They suit your personality better, I think."

"But I didn't fit in with the other folks around here," she confided. She felt a wave of disappointment that he hadn't appreciated the gesture she'd tried to make for him; then she told herself she was being silly. He wasn't even aware she'd worn the dress to try to show him she could be respectable.

Adam tipped his head to one side, studying her. The motion pushed their bodies into closer proximity. A warm, heavy sensation flooded Brandy's middle and her heart jolted. The air around them, though chilled with fall, seemed to crackle with electricity.

"No, you aren't like most folks," he admitted, resuming their dance at a discreet distance. "Not at all."

His words didn't sound critical, and Brandy thought perhaps he didn't mind her being different so much anymore. In fact, when he gazed down at her, his emerald eyes held a hot, bold look that swept the chill from the air and heated her skin.

From the corner of her eye, she saw Jean and Hershall dance past them. The couple laughed and spun, seemingly delighted with each other's company. Apparently Hershall had learned the hard way that there was more to being pretty than how a person looked. Suzanne, for all her beauty, was beginning to show her real self, and the sight had displeased both Hershall and, thankfully, Adam.

Off to the side, Brandy watched Earl Hawkins bring Maggie a cup of lemonade. Maggie wouldn't dance with him, feeling it wouldn't be proper as long as she was still married, but she accepted the cool drink and they spoke together softly. Carmel sat in her chair, eyeing all the people around her as if they were players in a drama, all the while tapping her toe to the music.

Brandy thought she'd never been happier than she was at that moment, with Adam McCullough holding her in his arms, and her sister off having fun with her friends, seemingly happier than she'd ever been. Life was good, and she suspected it would only get better if Dani and she stayed in Charming.

As Adam smiled down at her, she couldn't help thinking it was largely because of the way she'd come to admire and respect the sheriff.

Adam had been charming and polite tonight, making her feel as though he actually enjoyed her company. She'd recognized almost from the first that he was basically kindhearted. And even though he'd rarely shown that side of himself to her, she knew it was because of his dislike toward those other peddlers who'd hurt Carmel with their false encouragement and claims.

Tonight, she didn't feel any of his earlier hostility. Could he be softening toward her and Dani, despite his doubts? That thought brought her more pleasure than it should have.

She smiled up at him and settled closer in

his arms. He didn't smile, but his lips relaxed and the hard planes of his face softened.

As the night wore on, her feet ached, but Brandy never complained. She danced almost every dance.

When it came time for the bake sale, her carrot-and-raisin cakes sold right off, bringing in two dollars. Adam bought two himself, raising several eyebrows in the crowd. Earl bought Maggie's applesauce cake.

Dani popped by every now and again to tell Brandy about her adventures or to ask for another penny. And all through the evening, Adam stayed by Brandy's side. She couldn't deny the pride she felt at having such a handsome and attentive escort.

Suzanne had gone home early, pleading a headache, and Hershall, deserted by his date, offered to escort Jean home. Dani, her eyes growing blinky, climbed into Carmel's lap and settled close.

"Would you like a cup of hot apple cider?" Adam asked Brandy as they stepped down from the platform. He could barely take his eyes off her, because she looked so lovely. The dress had surprised him. It didn't suit her at all, and he found he missed her usual colorfulness. But even in such a nondescript garment, she was still the most beautiful woman at the festival. He couldn't keep his anticipation from growing. Anxiously he waited until he could get her alone to tell her his idea.

"Oh, cider sounds wonderful," she told him,

staring into his green eyes. He'd been the perfect escort. She knew tonight would be a night she'd never forget, no matter what happened in the future. Glancing over at Dani's nodding head, she smiled softly. "But I really can't. I think Dani's had enough fun for one night. I better get her back to the wagon."

"I'm about done in myself," Carmel said, stifling a yawn.

Maggie juggled Davey on her hip while a cranky Darrel tugged wearily at her skirt. "Us, too," she added.

"Maggie, why don't you and the boys stay over at my house and go home in the morning?" Carmel offered. "Those little ones look played out."

Brandy noticed Earl looked disappointed, and she suspected that he'd intended to ask Maggie if he could see her home.

Maggie didn't seem aware of his frustration when she answered Carmel. "Thank you," she said. "That would sure be better than trying to get the twins back out to the cabin by myself."

"And if you come along and help me with Dani," Adam's aunt offered slyly, "then Brandy and Adam can have their cider before calling it a night."

"Oh, no," Brandy protested. "I can't let you do that. I'll take Dani on out to the wagon."

"Nonsense, I have plenty of room. She can sleep in one of the guest rooms tonight. In the morning, Maggie can drop her off at the wagon on her way home."

"And I'll see the ladies home and then come back to help with the clean up," Earl offered, ducking his head shyly as he smiled at Maggie.

"Thank you, Aunt Carmel, Earl." Adam took Brandy's arm quickly, seeing she was about to protest further. "That sounds like a fine idea."

Brandy shot him a startled look, but he only took her hand, leading her across the grassy square.

She turned back to see Maggie set Davey on his feet and take the handles of Carmel's wheelchair. Dani's sleepy head rested on the older woman's shoulder. Her sister looked content and cared for. Brandy told herself to relax and enjoy the rest of the evening.

The band had slowed down. Mostly soft, flowing sounds drifted from the harmonica and the fiddle now. Children of all ages slept on blankets beneath the few trees or tucked into the backs of wagons. The men smoked pipes and contemplated how soon they could start work on the church. Women visited with neighbors they didn't get a chance to see often, or swayed gently in their husband's arms to the last dying notes played by the makeshift company of musicians.

Adam's hand closed tightly around Brandy's fingers as they strolled toward the group gathered around the warm, spiced cider. A thrill darted up Brandy's arm, centering in the peaks of her breasts. Breathing grew difficult beneath the tight restraint of her bodice. Even in the thin paisley shawl, she suddenly felt warm, despite the chilly breeze whispering across the way.

Several men tended the fire set up in a barrel at the edge of the square. A kettle of mulled cider hung over the flames, and as Brandy and Adam approached, one of the men ladled the spicy brew into two punch cups. Adam accepted them with thanks, releasing Brandy's hand. She tucked her fingers into the folds of her skirt, trying to hold onto his warmth for another minute.

"Here you go, best cider this side of St. Louis."

She took the cup and sipped, closing her eyes as the mixture of fruit and cinnamon slowly warmed its way to her stomach. "Ummm, delicious."

Adam sipped his cider, watching Brandy over the rim of his cup. Then he took her elbow and led her to the steps of the pavilion. They sat on the second step, silently enjoying their refreshments.

"I think it went well," he said, surveying the remaining townspeople milling around and dismantling the various booths. "Reverend Battersby should be happy with the proceeds."

Brandy nodded and quietly finished off her cider. Adam took their cups and returned them to the man tending the barrel.

He came back and held out his hand to her. "I'll see you home. Then I have to come back to help with the clean up."

"I can help," Brandy volunteered, eyeing his fingers as they closed around hers. Again she felt a quiver surge through her body. Her skin heated and her pulse sped up. As she rose to her feet, she prayed Adam wouldn't release his hold on her. He didn't.

"It's getting late. Besides, the men usually take care of clearing the square while the women get the children settled for the night."

Brandy nodded, unable to trust her voice now that Adam was touching her again. She wondered how they'd come to this closeness after the animosity he'd first shown her. Did he believe her now, trust her? If so, why? What had changed his mind? And did she care what had changed his mind, as long as it had been changed in her favor?

The walk back to her wagon was too short. Before Brandy had gotten her courage up to engage Adam in witty conversation or to question him about her and Dani's future, they'd arrived. She couldn't invite him in, not without Dani there. He would go back to thinking she was a loose woman if she did that. But, she didn't want to see him go, either.

"Thank you, I had a wonderful evening," she finally managed to say.

Adam walked her all the way to the door of the wagon, eyeing it expectantly. She stepped between him and the orange wooden frame.

"Well, good night," she whispered, tucking the shawl tighter around her shoulders.

Adam glanced down at her curiously, then seemed to understand her hesitation. "I had a good time, too," he told her, surprised that he spoke the truth. He'd really enjoyed himself, for the first time in a long time.

Adam stepped forward. Putting his large hands on either side of Brandy's waist, he pulled her closer. Brandy took a deep, shuddering breath. Then his head lowered and his lips touched hers. His eyes seemed to ask permission, and she let her lids drop slowly closed as she leaned toward him.

His hands slipped up her back to her shoulder blades as he bent over her, deepening the kiss. Her hands wound around his neck, clasping beneath the length of blond hair at his nape. His lips swept hers again and again. Then she felt the hot tip of his tongue tease the seam of her mouth, and she parted her lips slightly.

He groaned and clutched her to him. His gentle assault urged a response from her. She opened her lips more fully, allowing him complete access. She wimpered as his tongue touched the sides of her mouth and her teeth, then merged with her own.

When he pulled back, her knees felt shaky. She clasped the front of his shirt to steady herself. He covered her hands with his.

"I would like if you could stay here in Charming, Brandy," he confessed, his own voice husky with desire. He was shocked and amazed how strongly he felt toward her without his distrust standing between them. If she agreed to his suggestion, he knew the possibilities for their future together were endless.

Hope, joy, and happiness coursed through Brandy. She'd gotten what she hoped for. And, oh, so much more than she'd ever dreamed.

"Yes, yes, I want to stay."

He clasped her hands and kissed first one, then the other. He'd been really apprehensive about broaching the delicate subject, but his happiness at hearing her easy compliance overrode his caution and he blurted out, "Good, I was hoping you'd say that. We'll put the wagon up for sale to get you through while I see if I can find you a position. A good job, where you'll have enough to support Dani and yourself. And maybe I could talk to Dorothy about renting you her daughter's house—"

"Wait, Adam, what are you talking about? Sell the wagon? Find me a position?"

Adam drew back and gazed down at Brandy's baffled expression. Her dark eyes were still heavy with passion, but they glinted suddenly with understanding and more than a touch of anger.

"I'm talking about helping you get a respectable job and a proper place to live."

"I have a business, and it supports my sister and me very well. Why would I want a different job? I enjoy selling my remedies, and I for one don't see anything disreputable about it. And for that matter, what's wrong with where we live?"

"Look, Brandy, I understand the hardship your parents' deaths must have placed on you. I was there one time myself, you know. And I don't blame you for doing whatever you had to to take care of your sister. But you don't have to go on with this hokey medicine show anymore. I'm offering you a real job and a real home in a town with good people."

Brandy glared at him, her eyes flashing. Fury threatened to choke off her words, but she forced them out through the veil of rage that covered her.

"Good people? What, I ask you, is your idea of good people? Those who live in houses without wheels? Those who dress like this?" she asked, snatching at the ugly blue dress. Scalding tears burned the backs of her eyes, but she refused to allow them to surface.

Adam took her hands in his. "Wait, Brandy. I didn't mean it like that—"

She shoved his hands away and stepped up onto the metal step below the wagon's door.

"My sister and I are good people, Sheriff McCullough. We may dress different from you, and we may not live in a fine house. But we try our best to ease some of the suffering in this world, and we try to treat people with kindness and respect. And if you ask me, Sheriff," she drawled haughtily, "that's a damn sight more than you've done."

She opened the door and disappeared inside, closing it hard behind her. Then she fastened the latch and let her tears fill her eyes.

Chapter Fourteen

Brandy longed to rip the plain, dull dress from her body and throw it as far as she could. Instead, she removed it carefully and folded it. Maggie could use the dress; there was no sense ruining it just because it hadn't accomplished what Brandy had hoped it would.

Adam still thought of her as a charlatan; only now he'd decided to reform her. Rage bubbled in her, sending a fresh wave of tears to her eyes. She was thankful, at least, that her sister wasn't here to see her pain.

Everyone had had such a wonderful night. Brandy had thought that Adam was coming to like her. Even now, her lips tingled with the feel of his kiss, and just the memory could send molten heat coursing through her. But it had all been a sham. He didn't trust her; he didn't like her for who she was. And he never would. Why had she thought a dress would make any difference to him?

She fingered the pink ribbon at the neckline of her worn cotton chemise. Without enough energy to even change into a night shift, she lay down on the bed and let the tears she'd held in check since her father's death flow.

Adam lay on his bed, staring up at the darkened ceiling of his room.

He'd made a mess of things; there was no doubt of that. Calling himself every kind of a fool, he propped his hands behind his head. Why had he bludgeoned Brandy with his plans? Why hadn't he gone slower, gauged her reactions better?

She believed in her remedies, of that he no longer had any doubt. She'd been furious at him for suggesting she admit to being a fraud. Angry, but also hurt. He'd seen the look in her beautiful dark eyes. His bumbling attempt to make things better between them had only suceeded in making them worse. She probably hated him now. God knew, he was none to fond of himself right now.

Softly pounding a fist against his forehead, he tried to think of a way to rectify the situation. He'd have to apologize, yet again. Of course, she might refuse to speak to him. He couldn't blame her if she did.

Facing her again wouldn't be an easy task. He was sorry he'd insulted and hurt her. For the last two hours, he'd lain awake asking himself if maybe she truly was what she claimed. But in the end, he had to face facts. Carmel was no better. Brandy hadn't been able to help his aunt. When she left Charming, he'd once more be left to pick up the pieces of his aunt's broken dreams.

But that was no reason to treat a woman of Brandy's sensibilities so harshly. Obviously she had no gift for healing, but she did have a tender heart and genuine caring for people. And if her remedies made folks think they were better, then what did they hurt? Except of course for his aunt. On that subject, he would have to remain firm. No matter how he'd come to care for Brandy Ashton, his aunt's welfare must be his first concern.

When Maggie's wagon rattled to a stop outside the next morning, Brandy was already up and dressed. She'd slept little the night before and she knew that her face was puffy and that her eyes were red rimmed and weary.

"Mornin'," she called, drawing the paisley shawl closer around her indigo shirtwaist. Her berry skirt was cinched in at the waist with a wide brown leather belt. Beneath her worn boots, she wore her customary black stockings. In her hand, she carried the blue dress.

"Brandy, Brandy," Dani called, scampering down from the wagon. "You just wouldn't believe the room I slept in last night. It had a huge four-poster with a canopy, and the spread was snow-white and soft as goose feathers. And I didn't even have to share it, neither. And this morning Jean brought me tea and biscuits in bed. You just wouldn't believe it all."

Brandy and Maggie laughed at the steady flow of chatter, but inside, Brandy's heart gave a crazy lurch. She'd never seen Dani so animated. And all because of a bedroom, in a house. Hadn't her sister always loved the outdoors and traveling from place to place? Or, Brandy thought with dismay, had she only assumed Dani loved it because it was the only life they'd ever known?

"Then I guess you've already eaten," Brandy said, forcing a tight smile. "I made a big pot of oatmeal."

"Yuck!" Dani made a face, then patted her tummy. "I had bacon and hotcakes, with lots of butter and maple syrup. And Aunt Carmel let me have all the biscuits and cream gravy I could eat."

Brandy didn't miss the new title Carmel had inherited. Her sister grabbed the boys by the hand, and the three ran to the tree and dropped down on their full bellies. Another large knot of something oddly like apprehension wedged in Brandy's chest.

"Brandy? Are you all right?" Maggie asked.

Brandy turned her attention away from her sister, telling herself she was still upset by last night's events. She'd never been all alone in the wagon before, and she'd found she didn't like the feeling much. She'd missed Dani terribly.

"Yes, I'm fine, now that Dani's back. We've never been apart before. I guess I was just lonely."

"I noticed Adam came in rather early last night," Maggie hinted.

The dress still clutched in her hands, Brandy nodded. "Yes, well, he—um, he didn't. . . ."

Her voice trailed off as fresh tears stung her eyes. She blinked them back and took a deep breath, but realized she had no explanation she could offer Maggie. And her pride wouldn't allow her to admit, even to her friend, that Adam had thought she'd admit to being a fraud and then stay in Charming. His actions still infuriated her.

"It's all right," Maggie said. "You don't have to tell me."

"Here," Brandy said, thrusting the dress into her hands. "The dress was real nice, but it just isn't me. You take it."

"Oh, no, I can't."

"Please, I feel better in my own clothes. But you did such a wonderful job I'd hate to see it go to waste. Take it."

"All right," Maggie said, eyeing the signs of fatigue and strain on Brandy's face. She accepted the dress, and Brandy twisted her empty hands in the ends of her shawl.

"Thank you for bringing Dani home."

"It was my pleasure. She's a wonderful little girl. You should have seen her face last night when Carmel showed her to her room. You'd have thought it was Christmas," Maggie laughed, missing the pained look that crossed Brandy's face.

"I'm really glad Dani had a good time. We'd better get to work, though. We still have a lot to do today," she said, trying to cover a tremor of distress with a brisk facade.

Maggie blinked her understanding and mumbled hastily, "Oh, of course. I'll just be on my way."

She called to the twins and they all climbed back onto the wagon. Brandy and Dani waved good-bye as they rode away, but the smile Brandy forced couldn't quite cover the fear in her eyes.

"We're going to Aunt Carmel's today, aren't we, Brandy?"

Worrying her bottom lip with her small white teeth, Brandy looked down at her sister. "What?"

Dani repeated her question, twisting a long blade of grass into a knot with her fingers.

"Why are you calling her that?"

"What? Aunt Carmel? She asked me to. It's all right, isn't it? I didn't think you'd mind."

"No, it's fine," Brandy murmured, touching her sister's thin shoulder. "As long as Carmel was the one who suggested it."

"She sure did," Dani told her. "And that's not all. She said she wished she had a little girl like me. Aunt Carmel is lonely in that house. She's by herself most of the time. She asked me how

I'd like to have a room like the one I stayed in last night forever."

The knife twisted in Brandy's heart. She felt real panic attack her, cutting off her breath and turning her limbs to jelly.

"What?" she whispered quietly.

"Yep, she did. She said I was a pure joy to have around."

Despite the chilly morning, sweat broke out on Brandy's forehead. She dabbed her temples and tried to steady her nerves.

"You must have been very good then," she said, thinking she was overreacting. Carmel was probably just making Dani feel welcome. Brandy had nothing to worry about. Dani was *her* sister.

"I promised I'd be good, and I was. But you should have seen the beautiful things in that room, Brandy. There was cut-crystal bottles full of smelly stuff. Perfume, I think. A real china dish with the finest face powder and a huge puffy ball to put it on with. And a silver mirror and a comb and brush that Jean used to brush my hair this morning. I felt just like a princess."

"But you didn't take anything, did you?"

Dani's eyes shot wide, and her little mouth opened and closed quickly. "'Course not, I'd never take nothin' from that beautiful house. It's just the most perfect place I've ever seen."

Dani darted into the wagon, and Brandy was left to ponder her sister's puzzling words. Why hadn't the pretties in Carmel's house brought

211

out Dani's urge to swipe things? What was it about the home that suppressed her sister's bad impulses?

All the way to Carmel's house that morning, Dani chattered. She told Brandy no less than twelve times about drinking from a china teacup with gold trim and blue flowers and sleeping in a bed with soft, cottony sheets that smelled of violets. And she talked about Jean.

"She was singing when she came in last night. I heard her 'cause she passed by my room on her way to hers."

"It isn't your room, Dani," Brandy reminded her gently, afraid her sister was getting too attached to the lovely things in Carmel's home.

"I know that," Dani said, tossing her head casually. "But it sure was nice to have it all to myself for one whole night."

"Tell me more about Jean." Brandy quickly changed the subject.

"She was singing, like I said. And it musta been real late 'cause I'd already been asleep. And then this mornin', she floated around with a dreamy look on her face. And you know what?"

"What?" Brandy asked, truly happy for the first time that day. She was glad everything seemed to have worked out for Jean.

"She was still singing the same song."

Dani laughed and skipped ahead, opening the gate to Carmel's yard and hopping up the porch steps. She sailed through the door without even knocking, and Brandy heard her excited voice call out.

"Aunt Carmel, I'm back."

Brandy's apprehension came flooding back and she stopped beside one of the large white pillars to gather her careening emotions. She felt as though her life were out of control. She knew her heart was. Adam made it flutter and race; Dani had it tied in anxious knots. Pressing her hand to her bosom, she breathed deeply.

"Brandy, are you all right?"

Whirling around, she gasped at the sound of Adam's voice. Her hand fluttered to her throat and settled against the pounding pulse point there.

"Adam, you startled me."

"I can see that," he said, stepping closer. He studied the lavender circles beneath her eyes and the trembling fingers pressed to her neck, and his behavior the night before returned to vex him. "I'm sorry. Are you all right? You don't look well."

His face lined with concern, he reached out for her arm. But Brandy stepped back, not wanting him to see the effect his touch had on her. Just standing close to him rattled her senses.

"I'm fine," she lied.

He noticed her withdrawal and tucked his hands into his trouser pockets. He leaned against the pillar and crossed his boots, one over the other.

"I wanted to talk to you about last night."

Brandy saw him swallow hard, his eyes sweeping past her shoulder as he spoke.

"I think you said more than enough. I really should be inside with your aunt." She took a step toward the door, but his hand snaked out and caught her elbow.

"Please, can we go somewhere to talk?"

His eyes shifted down the street again, and she followed his gaze. Several storekeepers had come outside to sweep the walkways in front of their establishments or just to enjoy the morning sun. From their vantage points on the main walkway, they could see Brandy and Adam clearly.

"I don't think so," she said, remembering the pain she'd felt last night after hearing his accusations. "That really would cause talk if we were seen going off together."

"I don't give a damn about gossip, Brandy. I need to speak with you, alone. Please. I have something to say, and I would rather not have an audience when I say it."

His eyes pleaded, and Lord help her, she was intrigued by his persistence. Glancing around, she tried to think of an excuse.

"I'm here to help Carmel. I really should get started with her exercises."

"Your sister is already doing that. She flew by me about five minutes ago, and they were already hard at work by the time I stepped out of the room."

"Adam, there's no point," she finally said, all efforts at pretense exhausted. She didn't think she could stand another confrontation like the one they'd had at her wagon. Even now, the memory brought a flush of humiliation to her cheeks and a threat of tears to her eyes. "We both said all there was to say last night."

He let his hand slide down from her elbow to clasp her fingers. His thumb trailed over her knuckles, reminding her of the kisses he'd pressed to the same spot last night. Memories of their heated embrace filled her. She could feel his warmth and smell his scent, and she could nearly taste the warm fruity flavor of his mouth once more.

"No, we didn't. Wait here, please," he whispered, squeezing her hand and taking her silence for consent. "I'll tell Carmel where we're going and ask her to look after Dani for a while."

He slipped inside the house, the sound of his boots drawing Brandy from her stupor. She realized she didn't even know where they were going. And she'd never left Dani in anyone's charge before last night. Now, for Adam, she'd done it twice in less than twenty-four hours. What was happening to her? What was this crazy madness that stole over her whenever Adam touched her or spoke her name?

Adam hitched up his wagon, and Brandy allowed herself to be driven out of town. They rode in silence for a long time, each steeped in his own thoughts.

Brandy worried about Carmel's attachment

to Dani. Should she put a stop to the relationship? She didn't feel she could without some
logical reason, and Adam's aunt had been
kindness itself. Even Adam seemed ready to
call a truce between them, a fact that more
than surprised her, considering the accusations
he'd made the night before. His sudden civility
brought other concerns.

Remembering the townsfolk eyeing them as
they rode away, Adam knew Suzanne would
hear of his outing with Brandy before the
morning was out. After last night, Suzanne
would be sure to get the message loud and
clear. He was glad, but that wasn't the reason
he'd asked Brandy to ride with him. No solution
to their dilemma had come to him last night.
But he knew he owed her an apology, and he
meant to see she got at least that much.

The wagon slowed to a stop in front of a
cabin. The house was small and built of rough
wooden planks, but it looked sturdy and well
cared for.

"Who lives here?" Brandy asked, in no mood
for visiting.

"I do," Adam answered. "Most of the time,
anyway."

"This is your cabin?"

She took another look. Two clear glass windows flanked either side of the front door. A
sturdy rock chimney climbed one side of the
structure. The front porch ran the length of the
house, and a heavy wooden rocker sat on it.

"It's very nice."

"Come on. I'll show you the inside."

He took her hand, but Brandy drew back. The two of them, alone, in his cabin? It didn't sound like a good idea to her. Already her heart had picked up its pace. Her chest felt heavy, and her uneven breathing seemed to draw attention to the scooped neck of her blouse.

"I've been staying with Aunt Carmel," he explained. "So I need to check on things here."

Brandy didn't take his proferred hand, but she followed him onto the porch. He released a rope hanging beside the door. The rope held a latch in place so animals couldn't get into the house. The door swung wide, and Adam went in first, waving Brandy in behind him.

"I need to open the windows. It's musty in here. I think the roof might be leaking again. Do you mind if I check it out while we're here?"

"Go right ahead. I think I'll just wait on the porch."

She turned to retrace her steps, but Adam reached out and stopped her with a hand on her arm.

"I thought you could make us some tea."

"Tea?"

"Yes." He waved to the back of the house. "I think you'll find everything you need."

He pushed open the glass pane in the tiny sitting room and then disappeared behind a wall that divided the front of the house into two rooms. She assumed the other half must be his bedroom. In a moment, he was back.

"I'll only be a few minutes. Then we can talk," he told her, going outside and leaving the door open behind him.

Brandy surveyed the small room. It really was quite cozy. A slightly worn divan sat opposite the large fireplace, and a rocker much like the one on the porch was next to it. A beautifully crafted woven rug covered the rough-planked floor. A small bookcase sat in one corner and she walked to it and found a Bible, a volume of Shakespeare, and several informative texts on farming and animal husbandry. Then she went to the doorway Adam had disappeared through earlier.

Inside was a lovely tester bed, which took up nearly the entire room. A small chest of drawers sat beneath the window, and a trunk rested at the foot of the bed. A huge brown velvet coverlet was spread neatly on the bed.

She ducked out of the bedroom and went to the back of the house. Whereas the front had been divided into two rooms, the back remained one. This room was a combination kitchen and dining area, complete with a modern wood-burning stove with two eyes on top and a reservoir for warming water. Opening the side door, she found several small pieces of kindling already set inside. Locating a cup of long wooden matches, she lit one and stoked the fire to life.

A pitcher pump was attached to the porcelain sink, and a large square table with four chairs sat in front of another window. This window overlooked a stream, and as she watched, Brandy saw a squirrel dart from the lone oak tree nearby and race toward the water's edge. The whole scene took her breath away and she stood watching for a full minute.

She found the tin of tea on a shelf over the sink and filled the kettle from the pump. Oh, to have such a kitchen! She found herself enjoying the domestic task. And she prepared a tray with small crackers she had found in another tin, strawberry jam from the larder, and cheese she'd uncovered in a barrel in the corner. When the tea was finished, she took two earthenware mugs down from a shelf by the table and laid out napkins and flatware she'd found in the top drawer of a cherrywood chest.

Adam's eyes showed his surprise minutes later when he stepped into the room. "What's all this?" he asked, an odd light in his emerald-colored eyes and a half grin tipping one side of his mouth.

Brandy flushed. "I got a little carried away. Your home is very nice."

He didn't widen the smile, but Brandy thought his face softened somewhat and he looked pleased by her comment. "It's never looked better to me," he told her.

She pressed her hand to her abdomen to stop the sudden flutter of nerves batting around inside her. How had his words, so simple and seemingly innocent, turned the blood in her veins to warm honey?

"Sit down," she said, nervously fluttering around the table.

This time, she thought a small quirk played at the edges of his full lips, and she flushed again with embarrassment. Silently, she chastised herself for telling the man what to do in his own home.

He startled her by pulling a chair out for her and tucking her beneath the table.

"Thank you," she whispered, then poured the tea.

"I wanted to apologize for last night, Brandy," Adam blurted out abruptly.

Brandy handed him a mug and poured her own tea, adding a half spoonful of sugar. She hadn't found any milk and remembered he'd been away for a while.

"I know now I was wrong to suggest what I did. But I truly thought you'd be happy to be offered more gainful employment."

She started to speak, but he held up his hand. When she sipped her tea and watched him over the rim of her cup, he let his hand settle atop hers on the table. Brandy's eyes widened and her startled gaze dropped to their touching fingers.

"I know that I insulted you. I'm sorry. I realize now that you really believe in the remedies you provide for people."

"Of course, I believe in them," she cut in.

His hand tightened on hers. "I wish I could believe, too," he confessed. "But I can't. However, I found myself liking you despite my belief that you were a fraud. I told myself you were just a young woman in a bad situation, trying to make the most of what you had. But I see now you wouldn't purposely cheat people even if it meant providing for your sister. Yet still, I can't believe in what you claim to be able to do."

She nodded and sipped her tea, trying to hide her pain and frustration, not to mention the strong attraction that threatened to overwhelm her.

"I understand, and I appreciate your telling me all this. You're not the first one who's questioned my gift. And that is the way I look at my talents. Healing is a gift. My mother possessed it, and I do. I'm trying to teach Dani everything I know so she can help people, too. And maybe one day, I'll pass on what my mother taught me to my daughter. I believe I can help people, and I know I have to try. No matter what you or anyone else thinks."

His features softened and he met her intense stare. "Again, it seems we're at an impasse."

"Yes, it does."

"Is there no common ground then?" he asked, surprised to find himself more disturbed by the idea than he'd have thought possible.

"We still have our bargain. It was a fair exchange, and I intend to prove my abilities to you."

He frowned down into his cup and slowly nodded his head, silently agreeing they should just hold to their original deal, even though it meant Brandy would eventually have to leave Charming.

Brandy watched out the window as the squirrel scurried back up into the tree, an acorn lodged in its fat jaws. Her eyes followed the squirrel up the trunk, out onto a branch where a large nest had been prepared. There, the animal would store up food for the coming winter. She glanced at the puffy clouds drifting across the bright blue of the sky.

The squirrel wouldn't have long to wait. Neither would Adam. If Brandy couldn't produce results from Carmel's treatment soon, she and Dani would have to leave town. As she sat across the table from Adam, still warm and cozy in the wonderful little cabin, she silently prayed that wouldn't happen. Now, more than ever, she wanted to stay.

Chapter Fifteen

"Come on, Father. You must remember!"

Suzanne paced across the elegant front parlor in the combination house and office that she shared with her father. Across the foyer were the waiting and examination rooms, but Suzanne avoided those areas. She hated the medicinal smell and the sight of all those ghastly metal instruments. She would never understand how her mother had stood acting as assistant to her father for all those years, but Suzanne refused to do the same.

"I remember when you were two, you fell and cut your knee on the side of a metal washbasin in the yard. You surely did howl that day while I stitched up your knee." For a moment, the doctor's eyes seemed to focus on her angry expression, and he frowned. Then his smile reappeared and the light in his eyes dimmed. "You might have a bad scar from that. Mother worried herself sick you were gonna get lockjaw."

"Father, please," Suzanne pleaded, rolling her eyes heavenward. She didn't understand all the things he'd told her about his illness and the spells he seemed to be having more and more lately. Today was the worst she'd seen him. He couldn't seem to stay in the present for more than a few minutes. And she desperately needed him to remember something about that little peddler. Something that would convince Adam once and for all to run the twit out of town.

"Try to think," she said, fiddling with the wide China-blue sash at the waist of her white day dress.

"About what?" he asked, glancing blankly up at her.

Suzanne heaved a great sigh and knelt in front of his chair. "About the wagon, father. Think about that ridiculous carnival wagon. You said you thought you recognized it. From where? Where did you see it before?"

"We took you to the carnival in Paul's Valley the summer you were five. Do you remember that? You insisted on having everything you saw, and when I put my foot down, you would shriek and stomp your little foot. Mother always gave in to you. I told her you'd end up with a tummy ache, but she couldn't refuse you anything."

Suzanne reached out and grasped her father's bony shoulders, shaking them hard. "Listen to me, old man," she hissed. "You haven't had a single patient in three days. Every last one of those ungrateful yokels is going to that peddler for remedies. And Adam, damn him, is totally besotted. He's making a spectacle of himself over the girl. Now snap out of it and tell me what you know."

Desperately she shook her father's shoulders once more. His eyes met her angry gaze and he frowned. Then he patted her knee and shook his head. "No more treats, Suzie. You remember the last time. What an awful tummy ache you had. The answer is no, not this time."

This morning it was too cold for the paisley shawl, and Brandy finally had to give in and don her old brown coat. The sleeves were rolled twice, so her hands weren't covered. And the pockets had holes in them.

The clouds in the sky hung low and threatening. "Bundle up," she told Dani as they started toward Carmel's. Her sister's coat was a hand-me-down from Brandy's youth, and it hadn't fared much better than Brandy's. Shame filled Brandy. She hoped Adam would be busy elsewhere today, then chastised herself for her vanity. What did she care if he saw her shabby coat? Why should it matter to her if her attire didn't please him? It shouldn't. But deep down, Brandy knew it did.

She wanted him to like her, to believe in her.

But if that wasn't to be, she would have to settle for his admiration.

As the wind whipped an icy breeze along the main street, she shivered and hurried the last few steps to Carmel's gate.

"Come in, come in," the older woman greeted them from the doorway. "Hurry, before you catch a chill."

Brandy and Dani scurried through the door, closing it against the wind. They shucked their coats and hung them on the hall tree inside the door.

"Where did this bitter wind come from?" Brandy asked, basking in the warmth of the house.

Carmel led them into the parlor, where a fire glowed brightly in the marble fireplace. Brandy and Dani stepped forward, holding their hands out to warm them.

"Adam says a cold snap is moving in. Maybe even the first freeze."

"So soon?" Brandy gasped, realizing her time might have run out. She'd hoped for a few more weeks before winter turned bitter.

"Yep. He's already out this morning making sure the folks farther out are prepared. I don't expect him back until late." Rubbing her hip, she added, "My joints are in agreement with him."

"Well, let's see if we can't do something about that. I can't control the weather, but a nice warm wintergreen rub should help ease your joints."

Later, after the rubdown and exercises, Brandy and Dani stayed for dinner. It had become a routine, and Brandy had to admit that she didn't mind accepting Carmel's gratitude in this way. It saved her having to prepare the noon meal, and it would save them supplies in case winter did decide to make an early appearance.

"I had a thought," Carmel said over coffee. "You know Adam's sisters were both very stylish. Why, they bought clothes nearly every time they went to Oklahoma City. They outgrew everything long before they wore it out, and all their trunks and such are still upstairs. Some of those things would fit Dani, real good. They left a lot behind when they married and moved away, too. Those things might just fit you."

Brandy set her cup aside, ignoring the excited look on her little sister's face. "No, thank you," she said. "Dani and I have enough clothes."

The conversation brought to mind the failed attempt she'd made to impress Adam with the blue dress. Again, her pride stung at the memory. She and Dani would have to be accepted as they were. She wouldn't try to change herself again, not even with fancy garments.

"But the things are just wasting away up there, and Dani would look precious in the soft blue wool coat Beth wore the winter she was ten. It might be a tad big at first, but I'm sure she'd grow into it."

Brandy didn't want to hurt Carmel's feelings

by refusing her gesture, but the woman had already done too much for her sister. "That's very sweet of you, but it isn't necessary. Dani and I both have winter coats."

Dani's smile died, and she fussed with the silver coffee service in the center of the table. Brandy watched as her sister straightened the lace doily beneath the tray and arranged the long thin spoons alongside. She'd picked up many tidbits of etiquette from being around Carmel. Brandy had noticed her placing her napkin in her lap and automatically choosing the correct fork now, without waiting to see which one their hostess chose.

Her sister almost looked as if she fit in the grand house. If it weren't for her colorful clothes, worn beyond their prime, she'd look right at home. The knowledge cut deeply into Brandy's haven of security. Was she losing her sister to this place? This woman?

"Don't think of it as charity, Brandy. I want you and Dani to have the things. Adam's sisters took what they wanted when they moved to their own houses. They won't be coming back for anything."

"Really, Carmel, we couldn't. Thank you anyway."

Dani slumped back in her chair, and Brandy watched Carmel studying the girl's dejected expression. Carmel slowly laid her napkin aside and cleared her throat.

"Dani," she said, "would you go and ask Jean to bring me a clean cup? Mine seems to have gotten something on the rim."

"Yes, ma'am," Dani muttered, pushing away from the table and laying her napkin beside her plate. She shuffled toward the kitchen, and Carmel turned to face Brandy.

"I know you're a proud young woman, Brandy. And you have reason to be. You've done a wonderful job of taking care of Dani. But she isn't like you. She doesn't thrive on a life spent outdoors and the thrill of traveling from town to town. She wants to be an ordinary little girl. She wants to play with children her own age and go to parties. And she appreciates pretty things—things maybe you can't afford to give her right now. But I can. Don't allow your pride to keep Dani from enjoying her youth, and the small things I can offer her, even if it's only for this winter while you're here."

A lump of shame and chagrin welled in Brandy's throat. She couldn't bear to accept charity from Carmel or anyone. And she didn't want to admit that she herself had thought their clothing was inappropriate for the festival. Could she refuse Dani the chance to experience, just once, the life most little girls took for granted?

And her sister did like pretty things. Could that be why Dani stole? Was it that simple? Did her sister want nothing more than to be like other children? Brandy had been happy at Dani's age traveling from place to place. But, she remembered, she'd had their mother to be her anchor. Dani had lost both parents at a terribly young age. Of course, she wouldn't feel the security Brandy always had while growing up.

Brandy's shoulders bowed, and she felt a burning in the pit of her stomach. But she was strong and realistic. It hurt to think Adam's aunt could do better for her sister than she could. But facts were facts. And Brandy would not let her own feelings stand in the way of Dani's being happy.

"All right. If it'll make Dani happy, I won't object to her having them."

Carmel laid her hand over Brandy's and squeezed. "I know how you feel, but I wish you'd think of it as payment for all you've done for me. Take some of the things for yourself, too."

Brandy shook her head, raising her chin a notch. "No, thank you. I'm fine." She tried to convince herself of that fact, but vivid pictures of Suzanne's stylish clothing taunted her. She pushed aside the twinge of self-pity. "But as I said, you may pick out whatever you like to give Dani."

Her sister had just come back into the room and she heard Brandy's statement. With a little cry of joy, she set the cup she carried on the table and threw herself into Brandy's arms.

"Thank you, Brandy."

"Thank Carmel," Brandy instructed, loosening her sister's arms from about her neck. She gently turned Dani toward the older woman and Dani went, without hesitation, into Carmel's embrace.

"Thank you, Aunt Carmel. Can we get started right away? Jean will help me bring down the things that fit, and I can put on a show for you and Brandy in the parlor."

Carmel laughed and nodded quickly. "That sounds like a wonderful way to spend a cold afternoon. Go and tell Jean to show you the trunks."

Dani shot out of the room like a bullet, calling loudly to Jean as she went. Brandy set her cup aside, certain nothing else could possibly get past the hard knot of fear constricting her chest. Brandy knew Carmel meant well, but she couldn't help feeling her sister had just taken another step on the road away from her.

Jean brought down a silk screen from one of the girls' bedrooms and set it up in the corner of the parlor. Dani went behind it and stripped down to her chemise. Carmel positioned her wheelchair beside the settee, and Brandy sat next to her, forcing a smile.

As the afternoon wore on, Jean carried down everything the girls had left behind that either fit Dani or could be easily cut down. Several times, Brandy shook her head, declaring the particular item too grown up or too delicate. But the pile of clothing she'd approved continued to grow.

A small shrill cry from behind the screen alerted Brandy that her sister had discovered a particular treasure. She found herself scooting to the edge of the cushion in anticipation. When Dani stepped out, twirling and prancing, Brandy's breath lodged in her throat.

Her sister wore the baby-blue wool coat Carmel had mentioned earlier. It truly was the most beautiful thing Brandy had ever seen. With a white fur collar and brass buttons down the front, it fell to her sister's knees, and Brandy had to admit it would keep the little girl warmer than Brandy's old woven coat. Along with the coat, there was a matching muff, hat, and scarf. Dani looked like a doll in a shop window as she struck a pose.

Carmel clapped her hands and issued high praise. Brandy tried to laugh and enjoy the afternoon, but inside, her heart lurched with every outfit Dani donned. Her sister's smile and bright gaze tugged at her conscience, and she finally admitted to herself she did want the best of everything for Dani. Whether or not she could give it to her was another matter altogether.

Suddenly the wind whipped into a frenzy, rattling the panes of glass in the parlor window. Carmel wheeled over to have a look. Following her, Brandy and Dani glanced over her shoulders into the fading light. Dirt, leaves, and debris somersaulted along the road, occasionally twirling in a tiny whirlwind of movement. The fire sputtered and sparked, glowing bright orange and red, but outside everything had turned steely gray.

"Wow!" Dani exclaimed, snuggling deeper

into the warmth of the blue wool. "Do you think it'll snow?"

Brandy's heart plummeted. Clasping her hand to her lips, she leaned closer to the window and stared up at the leaden sky. An early snow would mean her time was up. She'd have to leave Charming—and Adam. With a sinking sense of loss, she wondered which she would miss the most.

"No, not this time. Unless I miss my guess, it's already too cold for snow," Carmel said.

"Darn," Dani mumbled, her visions of fun in the powdery flakes dissipating.

"But I tell you what. If it stays this cold for a couple of days, the shallow pond will freeze for sure and you can go ice-skating. Adam's sisters used to spend all winter on the creek. They'd skate until their faces were chapped from the cold, and then they'd all pile into the parlor here and heat cocoa and popcorn over the fire. We had a lot more young folks here in those days. It'd be nice to have the parlor alive with happy voices again. Lord knows, Adam's a gloomy gus when it's just the two of us."

Brandy tried to picture Adam laughing and skating, but she couldn't. He spent so much time taking care of everyone else. She wished just once she could help him put aside his cheerless disposition and have a good time.

Dani's eyes sparkled at the picture Carmel drew with her words. Then her little chin dropped and she fiddled with the bright buttons of the coat. "I don't know how to skate," she said sadly. "And even if I did, I don't have any skates."

"Don't you worry about that. Jean knows just where Jenny and Beth's old skates are stored. And I predict you'll be doing turns and swirls on the ice before the week's out. Jean," she called, "take Dani up to the attic and scout out Jenny and Beth's old skates. Make sure you get the best-fitting ones."

"Yes, ma'am," Jean said, taking Dani's hand. Together the two hurried off in search of another treasure. Brandy watched, her despair almost a physical pain. But she had to admit she'd never seen Dani happier.

"Brandy, come and sit down. I want to talk with you about something."

Brandy turned from the chilly scene outside the window and took her seat on the settee. Watching Carmel's usually animated face turn serious brought a wave of foreboding over her. She braced herself for the woman's words, certain she wasn't going to like what Adam's aunt had to say.

"It's going to be freezing outside tonight," Carmel began. "I know you girls have lived out of that wagon all your lives, but I just don't think I can rest knowing you're staying there. Please," she said, as Brandy started to interrupt. "I know how proud you are. But for Dani's sake, I want you to consider the offer I'm about to make. I would like for you and Dani to move in here, with me, for the winter."

Again Brandy made a move to speak, but

Carmel shushed her with a raised hand. "Don't say no right away. I know that's your first instinct, and I don't blame you. But I have plenty of room, and it'll make it easier for you to continue my treatments if you're here."

"I can't do that—"

"I meant what I said about wanting young folks in the house again. I miss the laughter and the company."

"And what about Adam? What do you think he'll have to say about this?" Brandy could well imagine what the sheriff's thoughts would be on the subject. Her ears burned just thinking about them.

"My nephew needs it most of all. I told you that boy never laughs. He hasn't smiled in so long I've forgotten what his teeth look like. Having you and Dani here, along with some of the other young folks, would do him a world of good."

Brandy had to smile at that thought. Some of the tension left her shoulders, but too soon her trepidation came flooding back. "I can't. I appreciate the offer, but that wagon is my home."

Carmel studied Brandy's tense features and breathed a long sigh. "At least think about letting Dani stay. That child needs some stability in her life right now."

Grief and despair tore at Brandy's soul. Her sister was all she had left in the world. The thought of giving Dani up, even temporarily, would be like cutting her own heart out. But she knew in the depths of that very same heart that Dani would be better off with Carmel. The woman adored her, had from the first moment they'd met. And she could give Dani all the things Brandy never could. Every shred of her being cried out for her to take her sister and go, but she knew Carmel was right. And Brandy had always done what she thought best for her sister.

Slowly, she nodded her head. "If Dani wants to stay with you, I won't stop her. I love my sister," she said, facing Carmel, her head high. "Her happiness is the most important thing to me."

"She'd be happier if you would stay, too."

A warm smile touched Brandy's lips, but she shook her head. "I can't. The wagon has always been home to me," she repeated. "I wouldn't feel right anywhere else." Briefly her mind conjured a picture of Adam's cozy cabin, but she quickly shook the image aside. That was nothing more than a fantasy.

"I understand. And I know how hard this is for you. But you're doing the right thing for Dani. She'll be better off here with me for a while."

The finality of her statement made Brandy's heart slam against her ribs. She took a deep, shuddering breath. "It's only for a little while," she reminded Carmel and herself. "It's only temporary."

Carmel saw her distress and took her hand. "Of course, dear."

Chapter Sixteen

"Do you mean it?" Dani asked excitedly, her face alive with pleasure. "We can stay here the whole winter?"

"Not we, Dani," Brandy said. "You. I'll be staying in the wagon." At her sister's suddenly solemn expression, Brandy smiled and added, "Someone has to keep an eye on things. And I'm not promising the whole winter. Adam will still expect us to leave if I don't hold to my part of the bargain."

"Don't you worry about that," Carmel said, her lined cheeks pink with delight. "I can still handle my nephew."

Dani's rosy glow quickly returned, and Brandy didn't have the heart to tell them both that Adam had insisted on seeing results.

And so far, Carmel hadn't shown any grand improvement.

"I don't know, Brandy," Dani said hesitantly. "I want to stay, but at the same time, I've never been away from you before."

"And you won't be now," Brandy assured her, kneeling to look her sister in the eye. "I'll be right at the edge of town, and I'll still be coming here every day to treat Carmel. The nights are the only time we'll be apart."

"I guess that's okay then."

Brandy hugged her sister and choked back the stinging tears burning the backs of her eyes. Her throat closed on a sob, but she forced a smile and swallowed her pain.

"I better get going," she said, rising. "It'll be cold enough to freeze the devil himself when the sun goes down."

"Won't you stay for supper?" Carmel asked, obviously noting Brandy's despair.

"No, thank you. I have to get back to check old Sal. I'll see you tomorrow." She hugged Dani and pressed a kiss to her head. "You behave yourself," she whispered.

"I will," Dani promised.

Brandy huddled into her coat and walked briskly out of town. She forced herself to think of something other than Dani as she trod along, her breath a fog on the chilly air. She recited remedies she knew by heart until she reached the wagon. Then she went inside and shut the door.

And the tears came. She cried as she'd never

cried before. Great sobs wracked her body as she looked around at the dilapidated wagon. How had she convinced herself this was a good home? It wasn't even a home. It was an old wagon with a cot and a stove. The walls were covered with thick paper to keep the wind out, but already she could feel the draft seeping in. Soon, it would be cold enough to freeze the tears on her cheeks.

She stood up and lit the stove, checking to make sure she had enough sticks and twigs in the basket on the floor to get her through the night.

The flames shot to life and soon the little wagon filled with heat. She shrugged out of her coat and tossed it on the table. She'd declined supper at Carmel's, and now she felt too weak after her crying jag to prepare herself anything. Not that she had an appetite. Her stomach was tied in knots. Every time she glanced at Dani's cot, she felt a gaping void in her chest.

But she'd done the right thing, she reminded herself. It was what Dani wanted, and Carmel, too. Brandy had already admitted to herself that she hadn't been able to do what was best for her sister. Carmel would, and Dani deserved a chance.

Still, Brandy thought she'd never been so sad in her whole life. When she'd lost her mother, she still had Dani and her father. And although Wade Ashton wasn't a typical parent, he'd loved them and he'd taught them to laugh and find the good in life. They'd been happy. Or at least she had.

It hurt to think Dani's needs hadn't been met. Brandy had taught her sister to read and write just as their mother had taught her. And she was passing on everything she knew about healing so Dani would be able to help people the way she and their mother always had. And their father, never one to be serious too long, had nevertheless taught them both the value of family love. Somehow, she'd always thought they'd be together forever.

Wrapping a blanket around her shoulders, she crawled into the corner of her cot and sat there. Her tears had dried. She was being silly, she told herself. Dani was less than a mile away. If the loneliness got to be too much to bear, she'd simply go and fetch her. Of course, she'd never do that. The look on Dani's face when Carmel had told her she'd be staying there stuck in Brandy's mind.

They'd had laughter and joy, and Brandy had truly been happy all her life. But she felt certain that her sister had never been as happy as she was in that moment. And Brandy would not deny Dani the one thing that could make her eyes sparkle and dance and her face glow with happiness.

Over breakfast the next morning, Brandy told herself again she was being ridiculous. But her yawns and the kinks in her back and legs reminded her of her sleepless night. Every sound had jarred her; every puff of wind chilled her. Even now, the silence seemed deafening.

She pushed aside her bowl of oatmeal. Would she ever get used to staying here without her sister's constant chatter and bright spirit? If so, how long would it take? She wasn't certain she could stand too many more nights like the last one.

In trying not to think of her sister, she'd found her thoughts wandering more and more to Adam. Carmel was right; he was much too somber. Brandy thought he'd enjoyed himself at the festival, but then they'd quarreled. Could she show him how to have fun? She might not have much time left, if Carmel didn't show some improvement soon. But if she put her mind and energy into it, she believed she might actually be able to show Adam a good time. As long as they stayed off the subject of her profession.

Drawing from the wealth of cheer she usually possessed, she dressed and brushed her hair. Brandy wouldn't let Dani know how upset she'd been about her little sister's absence. Dani wanted to stay with Carmel, but Brandy knew she'd come back in a minute if she thought Brandy needed her. So she forced herself to look happy, donned her coat, and started for Carmel's.

Feigning a cheerful attitude had a positive effect on her, and by the time she reached the grand house, she was feeling better. Nothing had changed. Dani was still her sister, and she'd see her every day. There was no reason for her to be concerned. Her treatments *would* help Carmel. And she'd see Adam have a good time at least once if it killed her—or him.

The morning passed quickly and Brandy's good humor returned completely. Dani looked wonderful in a pastel plaid dress with white puffs of lace at the neck and cuffs. She wore snowy-white stockings, and her hair had been plaited into two neat braids. Her cheeks shone with pride as she pranced around in the dainty getup.

"And just look at these," she cried, presenting a pair of brown lace-up skates. "Aren't they the most wonderful things you've ever seen?"

"They're very nice. I hope you thanked Carmel for her generosity."

Instead of answering, her sister exchanged curious glances with Carmel and Jean, who'd come in to bring tea.

"Dani and Jean found another pair upstairs, Brandy," Carmel finally said. Jean reached behind the settee and withdrew a pair of black skates. "Dani said they're your size."

Brandy eyed the soft leather and shiny blades of the skates, which looked brand-new.

"I couldn't," she whispered, but her gaze lingered on the skates.

"I'd be more than pleased if you would accept them," Carmel insisted.

Dragging her attention back to Carmel, she shook her head. "Thank you, but I don't even skate."

Again, knowing glances surrounded her. Dani giggled and Carmel smiled, but it was Jean who stepped forward, holding the skates out to Brandy.

"A bunch of us are going to the pond tomorrow night if the temperature stays below freezing until then. I'd like you and Dani to come along."

"I've invited the young people back here for cocoa and popcorn," Carmel said, smiling. "It'll be just like old times around here if you and Dani go along."

Brandy wanted to refuse, but found herself looking forward to an evening of lighthearted fun. Learning to skate sounded like something she'd enjoy. And she'd never spent time popping corn and drinking cocoa around a warm, cozy fire. She tried to ignore the tiny thrill that coursed through her.

"Will Adam be there?" she asked, thinking of her plan to help him.

"He might be," Carmel told her, a knowing grin lighting her features. "Of course, he might get tied up."

A broad smile slipped slowly across Brandy's face. "That does sound nice. I'd love to join you."

Jean grinned and passed over the skates.

Brandy fingered the supple leather, admiring the craftsmanship. "I'll just borrow them," she said, gently caressing them as she spoke to Carmel.

"Whatever you like," the older woman said with a bright smile.

Afternoon gave way to evening, and Brandy knew she couldn't put off leaving any longer. She had to return to the wagon before full dark. Tonight, she told herself, she wouldn't fret over her sister. Carmel was doing wonders for Dani.

As Brandy buttoned her coat against the wind, she hoped her treatments were doing Carmel as much good. Winter, it seemed, had hopscotched fall and come to Charming with a vengeance.

As Brandy approached the gate, she heard her name called and looked down the street. Her heart fluttered and raced as she saw Adam hurrying toward her.

Adam stopped outside the gate, and they faced each other, with nothing but the low iron fence between them. Lord, but she looked beautiful with her hair blowing slightly in the wind and her cheeks pink with cold. He'd thought of little else since their trip out to his cabin, and he'd found himself impatiently going about his business, wishing he could think of an excuse to see her again.

The silence held for several awkward moments, then he cleared his throat, and said, "Hello."

"Hello," she answered, smiling a little. She was glad they'd called a truce, even if it was only temporary.

"How are things going?" he asked, motioning his head toward the house. "With Carmel, I mean."

"Fine." She looked up at the darkening sky. "These things take time."

He only nodded, and Brandy wondered if she should steer their conversation away from this possibly explosive subject. His next words took the decision out of her hands.

"I had to go out to the Cooper's farm. Someone smashed all their pumpkins in the field. Probably just kids looking for fun."

Brandy nodded, not certain what to say. She suspected he was just making small talk and wondered if he felt as nervous and jittery when they were together as she did.

He noticed the skates she carried over her shoulder and frowned. "Those look like Beth's skates."

"I hope you don't mind. Carmel lent them to me for tomorrow night."

"The skating outing," he said, as though just remembering. "So you're going?"

"I told Jean I would."

"Good. I would have mentioned it, but I'm afraid I'd forgotten."

"You'll be there?" she couldn't stop herself from asking.

"Yes, I don't skate, but I usually show up just to keep an eye on things."

245

"Then I'll see you there."

"I could pick you and Dani up in the flatbed. I usually take it along to haul some of the kids home in."

"That would be nice." She bit her lip to keep from grinning broadly at the thought of spending another evening with Adam. They'd had a good time together at the festival, despite what had happened later. And now she had a plan to see that he enjoyed himself as well. She could hardly wait.

"So where is your little sister?"

Brandy pulled her attention back to the conversation, pushing aside her daydreams of the coming outing. "Dani? Why, she's with your aunt."

"With Carmel? I don't understand."

A thread of apprehension wound up her spine. "Carmel didn't tell you?"

His eyes narrowed and lines of suspicion etched furrows between his golden brows. "Tell me what?"

The thread knotted and settled in her stomach, and Brandy knew real fear. Adam didn't know of their arrangement, and by the look on his face, she guessed he wasn't going to like it.

Bolstering her resolve, she looked him in the eye. "Dani is staying with your aunt."

"Staying with—What are you talking about?"

"Carmel invited Dani and me to move in with her. I couldn't—"

"Dammit," he swore, slamming his hand

against the fence rail. He plowed his fingers through his hair and glared at her. "I should have known you were up to something like this."

"Up to what? I didn't—"

"I turn my back for one day, and you two weedle your way into my house. How did you do it?"

Brandy opened her mouth, but again he cut her off.

"What? Did you play on her sympathy, using your little sister as a pawn to get you in the door? Or did you tell her how much easier it would be to help her if you were living at the house?"

"Neither," she told him coldly, stiffening at the accusations. "I didn't—"

"Well, let me tell you something. It won't work. I'm not the soft touch my aunt is. I won't mind a bit tossing both of you out on your behinds. In fact, I think I'll enjoy it. Maybe now she'll listen to me when I tell her what a fraud you are."

Steamed beyond rational thought, Brandy yelled, "Stop it! Just stop!"

Startled, Adam blinked, then seemed about to regain his thoughts and continue. Brandy didn't give him the chance.

"I'm tired of you calling me and my sister names and throwing accusations around. For the last time, I am not a fraud, a charlatan, or a cheat. I'm just a plain herbwoman. And if I can help Carmel, I will. If I can't, I'll say so and move on. But no one is going to treat Dani and me this way when we haven't done anything wrong. Your aunt invited us both to move in. I refused, but she insisted Dani stay with her."

That surprised Adam, but he recovered quickly. "I haven't seen any signs to indicate you're anything but what I've called you. My aunt isn't walking. She's no better than when you started. And I saw Maggie this morning. She told me Davey has had another seizure. So your booze brew obviously didn't cure him. Look around you, little Gypsy. The clouds are dark and the wind is sharp. Winter's on its way," he told her, a hot gleam turning his eyes to emerald chips. "And so are you."

Chapter Seventeen

Adam watched as Brandy wobbled to her feet, laughing and shrieking, Maggie and Jean beside her offering balance. Across the ice, he could see Dani, tottering unsteadily on the skates. The little girl had taken to the sport better than Brandy had and was already making her way across the pond with Maggie's two little boys running along beside her. The twins didn't have skates, he noticed, reminded of Maggie's situation.

But his mind couldn't stray from Brandy for long. Once more he'd allowed his suspicions of her to override the fondness he'd begun to feel.

Carmel saw through him, too. She'd nailed him to the wall after his argument with Brandy, telling him it had been her idea to take Dani in. An idea, she added, that had caused Brandy deep pain. But Brandy had once again put aside her own feelings to do what was best for her sister.

That had been enough to make him feel like a heel, but his aunt wasn't through. She told him if he opened his eyes he could see that it was his own growing feelings for Brandy that had him running scared.

Again, he turned to watch her on the ice. She was indeed the most beautiful woman he'd ever seen. Unlike himself, she always had a ready smile that somehow made him ache to share her joy, despite his doubts about her. And somehow Brandy managed to remain cheerful through whatever went her way. He had everything a man could want, but had never let go and embraced life the way she did.

Dani skated up to her sister and spoke, sending the two off into fits of laughter and causing the little girl to lose her balance. She swayed and Brandy made a grab for her, toppling onto the ice in a heap. Dani landed atop her, and Brandy merely laughed harder. Then Brandy ruffled Dani's hair and raised the girl to her feet.

Beautiful, vivacious, loving. More than anything in the world, at that moment, Adam wished he could have Brandy for his own. He longed to say to hell with his doubts and join the ranks of her admirers. He couldn't do that, but he could at least apologize for his inexcusable behavior the previous day.

He skirted the perimeter of the pond and came up behind Brandy as she inched her way toward a log seat nearby. She plopped down, her moss-green skirt flaring out beside her. Pushing the fabric up to her knees, she retied a skate lace that had come undone. Adam stopped and watched as she unconsciously offered him an intimate view of stockinged legs. Her shapely calves rose above the top of the skates, and her slender knees were outlined beneath the cotton wool. Her wave of blue-black hair, tied at the nape with a ribbon and left to hang down her back, fell over her shoulder and curled around her left breast. Flushed and mussed from skating, she could easily have passed for a woman who'd just been made love to. As he felt his body's response to the picture his mind conjured, Adam admitted to himself that he wanted to be the man who ran his fingers through her hair and put the rosy glow on her face.

"Brandy."

She turned to face him, the smile slowly slipping from her lips. His heart ached at the loss of her smile, knowing he was responsible.

"Adam," she said, tossing her skirt back down as she rose shakily to her feet. She hadn't seen him approach, and her heart danced a jig at his sudden appearance. Was he still angry? Would he continue their argument here, in front of half the town? She met his gaze and saw the minute softening of his eyes.

"I'd like to talk with you a minute," he said.

She stared across the ice and then glanced back at him. She could read the remorse on his face, and she decided to use his contrition to carry out her plan.

After their confrontation the night before, she'd wanted nothing more than to go back in the house, collect Dani, and return to the wagon to lick the wounds of her injured pride. But she'd thought first and decided Carmel would explain everything to Adam. And he'd listen to his aunt no matter how enraged he was. Brandy also knew the older woman would never allow Dani to be hurt by his anger.

Understanding Adam's reaction had taken a little longer. She'd been up late, battling her own ire and hurt. However, sometime around daylight, she'd come to the conclusion that Adam could not put aside his mistrust overnight. If Brandy expected him to see her for what she truly was, she would just have to be patient. And she very much wanted to return to the pleasantness of their too brief truce.

Deciding the best way to do that was to simply pretend their quarrel had never taken place and follow through with the plan she'd devised at Carmel's, she arched one brow impishly.

"If you want to talk to me, then you're going to need skates," she challenged, her smile gliding once more into place. Her arms flailing the air, she started across the pond, toddling forward and back.

Adam cursed, but he couldn't help the

measure of amusement he felt at her challenge. Looking around, he spotted Earl nearby unlacing his skates.

Within minutes, Adam stomped onto the ice, with Earl's skates pinching his cramped toes. He hadn't skated in years and didn't want to try now. But the gauntlet had been tossed, so he carefully walked toward Brandy.

"As you requested," he said, holding his hands out to the sides and jerking crazily as the motion upset his balance. She laughed and eyed his wide-spread feet.

"All right, so talk," she told him, taking his hands. He tried to pull back, but she held firm, moving her feet backward and drawing him along.

"No, wait. I don't skate anymore."

"You do now," she said, nodding toward his moving feet.

Adam let her pull him slowly across the ice, each bracing the other as they struggled to master the awkward sport. For several minutes, his attention focused on staying on his feet and off his rear, but soon he relaxed and the skills he once possessed came slowly back to him.

"This isn't so tough, once you get the hang of it again," he said, taking her arm in his as they eased along side by side. He immediately regretted his sudden movement when he wobbled to and fro. His arm slipped around her waist, and he grasped her elbows. As he balanced them, her back to his front, he gripped the slender bend of her arms through her worn coat.

"You wanted to talk," she reminded him as they moved slowly but gracefully across the ice.

He looked down into her upturned dark eyes, certain all the regret and chagrin he felt showed on his face.

"Aunt Carmel set me straight when I went in last night," he began.

Continuing around the pond, Brandy nodded wordlessly.

"I'm sorry. Again. It seems I'm always apologizing to you. I jumped to conclusions when you told me Dani was staying with Carmel. I acted like a jackass, I know. You have every right to be furious with me."

Brandy smiled and released his hold, turning carefully to face him. Touching his cold cheek with her fingertips, she shook her head. "I'm not angry, Adam. I admit I was hurt. After you stormed away, I wanted to take my sister and leave. But I knew that would do no good. So I thought about it for a long time and decided to try to understand your feelings. You've made your views clear from the start. I never had any illusions about how you felt toward me and Dani."

"I've tried—"

She moved her fingers to his lips, silencing him. But as the warmth from his mouth seared her cold, sensitive skin, she drew them back again, placing them safely on the sleeve of his jacket.

Heat rushed up her neck, warming her windblown skin. Her cheeks flamed, and she hoped the cold would disguise her blush. She swallowed hard and forced her voice to sound normal.

"I know," she said. "But it just isn't any good. You can't make yourself believe something any more than I can make myself be something other than what I am. Out at your cabin we agreed to disagree on the subject of my occupation. I see no other way."

She tipped forward and he steadied her, reveling in the feel of her breasts brushing against his chest. Even through their layers of clothing, he thought he felt her heat, her form. Swallowing hard, he drew back, trying to look unaffected.

"Still, we did make a deal. I intend to keep my word. I'll leave you alone until winter officially arrives. You're entitled to a few more weeks despite this unusual cold spell we're having."

"Thank you. That's all I can ask," she said, releasing his arms altogether. She had to get away from him before he noticed her discomfort and guessed that his closeness was the cause of it. "I better go check on Dani," she whispered, turning unsteadily away and leaving him standing alone on the ice.

Adam felt the loss of her touch immediately, and he longed to pull her close once more and hold her tight in his embrace. But he let her go, watching her wave jauntily and skate off across the frozen pond.

Despite his attraction, he knew he still did not believe in her healing abilities. And when winter arrived on the calender as well as in the air, he had no doubt his aunt would still be an invalid. He wouldn't go back on his word now, and he wouldn't go back on his promise later. If Carmel wasn't healed, Brandy and her sister would have to go. Even though he realized just how much he would miss her.

From the edge of the pond Suzanne watched the exchange between Brandy and Adam, her temper simmering. She had dressed in her new skating outfit, made of soft cashmere with fur trim around the neck, sleeves, and hemline. In her hands, she twisted a beautiful white muff viciously. She had taken pains with her appearance tonight, determined to show Adam what a treasure he'd given up. In her mind, she'd envisioned him walking across the brittle grass, his boots quickly closing the unbearable distance between them. He'd take her hands, perhaps kiss them. She'd smile and his heart would melt. He'd be hers once more, and the shabby little peddler would watch from afar as they strolled off, all thoughts of skating chased from their minds.

Instead, Suzanne glared through narrowed eyes as Adam seesawed his way toward the edge of the ice. Several people called out encouragement to him as he made a spectacle of himself. And all because of that wretched cheap-jack. Suzanne had tried to get Adam onto the ice for years. But he'd refused her pleas, choosing to watch from the shore as she performed graceful maneuvers just for him.

Damn the woman, she thought, snatching her skates from the low bench. All the pleasure had gone out of the evening for her, and it was Brandy Ashton's fault. Every miserable thing that had happened to her in the last few weeks was due to that black-haired witch.

Well, she'd had all she could take. Tonight she'd press her father until he remembered what he knew about Brandy's past. And if he didn't know anything, she'd just have to come up with something of her own design.

After the sun sank below the horizon, the wind turned bitter. Brandy shoved her hands into her pockets, fingering the loose threads surrounding one of the many holes there. She watched Adam return Earl's skates and shake the man's hand. He said something and they both glanced toward Maggie and her boys. Maggie had rigged a makeshift sled out of a scrap of sheet metal, and the boys giggled wildly as she pulled them across the ice.

Brandy saw Earl's gaze light with inner fire as he watched the trio. Adam nodded slowly and turned away, but Earl continued to stare at Maggie, his heart in his eyes.

Just then someone called Maggie's name, and both Earl and Brandy turned toward the new arrival. Bill Owens, the storekeeper, crossed the street and hurried toward the pond, waving something white in his hand.

Maggie handed Dani the rope attached to the sled and started toward Bill.

"Hello, Bill," Brandy heard Maggie say, her voice polite but reserved.

"This came for you today. It's from Californy, but not from your man. Still, I thought you might want it right away so I brought it over."

Brandy suspected the storekeeper's motives. Obviously he thought the letter might contain money, and he had his eye on collecting what Maggie owed him. Brandy wandered closer, not wanting to intrude, but not about to leave Maggie alone with the miser.

Maggie frowned as she read the front of the well-worn envelope. She turned it over in her hand and loosened the flap. Extracting a single piece of paper, she looked apologetically at the storekeeper.

"Nothing this time, Mr. Owens," she told him, as she quickly scanned the address on the outside of the envelope.

The man huffed and sauntered away. An icy premonition that had nothing to do with the weather swept through Brandy. She stepped beside Maggie.

Maggie looked back at her boys, who were squealing in delight as Dani skated around the pond with them in tow. Finally, as though she too sensed something was amiss, Maggie opened the page.

Her eyes lingered on the letter until Brandy thought it must be rather long. But as she leaned closer she could see the letter was no more than a few lines. Her gaze swept Maggie's ashen face. The paper shook in Maggie's hand, and her whole body trembled.

"Oh, Lord," she whispered, the page crackling as her fingers jerked with emotion. "Oh, no."

Brandy looked up to see Adam striding in their direction. She urged him to hurry with a desperate glance as she took Maggie by the elbow. Adam sprinted the last few steps and together they led Maggie to the log bench.

"Maggie? Is everything all right?"

Brandy heard Adam's tender words, but his soothing tone had no effect on Maggie. Kneeling beside her friend, Brandy took the letter and quickly read it. Her heart slammed against her ribs, and she sucked in a ragged breath.

"Oh, Maggie," she said, clasping the woman's hand. "I'm sorry, so sorry."

She passed the page to Adam, and he scanned it before stuffing it into his pocket. "Come on," he said, motioning Brandy to take Maggie's arm. They helped her to her feet and started for Adam's wagon.

Earl rushed up to them as they approached the wagon. Adam hefted Maggie onto the seat and then lifted Brandy up beside her. He turned to Earl, a grim line around his mouth.

"Give us a little while and then bring Dani and the boys to Aunt Carmel's," he said as he jumped onto the seat and settled beside Brandy.

Earl nodded his compliance, but already the wagon was moving at a good clip toward the other end of town. Brandy put her arm around Maggie's shoulder and drew her closer. Since the three of them were on the seat, they had little room left for movement, and Brandy's gesture pressed her more firmly against Adam. She could feel the warmth of his hip against hers. Leather scraped across heavy cotton as his shoulder brushed her arm. An awareness she shouldn't have felt at such a time crept over her nevertheless, and she wiggled nervously on the seat.

As they arrived at Carmel's, Maggie seemed to get hold of herself. They helped her into the house, and Adam poured her a hefty shot of brandy as Brandy led her toward the waiting fire.

"Drink this," Adam ordered.

Maggie took the glass and swallowed the liquor in two gulps, coughing and choking as it burned its way down her throat.

"What's happened?" Carmel asked from the doorway. She rolled into the room and glanced from the glass in Maggie's hand to the couple standing anxiously nearby.

"Jim's been killed," Adam stated baldly.

His words brought a strangled gasp from Maggie, and he cursed himself as he helped her to the settee.

"I'm sorry," he mumbled, cursing his insensitivity as he went to the sideboard and refilled her glass.

This time she waved away the brandy. Clutching her hands together in her lap, she looked up at the group gathered around her. "I'm all right now," she said. "Really, I am."

Brandy and Adam exchanged doubting glances and Carmel sat, wide-eyed and shocked. Maggie laughed dryly and pushed the loosened strands of hair from her face.

"I know I'm supposed to be the grieving widow," she said slowly. "But I'm not." She reached for the glass Adam still held. "On second thought, I will take that drink."

This time she sipped the liquor. "Do you know the first thought that crossed my mind when I read that letter?" She didn't seem to expect an answer. None was forthcoming. She continued. "I thought, 'Oh, God, how are we going to make it through the winter.' Isn't that terrible? Someone I don't even know tells me Jim was killed in a fight over a card game, and all I can think of is that he won't be sending any more money."

"You're in shock, Maggie," Carmel said, coming farther into the room.

But Maggie only shook her head. "No, I'm not. I suppose I always suspected something like this would happen."

"He was your husband, it's only natural you're upset." Brandy sat beside Maggie on the settee and laid her hand on Maggie's shoulder.

"But that's just it. I'm not upset that he's dead. I'm worried about the boys."

"Don't worry, Maggie. Everything will be all right," Adam told her, sipping his own brandy.

"I know how this must sound," Maggie said. "But I can't help it. I loved Jim when we married. I vowed to be a good wife, and I was. But when the twins were born and Jim saw that Davey wasn't, well, normal, he couldn't deal with it. He withdrew from me and the boys more and more until finally he left. I tried to understand, but Davey was our son and I loved him. I never forgave Jim for turning his back on his children. When he left, all the old feelings I'd tried to keep alive left with him. I just felt empty. Except for the twins. The boys became my whole life. That's why I took the money Jim sent. I couldn't remarry, and I had no skills to get a job, even if there had been a decent position open in town. I had no choice."

"You did the right thing, Maggie," Carmel said. "You've always done what's best for the boys. No matter how farfetched it seemed," she added, cutting a sharp look at Adam.

Brandy saw Carmel's silent admonishment and fought a grin. Adam's aunt never missed an opportunity to defend her. Brandy appreciated the support and the warm feelings of belonging that accompanied it.

Turning back to Maggie, she patted her shoulder. "You can't help how you feel. Your husband's been gone a long time."

"But I should feel something. Our marriage

was good before the twins were born."

"But you're their mother. No one can blame you for being angry that Jim deserted the three of you."

Maggie shook her head. "I'm not angry. I simply don't feel anything at all," she confessed. "Except concern for my boys."

"And they're all that matter now," Adam said, hunkering down in front of the seat. He took Maggie's cold hand and rubbed it briskly between his own. "Jim is gone, but he's been gone in all the ways that count for a long time. You and the boys are here, and you need to focus on your future."

The shaking took hold of her again, and the amber liquid sloshed in her glass before she passed it to Brandy. Brandy set it aside and knelt beside Adam, taking Maggie's other hand.

"What future?" Maggie whispered. "Oh, Lord, I'm so frightened."

"Maggie?"

The voice from the curtained doorway startled them all, and Adam and Brandy both tried to turn on the balls of their feet at the same time. They collided and he reached out, capturing her in his embrace. Maggie looked over their bent heads to where Earl stood awkwardly twisting his hat.

"Jim?" was all he said.

Maggie nodded and rose slowly to her feet. Adam pulled Brandy up beside him, his arm still around her shoulders.

"I'm sorry," Earl said.

Maggie shrugged.

Earl's eyes softened and he shook his head slowly. "That's a lie," he said. "I'm not sorry. I love you, Maggie. You deserve better than what Jim gave you. If you had been mine—" He seemed to notice the others for the first time and his words trailed off.

Maggie stepped closer, her eyes filled with the tears she hadn't shed over her husband. "Yes?"

With an embarrassed flush, he continued. "If you were mine, I'd do everything within my power to make you happy. You'd never have reason to cry."

"Thank you, Earl. That's real kind of you. But it's just too soon for me to think about another man in my life right now."

"I could take care of you and the boys. You wouldn't have to worry about anything."

Maggie shook her head, sniffling. "I can't. I care for you, too. But I haven't even gotten used to the idea that I'm a widow yet."

He lowered his head, nodding his understanding, but unable to hide his disappointment.

Behind them, Dani appeared with the boys. They all had a fresh-baked cookie in their hands, and Brandy surmised Earl had let them off at the kitchen door with orders to have a snack before coming to the parlor.

"What's wrong?" Darrel asked, seeing the tears on his mother's cheeks.

"Nothing, son," Earl said.

Darrel stepped next to his mother and took her hand. Davey, not wanting to be left out, crowded in, too.

"Come on. I'll take ya'll home," Earl offered. "We can have a talk with the boys on the way."

Maggie turned back. "Thank you all for your concern. I think you were right, Adam. Everything is going to be just fine."

They filed out of Carmel's house, leaving an expectant silence behind. Dani frowned in confusion. Carmel smiled knowingly.

Suddenly Brandy became aware that Adam's arm still held her against his side. Instinct urged her to lean into his warm, solid form. But she knew that would be a mistake. They'd tried to find common ground where they could peacefully coexist. But there was none. She was what she was. He would never accept that, and she could never change.

With tremendous regret tugging painfully at her heart, she stepped away from him.

Chapter Eighteen

"I'll see you home."

Adam held Brandy's coat as she tucked her arms into the sleeves.

"That isn't necessary."

His hands lingered a moment on her shoulders, then slid slowly down her arms. She could feel his warmth against her back, and a hot wave of desire shot through her.

"It's on my way," he said, stepping around in front of her. In his gem-green eyes, Brandy saw her feelings of desire mirrored. "I'm staying at the cabin tonight."

A delicious shiver of longing swept over Brandy. For the first time in her life, she wanted a man. Not any man, only Adam. Again his gaze met hers and her heart turned over. "That would be nice, then."

"Dani's all tucked in," Carmel said, rolling into the front hall.

"Is she still upset?"

"She was still a little sad, thinking of Darrel and Davey losing their father. But I explained to her that they really didn't know him that well. She's sleeping now."

"I'd better get going, then."

"I'll see Brandy home." He bent to kiss Carmel's cheek. "And I'll see you tomorrow. You'll be all right?"

She nodded. "Jean is here, so I'll be fine. Go on before it gets any later," she said, shooing them to the door. The wind blew in and she shivered. "Or any colder."

The frigid air curled around Brandy's ankles. Her skirt whipped against her legs, fluttered, and snapped back into place. She buttoned the heavy wooden buttons on her coat and turned up the collar.

"It's getting colder by the minute," she said, chafing her arms with her hands to warm them.

Adam shrugged into his leather jacket and pulled it closed. "I thought this cold snap would be letting up by now. But I think we're in for an early winter after all. Wait here. I'll be right back."

He jogged around the side of the house, and Brandy watched the soft leather pull tight across his shoulders. The form-worn denims swished as his muscled legs pumped. Despite the cold, Brandy felt as though she'd sipped sweet wine. Her stomach clenched, and her blood flowed like warm caramel.

Soon, he came back leading his gray horse. "Would you like to ride?" he asked.

Brandy felt a flame of passion sear her reasoning. More than anything, at that moment she wanted to be cradled against his thighs on the back of the massive animal, their bodies pressed tight as they swayed with the horse's movement. She cleared her throat, feeling icy sweat dot her brow.

"No, thank you," she whispered shakily. "I'd rather walk."

He held the reins, and together they headed for the end of Cherry Blossom Street.

Watching her rapid breathing make little clouds on the cold air, Brandy told herself she had to get hold of her wildly careening emotions. Every time Adam glanced in her direction, a rocket of desire exploded through her. Her middle felt heavy and her limbs leaden. Her senses hummed with a current of awareness.

The horse snorted and sidestepped, jarring Adam's shoulder and knocking him into Brandy. Adam reached out his hand to steady her, and Brandy jumped away nervously, afraid actual physical contact at this point would be more than she could handle.

He cleared his throat. "Sorry," he murmured, jostling the horse with his elbow, an embarrassed frown creasing his brow.

As they approached the outstretched

branches of the live oak, Brandy knew she didn't want Adam to leave yet. They stopped beneath the branches, and she stared up at his features, which were lit by the dappled moonlight.

"I hope everything works out for Maggie now," she said, trying to prolong their time together.

"I'm sure it will. Earl loves her. He has ever since they went to school together, I think."

A sharp wind whistled around them and Brandy shuddered. Adam step closer and immediately all thoughts of the cold fled her mind.

"You should go on in. It's getting colder."

Nodding, she tipped her face up to look into his eyes. Her breath caught in her throat and she gasped. Suddenly the undeniable fact hit her, shocking her with the depth of emotion she felt. God, she was in love with Adam!

His face was handsome, his magnetism potent. All of that could account for the overwhelming attraction she felt. But she knew it was his soul, so kind and giving, that made her heart pound against her breast.

Certain he could read the revelation on her crimson face, she looked away. "Would you like to come in for a cup of hot tea?"

His eyes snapped back to her face and he seemed surprised. Two tiny lines appeared on the side of his lips and between his brows.

"I better get going."

She nodded, ready to withdraw, then

stopped. No, she didn't want him to go. "It's going to be very cold by the time you reach your cabin. Are you sure you wouldn't like to come in for just a minute and get warm first?"

He hesitated, studying her face in the obscure light. Brandy held her breath as she waited, then released it when her chest began to ache. The tiny puff made a cloud on the cold air and he chuckled.

"Yeah, I guess I will."

Her knees trembling, she walked to the door. Pushing it open, she motioned him inside.

Adam ducked to get through the small doorway, his eyes trying to focus in the pitch-blackness of the wagon's interior. He felt Brandy brush past him, heard the sound of a match against a rough surface, and smelled the sulfur at the same time he squinted against the bright flame from the lamp she'd lit.

"It'll just take a minute," she said, removing her coat and opening the tiny door on the side of the wood-burning cookstove. She dropped several twigs into the black belly and stoked the banked embers. Adam eyed her bottom, which was outlined against the thin fabric of her skirt, and turned away. He released a heavy breath and watched it form a white cloud in the air.

"Damn," he said, rubbing his hands together. "It's cold in here."

She fastened the latch on the stove door and straightened, wiping her hands on her skirt.

"It'll warm up in no time," she told him, dipping water from a small bucket beside the stove and filling the kettle.

Adam's eyes, accustomed to the light, scanned the cramped wagon. The table, though well made, was old and small. Only two crude seats flanked the oaken surface. He reached up to remove his hat and noticed for the first time the ceiling barely over his lowered head. The bunks were narrow and short. He thought of his outburst when he'd learned Dani was living with Carmel, and a wave of shame washed over him. No wonder Brandy allowed her sister to stay with his aunt.

True to Brandy's word, the little space soon warmed up, but Adam's distress grew. He removed his jacket. If it warmed up this fast in the winter, what would it be like in the heat of an unrelenting summer? The place must be an oven.

"Why didn't you move into Carmel's, too?" he asked. "She has plenty of room."

Brandy laughed and rubbed her hands together once more as the warmth finally began to seep into her. "I can just imagine what your reaction would have been to that."

Flushing with chagrin, he took an awkward step toward her and bumped his head on a cross beam anchored to the ceiling.

When he cursed, Brandy smiled. Damn, but she was beautiful. Her needs were so simple she could find happiness in calling such a place home. Realizing he wanted so much more for her, Adam had to finally admit the truth. Somewhere along the way, despite his objections and proclamations, he'd fallen under Brandy Ashton's spell. He cared for her more than he could ever remember caring for any woman other than his family members.

And he desired her. Never had he ached for a woman so long or so intently. Just her laugh or her smile could shoot hot shards of passion through his loins. Even now, he felt his body's reaction to her closeness. Her lips beckoned, and for once he didn't argue with his conscience.

"What are you laughing at?" he asked, wearing a mock frown and rubbing his forehead.

"I'm sorry," she said through her mirth. "I never thought of my father as a small man. In fact, most of the time, he seemed larger than life. But he certainly didn't fill the place up like you do."

"Yes, well, he must have been a midget then."

Another spurt of laughter exploded from Brandy, and she covered her mouth with her hand. Turning back, she gathered cups and her best tea cozy and set them on the table.

Adam came forward and drew out a chair, but when he tried to sit, his knees bumped the table and the cups rattled and teetered dangerously. He slid out again and stood.

"Oh, dear," Brandy said, a huge smile spreading over her rosy lips. "You really are taller than I realized."

Her gaze swept the tiny room.

"I'll just sit here," he said, easing the seat of his pants toward her bunk.

"On the bed?" she exclaimed.

He straightened so quickly his head brushed the ceiling, and he ducked to avoid another nasty crack on the skull.

"If you'd rather I didn't—"

"No, of course not," she assured him.

Brandy fought for breath as she imagined Adam on her bed. His body touching the same blankets that had touched her as she'd dreamed about him the night before. The dream had been very real, very vivid, and very disturbing. She swallowed hard and whirled to face the stove.

"I've been a damned fool," he suddenly exclaimed without preamble.

Brandy, holding the steaming kettle with a woven oven mitt, faced him slowly. "What?"

He met her startled gaze and his eyes softened to a warm jade. He shook his head, raking his fingers through his hair.

"My accusations toward you were based on prejudice. I disliked medicine peddlers, and so I attributed you with all their unsavory qualities."

"You did what you thought you had to do. I understand that."

"I've been a fool," he repeated. "In trying to protect this town, I acted like an ass toward you and your sister. You haven't done anything the people of Charming didn't want you to do.

And you haven't done anyone harm as far as I can see. I didn't want to admit I was wrong about you, that you weren't like the others who'd come through here before. I was afraid you'd hurt Carmel, and because of my fear, I intentionally made things difficult for you."

"Are you saying you believe in my remedies now?" she asked, setting the kettle aside, her dark eyes narrowed in doubt.

Adam heaved a sigh and slowly shook his head. "I wish I could say that, Brandy. That would solve everything, wouldn't it? But I just can't. I no longer think you'll cheat my aunt or intentionally hurt her in any way, but I'm afraid I don't hold out much hope for your ability to heal her, either."

Brandy came and sat beside him on the bed. He couldn't trust her, but at least now she understood where his emotions originated.

"You can't help how you feel."

"No, but I could have acted better. I'm—"

She pressed her fingers to his lips. "Don't. You've said enough. It doesn't matter now. None of it. I've seen how much you love your aunt. How you care for Maggie and the other folks in town. I admire you for standing up and trying to protect them."

He took her fingers and pressed a kiss to the sensitive tips. Brandy felt a swirl of longing race all the way to her toes.

"If I had shut my mouth and opened my eyes, I would have seen the truth. I don't need to protect anyone from you." He closed his eyes briefly and lowered her hand to his chest, where she could feel his heart thumping madly. "Except perhaps myself."

Brandy sucked in her breath and clamped her teeth on her lower lip. Did he mean what she thought? Could it be?

"You?" she whispered.

He nodded. "I've grown used to you being around. And I'm afraid I didn't hide my attraction very well. I told myself it was crazy, but I couldn't help it. So many times I was angry with you; while at the same time I found myself wanting to share your laughter." He caressed her cheek. "I searched for a hint of your smile like the first rays of morning sunshine."

"Oh, Adam."

He smiled, finally, and the unfamiliar expression warmed his usually cool mien. His emerald eyes sparkled, and his full mouth parted to show his straight white teeth. The transformation took Brandy's breath away and she gently cupped his chin.

"You have such a beautiful smile," she told him.

They sat for several moments, each touching the other, looking their fill. Slowly, Adam's head lowered toward hers, and Brandy arched to meet his seeking lips.

Their kiss burned hotter than white flame, instantly ardent and eager. He wrapped his arms around her back and she encircled his neck. And still the kiss lingered.

Neither hurried. They explored slowly, tasting, touching. When Adam's hand slid around her ribs to brush against the soft fullness of her breast, she opened her eyes and gazed at him.

"I want to touch you."

She took his hand and led it to the hard nub of her nipple. She couldn't hide her reaction. She didn't want to.

"Yes," she said against his lips as he kissed her once more.

Kneading her breast gently, he sought the deepest recesses of her hot mouth. Letting his tongue delve into the sweetness, he pleasured her.

His hand sought and found the waistband of her skirt, and he slipped his hand beneath her blouse.

In a move that shocked him to the core and aroused him beyond endurance, she crossed her hands and boldly lifted the loose garment over her head. Only her ribboned lawn camisole protected her upper body from his questing eyes and hands.

In return, he tugged his own shirt off and took her hands, indicating his need for her to touch him as he had touched her.

Trembling, she let her fingers roam the steely contours of his chest. A small patch of soft golden hair started between his nipples and trickled down to the buttons of his fly. Her eyes lit on the bulge beneath, and she quickly averted her gaze.

"I want you," he confessed, seeing her blush.

"I've wanted you since the day I stood and watched you hawking your remedies in the square. I'd never seen anyone so lovely, so full of life. I craved you, as though your vivacity was a drug I could draw from."

Brandy couldn't speak. Never had she thought she'd love a man this way. Nothing mattered, except their time together. Their differences couldn't temper their passion. She wanted him, too.

With her seeking lips, she showed him how much and they both fell victim to the raging emotions they'd held in check for weeks. His passion gained momentum, and he leaned over her, pressing her into the blankets. He followed her down, his lips never leaving hers.

"Love me," she murmured, between feathered kisses.

Adam drew back, only slightly, and met her heavy-lidded gaze. "Are you sure?"

"Yes, oh, yes. I'm certain."

He clasped her to him and stretched out along her side. His booted feet hung over the edge of the cot, his elbow bumped the wall of the wagon. But he didn't mind the close quarters. Nothing could lessen the sweetness of this moment in her arms. Slowly, he unfastened the buttons on the side of her skirt, and she rose so he could remove it. Beneath she wore only her sleeveless camisole and a simple pair of ruffled pantalets. He unbuckled the tapes on either side of her waist and hesitated a moment in case she should change her mind.

When she made no move to stop him, he removed the undergarments and rolled down her thick black stockings. She lay naked before him, unabashed and radiant in her beauty.

"God, you're the sweetest thing I've ever seen," he said, his voice rough with longing.

Her cheeks flushed, but she didn't turn from his heated perusal. After a lingering caress, he rose and quickly removed the rest of his clothing. She watched, silent but wide-eyed.

"Brandy?"

"You're magnificent," she whispered, her hands reaching for him. He rolled atop her and she let her fingers explore his scorching flesh. A sheen of perspiration broke out along his spine.

"You're hot."

He groaned and lowered his body to press fully against hers. "Oh, God, yes."

Again his mouth covered hers, his weight bearing her down. The feel of flesh against flesh was a wonderful new sensation she'd never imagined.

His hand skimmed her stomach and eased between their bodies until he located her upper thighs. Making tiny circles with his blunt nails, he teased her, drawing closer and closer to the core of her womanhood.

Brandy gasped as he reached his destination and touched that part of her no one had ever touched. She cried out against his mouth, her exclamation drowned in another soul-jarring kiss.

Her stomach coiled around a feeling she couldn't fight or understand. Trying to pull her lips from his, she longed to ask him what was happening to her. The stroking of his fingers caused the knot in her middle to tighten.

Whimpering a need she couldn't identify, she arched against him and felt the proof of his desire press into her pelvis. Suddenly she knew what she hungered for. Running her hand down his back and around his hard, muscled hip, she led the male part of him to her opening.

Adam made a strangled sound deep in his throat and tried to pull back, but Brandy lifted her hips and he was lost. He sank into her with a cry of unleashed desire.

Almost as soon as the slight pain subsided, the burning need returned, and Brandy felt herself lifted to the precipice of fullfillment once more. Adam thrust into her over and over until she soared on a wave of sensuous pleasure.

Cupping her cheeks with his palms, he stared into her face as the sensation gripped her. Seeing her reach the pinnacle, he surged forth, joining her in the riotous assualt on their senses.

They lay silent, only their labored breathing and the pounding of their hearts disturbing the stillness around them.

Racked by a depth of emotion she hadn't known existed, Brandy began to tremble. Adam clutched her tighter and reached for the quilt they'd shoved to the foot of the cot in their tussle. He drew it over them both and shifted to the side, taking some of his weight from her small frame, but not removing his warmth.

"Words escape me," he whispered against her hair, as he pressed a kiss to the crown of her head.

Brandy cupped the back of his neck and led his face into the curve of her shoulder. No words were necessary. Their bodies had spoken volumes.

A bitter cold nipped Brandy's toes, and she snuggled deeper into the blankets. But the pounding that had roused her from her slumber now pulled her fully awake.

Someone was knocking on the door!

She sat up quickly and gasped, turning to look at Adam. Only an empty pillow greeted her. He'd gone. Sometime during the night, he'd slipped away without her knowing it. She felt both anguished and, considering her early visitor, relieved.

"Just a moment," she called, throwing the covers aside. She reached for her heavy chenille robe and drew it around her, shivering in the chilly morning air.

Swiping the tangled mass of hair from her face, she opened the door a crack.

"Suzanne?"

Brandy couldn't have been more surprised. She glanced back at the rumpled cot, still warm and scented with her and Adam's lovemaking.

Ignoring the blast of cold air that swallowed her up, she stepped out the door.

"What can I do for you?"

The blonde studied her for a long minute, and Brandy wondered if Suzanne suspected how she'd spent the early hours of the morning. Of course, that was ridiculous, she told herself, clutching the robe closer to ward off the bitter cold.

"I wanted to speak with you before going to Adam," Suzanne said, drawing a slip of paper from her cloak pocket. She handed it to Brandy.

"What is this?"

"That's the proof Adam has been looking for. The evidence he needs to send you away."

Stunned, Brandy stared at Suzanne. "What are you talking about?"

"My father recognized your wagon the first time he saw it. It took a little persuading, but I finally got him to recall where he'd seen it."

Foreboding chased away Brandy's thoughts of the cold. Apprehension slithered up her spine bringing a chill of its own.

"I don't understand."

"Neither did I at first. But I wired St. Louis after Papa finally remembered a few of the details, and the marshall there filled in the blanks for me. It seems," she said, an evil grin of malicious pleasure crossing her face, "that your father spent some time in his jail."

"Jail?" Brandy parroted, feeling half-witted

as she struggled to follow the thread of this bizarre conversation.

"Yes. He was arrested and sentenced to fourteen months for fraud and corruption."

"I don't believe you. My father was never in jail."

"Look at the paper and see for yourself," Suzanne taunted. "It's all there. A long time ago, your father ran a counterfeit revival, bilking people out of money with his false claims."

"False claims?" Brandy whispered, her hand trembling so she couldn't make out the words before her.

"Yes. Claims that he could heal people." Suzanne chortled wickedly and shook her head. Pressing her fingernail to her lip, she added, "Now where have I heard that before?"

Chapter Nineteen

Throwing back her head, Suzanne went off in peals of laughter, and the sound echoed through the winter-bare branches of the big oak.

Brandy tried to focus on the words shifting and wavering before her damp eyes. It couldn't be. Suzanne had to be lying.

"The marshall was only too happy to wire that statement when I explained what you and your sister were trying to do here. It's all there. Wade Ashton's arrest, the subsequent trial. It was a big scandal. So many people had donated money to your father's coffers. Everyone attended the trial so they could see justice done. And now, it's my turn for justice."

"You're wrong. This marshall must have

285

made a mistake or confused my father with someone else."

"It's not likely," Suzanne said with a snort. "Your father's name, his description, as well as a description of that trashy wagon. I don't imagine there are many around like that."

Brandy rapidly scanned the first few lines on the paper. The date of her father's arrest was two years prior to her birth.

"Why are you doing this?" Brandy asked. "Why bring it all out now?" She suspected Suzanne's motives, but couldn't understand the woman's hatred.

"Why? To help Adam of course. He's been wanting to get rid of you ever since you arrived. And now he has the ammunition to do it. No one will trust you or defend you after they see this."

She snatched the page from Brandy's trembling fingers and pretended to read it again. "Umm, umm, umm," she said, shaking her head. "Imagine, having the daughter of a criminal camping right in our very own town. A charlatan posing as a healer. Why, it's a wonder we haven't been robbed blind while we slept."

When Suzanne trilled another high-pitched laugh and turned to go, Brandy rushed forward.

"Suzanne, wait," she called. "Don't do this, please." Brandy hated to beg but she couldn't stop herself. Last night, she'd enjoyed pure bliss. This morning, she'd glimpsed pure hell. She couldn't lose Adam now. Not like this. She didn't care if the whole town shunned her. Only Adam's reaction mattered to her now. And she knew his honor would never allow him to forget her father's crimes once he found out. She couldn't bear to see the censure she knew would be in his eyes once more. Desperately, she reached out and grasped Suzanne's arm.

Snatching her cloak from beneath Brandy's fingers, Suzanne sneered. "Take your hand off me, you little tramp. Do you think for a minute I would help you even if I could? I want you gone more than anyone. And now," she said, waving the paper triumphantly, "I can finally be rid of you."

"This is about Adam, isn't it?" Brandy rushed on, her toes sinking into the dew-covered ground. Icy cold pierced her bare skin and sent needles of pain up her legs, but she paid her discomfort no mind.

"You don't have to do this. I'll stay away from him. I swear, if you promise me you won't show that paper to anyone, I'll stay away from him."

Brandy hated making the promise, but more than her pride and her heart was at stake here. She had to consider Dani's feelings, too. What would the news do to her sister? Dani had blossomed since they'd arrived in Charming. What would this scandal do to her newfound security?

Suzanne rolled the page in her hand and tapped it against her palm. "I'm going to take great pleasure in showing this not only to Adam but to every person in Charming. Starting this very morning."

She turned and strolled away from the tree, humming a lively tune as she walked jauntily toward the main street of town.

Brandy's heart fell to her stomach, and she clutched the chenille robe tighter around her to forestall the violent shaking that had overtaken her. Tears coursed down her face, stinging her frigid cheeks. She couldn't move, couldn't breathe. Her legs quivered unsteadily beneath her. What would she do? How could she face Adam after he learned of this?

Seeing her cold-reddened toes peeking from beneath the robe reminded her of the dampness, and she went back into the wagon. Stoking the fire by rote, she numbly went about heating the tea she and Adam had never gotten around to drinking the night before. Wrapped in a cocoon of anguish, she sank into the corner of her disheveled cot. Her throat ached with despair. Sobs bubbled up, blocking her breath. Her lungs burned and she doubled over in physical pain. She knew what she had to do. And she knew it would tear her heart out to do it.

"Brandy! Brandy, open the door."

Brandy roused herself from her stupor of hopelessness and went to the door.

Maggie stood outside, shivering in the cold wind that whipped furiously across the field.

"I just came from town," she blurted, trying

to catch her breath. She stepped into the wagon without waiting for an invitation. "Suzanne—"

"I know," Brandy said, conscious she still wore the robe and nothing else. She hadn't even been able to rouse herself enough to dress after Suzanne had left.

"Is it true, about your father?

Brandy shrugged. "I don't know. I suppose it must be. The statement Suzanne had looked official."

"You didn't know?"

Brandy met the spark of anger mixed with pity in Maggie's eyes and shook her head.

"I'd like to just tear Suzanne's hair out by the roots," Maggie cried, bustling over to the stove and reheating the twice-boiled tea. After it began to bubble, she poured them each a cup and handed one to Brandy. "How could she be so vicious?"

"She wants Adam. And she wants to be rid of me."

"Well, that's because a blind man could see Adam's interested in you. She's jealous. He never looked at her the way he looks at you, with passion and desire burning just below the surface." Maggie sighed wistfully and sat at the table.

Brandy cringed, certain Adam's expression would be far different the next time he faced her.

"I've been sitting here thinking over my life," she said, warming her hands on the cup. "I guess I should have suspected something like this. Papa always was a dreamer. He fell into one scheme after the other, always certain his latest venture would make him rich. Mama was his constant over the years. She brought in money-selling remedies and never let on that she doubted any of his ideas. But she was always stressing the value of honesty. I didn't know it was Papa she constantly felt needed warning."

"That doesn't necessarily mean he was a bad person, Brandy. Lots of people suffer flights of fancy."

Maggie's eyes shone and Brandy thought her friend had forgiven her wayward husband and maybe even had a few dreams of her own now. She hoped they'd all come true. Maggie deserved some happiness.

"I suppose if Mama knew of his past that would explain why she was so scrupulously honest. After they met and married, she must have tried to keep him on the right side of the law. But after she died, I just don't know. He was the one who convinced me I had the gift for healing. I hadn't thought so before Mama died, but Papa vowed he could see it. He pressed me until I agreed to take Mama's place. Now, I just can't be sure."

"Don't think like that," Maggie admonished. "You do have a gift for healing. Just look at all the good you've done here."

"What? Cured a few cases of bunions and cleared up Jean's blemishes? Anyone with minimal knowledge of herbs could have done the same."

"What about Davey?"

Brandy rubbed a tear from her cheek and looked into Maggie's eyes. "I didn't do anything for Davey. Adam told me he's still having seizures."

"But they aren't as bad. He's lots better."

"That's just because he's getting better nourishment now. The milk and eggs and such did that, not me."

"You can't believe that?"

"I have to. It's what Adam will believe." Brandy pressed her hands to her eyes. "It's what he's believed all along and he was right."

"There must have been other people in other towns. Folks you helped."

"We never stayed in one place long enough to see the results of my remedies. I guess now I know why," she said, lowering her head. "Papa never stayed anywhere more than a few days. Dani and I hated traveling in the winter months, but he'd insist we keep going. Usually south, where we didn't have to worry about the weather slowing us down. This was going to be our first time staying in one place for the winter. I wanted to give Dani that; she's been through so much."

Brandy's tears flowed freely now, falling onto the wrapped bodice of her robe. Black grief such as she'd never known encompassed her. Why hadn't she seen her father for what he'd been? He'd used her, just as he used the people in St. Louis, to make a quick dollar.

"Come to Carmel's," Maggie urged, taking her hand.

Brandy released her hand and scrubbed the moisture from her face. "No, I can't. I can't face her. God, she was counting on me to make her well."

"Carmel will understand, Brandy. You're not responsible for something your father did more than twenty years ago. She really cares about you. And she loves Dani like her own."

Brandy slowly lifted her head. A thought seared her brain, but she quickly discarded it. No, she couldn't. Just the idea stole her breath and caused a wrenching pain in her gut.

"I'll be all right," she lied, certain she'd never be happy again. Her whole world felt as though it had shattered into a million tiny, jagged pieces.

"I left the boys with Dani and Carmel. I have to get back."

Brandy forced a tight smile. "You go on. And don't let on to Dani anything's amiss. I think I should be the one to tell her."

"You'll come then?"

Brandy nodded. "But later. I can't go to her like this. It'll frighten her. Explain to Carmel for me?"

Maggie pressed her hand. "I will. And don't worry. Folks'll understand. Everyone likes you and Dani."

Brandy watched her go, depression weighing her down. She knew it didn't matter what anyone else thought. Adam's opinion was the only one that counted. And she already knew what he would think.

It was late afternoon, and Brandy hadn't yet been able to muster the strength to go to Carmel's. For the first time in her life, she couldn't shake off her sorrow and depression. It hung around her like a suffocating cloak, cutting off her will to prevail. She'd spent the day crying and considering her options. They were limited. Worse, they were all too painful to even consider.

She'd managed to get dressed, but she was barefoot and her eyes were bloodshot from her tears.

She'd reheated her tea for perhaps the tenth time, but still could not take more than a sip. Every time she tried, her stomach roiled and clenched.

She heard the sound of approaching hoof-beats and tensed. Shaking her hair out of her face, she went to the door and peeked out.

The sight of Adam, tall and proud on his gray mount, shattered her fragile control. Panic rioted within her breast. She wasn't ready for this! She couldn't face his anger yet.

He looked up and smiled warmly as he dismounted. Brandy narrowed her eyes. He looked . . . happy. He tied his reins to a low-hanging branch and came to the door of the wagon.

"Hey, darlin'. Can I come in?"

Brandy stepped aside dumbly, wondering why he wasn't demanding answers.

"I'm sorry it took so long to get back. I've been out to the Cooper's farm." He kissed her cheek and warmed his hands over the stove. "Their pumpkins were vandalized again last night. Only this time old Harold was waitin' for the varmints. He had 'em trussed up in his barn when I got there. A couple of kids from the next county. I convinced him to let them go, and I took them home, with a warning that should keep them out of trouble for a while."

He turned back, his smile fading as he got his first good look at Brandy. "What's the matter, darlin'? You sick?"

Relief rushed through Brandy until she thought it would explode right out of the top of her head. He didn't know! He had no idea! He'd been gone all day.

"Hey, have you been crying?" he asked, stepping closer and taking her arms. He studied her face. A look of chagrin cut across his expression. "You didn't think I'd run out on you, did you?"

"No, I'm fine," she whispered, her eyes filling with happy tears. She offered a silent prayer of thanks to God for being generous enough to give her this one last moment with Adam.

He pulled her into his embrace. "Come here," he said. "I've been waiting all day to hold you again."

She went eagerly into his arms, her mouth searching for his. She kissed him with all the love she'd thought lost to her. He drew back, grinned, and swept her up. Lowering his mouth to hers, he settled her gently on the cot.

"I want to take you to my cabin," he said, already reaching for the buttons on her shirtwaist. "This damned bed is too short."

Brandy forced a light laugh, hiding her broken heart. They'd been blessed with a brief reprieve. And she meant to make memories they'd both hold in their hearts forever.

With desperate haste, they stripped off their clothes. Brandy ached with a need so great she could barely contain herself. Adam tried to soothe her, but his need was as great as hers and soon they came together. Fast and hard, he drove into her. She responded in kind, rolling him over and straddling his hips. He cursed low, and she reveled in the power she felt as she took control.

"Oh, darlin'," he moaned, holding her hips as she rode him. "Do you know what you're doing to me?"

Brandy knew. For the first time in her life she loved a man enough to share her body and soul with him. And she had only one chance to show him how much she loved him before fate would part them.

It was over too soon and they both sank into the blankets, exhausted.

"Lord, girl. I guess I don't have to ask if you missed me," Adam teased, his pulse and breathing still accelerated.

Brandy pillowed her head on his shoulder

and snuggled closer. "I missed you," she said, thinking, *God, how I will miss you.*

"We didn't talk much last night," he said, a smile in his voice. "I guess we'd better."

"Not now," she whispered, pressing kisses against his neck and chest. "We'll talk later."

She knew they wouldn't. There would be no point. Right now she just wanted to savor their time together. She knew she ought to tell him the truth, but she couldn't bring herself to spoil these last moments together. He'd know soon enough, and then there'd be nothing to talk about anyway.

For several minutes they lay there, silently exploring their love for each other. Adam's caresses grew bolder, and Brandy could feel his renewed passion stirring. Bitter tears threatened to fill her eyes, but she blinked them back and forced a smile as he rolled her onto her back.

Much later, he sat up and pulled his trousers on. Brandy drew the blankets against her bare chest and touched his back.

"Are you leaving?"

He turned and kissed her full on the mouth. "I have to ride out to Cooper's to fill him in on his vandals. It'll take me a couple of hours, but I'll be back." His stern countenance had returned and he cupped her cheek. "Then we're going to have to talk seriously. About us, about this," he said, motioning to the rumpled cot. He tucked his arms into his shirtsleeves and hastily fastened his shirt up the front.

She smiled and nodded, trying to pretend for a moment that everything could be worked out with a few words. The lines of tension eased from his face, and he leaned forward for a long, sweet kiss.

"I want you to move in with Carmel, for a while. I didn't realize how—unsuitable this wagon was."

Brandy glanced around at the home she'd lived in her entire life. She shook her head. "This is where I belong," she said.

He stoked the fire, which had died, and turned back toward the cot. "It's too damned cold for one thing. Besides, Carmel has plenty of room. At least think about it?"

"I have," she told him honestly. In the last twenty-four hours, she'd thought of little else. She'd have given anything to live with Adam. Either at Carmel's or at his own cozy cabin. Now, it would never be.

He frowned darkly. "Just agree to think about it. If this is going to work out we're both going to have to make some big changes."

Unable even to speak, she nodded her head. It wasn't a lie. She'd probably think about Adam, and Charming, for the rest of her days.

"Good. I better go." He leaned close again. "'Bye," he whispered against her lips.

"Good-bye," she said, her heart breaking. She saw his frown and forced a smile. He still looked uneasy as he pulled on his boots and coat and left.

Brandy listened until she could no longer hear his horse's hooves. He hadn't mentioned marriage, but she knew he would when he returned. Adam was too honorable to have made love to her without having made a commitment, at least in his own mind.

Last night, she'd thought of their future together. But that was all changed now. A future with Adam was out of the question. She knew what she had to do. But, God help her, she didn't know how she'd ever be able to do it.

Chapter Twenty

With her resolve firmly in place and her tears in check, Brandy donned her coat and started for Carmel's house. She checked Sal's leg before she left. The swelling was gone, and no tenderness remained. She hoped the mare would be fit to travel.

The icy wind whipped Brandy's hair around to slash against her cheeks. Heavy, moist clouds sat low in the sky. Time was running out.

Gaining the porch steps, she took a few seconds to look around. This house and town had become dear to her. A flash of wretched loneliness stabbed her heart. She'd miss Charming.

Carmel answered the door, her usually animated face for once showing every one of her years. Her green eyes, so like Adam's, lowered with sympathy.

"Come in, child," she said, clutching her shawl closely against the frigid air stealing into the hall.

Brandy stepped inside, but didn't remove her coat. She shivered from cold and despair. Carmel rolled toward the parlor, Brandy following.

"Dani's in the kitchen helping Jean make pumpkin cookies. We can talk privately."

Going to the welcoming flames of the fire, Brandy held out her trembling hands. But the cold that permeated her body came as much from the inside as out, and she feared no amount of heat could warm her.

"I've decided to leave," Brandy announced resolutely.

Carmel gasped and Brandy forced herself to face the woman she'd grown so close to. Her eyes stung, but she'd cried all her tears.

"There must be some other way," Carmel said.

Shaking her head, Brandy went to sit on the settee. She fiddled with the embroidered doily on the cushioned arm. "No, there isn't. I've thought it through. Really, I have."

"Does Adam know yet?"

Twisting her hands in her lap Brandy said softly, "No."

"Wait and talk to him at least. He cares for you. I know he does. You've been so good for him. You must have noticed the changes."

Yes, he'd changed. He even cared for her now. But he'd been honest about his doubts. Despite his feelings for her, he still had them. And when he learned about her father, they'd be confirmed as far as he was concerned. She could face the whole town and their suspicions, but she couldn't bear to see the hostility return to his eyes. Not after those Kelly-green orbs had gazed down on her with tender passion.

"We made a bargain. Despite his concerns, Adam held to it even when he'd have liked to have forced me to go. Winter's here now and I have to keep my end of the deal. It's time to move on. The sooner the better," Brandy added, looking out the window at the gathering clouds.

"At least wait to see what he has to say. Maybe he's changed his mind."

Brandy watched the icy moisture trickle down the window pane, reflecting the fire's glow in the diamond drops. So warm and welcoming inside, so cold and desolate out. A mirror image of her own self. Inside, her heart had turned to ice at the thought of leaving Adam. But outside, her body burned with memories of his touch.

"Don't you see? I can't face him. He's said all along that I was a fraud. Oh, he came to like me and Dani well enough. But there was always that mistrust."

Brandy looked over her shoulder at Carmel's bright eyes. "I can't bear to see his face when he learns about my father's crimes."

"Stop that," the older woman admonished, wiping at her eyes. "You aren't to blame for something your father did before you were even born. You couldn't have known."

"I think, deep down, I realized he wasn't all I thought he was. But I loved Papa, and he was a good father despite his faults. Dani and I worshiped him. I'm not sure it would have made any difference if I had known. I might have done everything just the same." Her uncertainty ate at her. She'd wondered a hundred times since learning the truth about her father if it would have really made a difference to her. Would she have refused his pleas had she known his only thought was to turn a profit?

Looking at Carmel's slumped form in the hated wheelchair, Brandy could only guess.

"I truly wanted to help you, though," she said, desperate for Adam's aunt to believe that if nothing else.

"And you did, you and Dani. Why, I've been feeling a lot stronger. I was just thinking yesterday that maybe it was time to try walking again."

"No," Brandy cried, her eyes flying wide. "You mustn't do that. You could hurt yourself even worse."

"Pshaw. My hips hardly hurt a bit, even as cold as it's been. Do you know how long it's been since I've made it through a winter without that awful pain?"

Recognizing Carmel's ploy to cheer her up,

Brandy summoned a small smile. "Thank you for saying that. But it doesn't change the facts. I don't have any healing powers. I wasn't ever as good as Mama. I can't keep taking money from people for something I don't possess."

"What will you do?"

Shrugging, Brandy fought off the wave of debilitating fear. What would she do? The only skill she'd ever learned had been a lie. She knew nothing else.

"I'll find something," she said, thankful she sounded more confident than she felt.

"And what of Dani?"

The steel band around her heart closed tighter. Could she do it? Even for Dani's sake?

Yes, she had to. Her mind was made up.

"I want Dani to stay here with you."

Carmel's face paled, and her hand fluttered to her breast. "You can't mean that."

"Yes, I do. She deserves better than anything I could offer her, especially now. I didn't realize it until just recently, but Dani never liked living the way we did. To me, our way of life represented freedom. But it must have been frightening to a child without even her mother to assure her. There's something about Dani you don't know."

"You mean her, um, hobby. I know about that."

Shock slipped across Brandy's features and she sat straighter. "How?"

"She told me. We had a little chat, and she agreed it wouldn't be a good idea to keep it up.

303

Living in a town this small, she knew someone was bound to find out. She didn't want to—"

Carmel's words trailed off and her eyes lowered. The lump in Brandy's throat grew and tightened, and she asked, "Dani didn't want to have to leave, did she?"

Carmel shook her head. "She didn't want to cause you any trouble."

"She's really a sweet child. She never meant to be bad," Brandy said. "But she's never been able to stop herself, either. Until now."

Their gazes locked across the small space. Brandy's heart did battle with what her mind told her would be best. Carmel watched her silent struggle.

In the end, her love for her sister won out, as it always had. "Which is why Dani should stay with you."

"She won't do it. That little girl loves you more than life itself. She'll never agree to this."

"That's probably true," Brandy conceded, smiling at the thought of her sister's determined spirit. "Which is why I've decided not to tell her."

"No," Carmel exclaimed. "You can't do that. It'll break her heart."

"She'll be hurt at first. But in the future, when she's older, she'll know I did it because I love her so much. And she'll have you. If you'll have her, that is," she added, realizing Carmel hadn't actually agreed to the plan.

"You know that I love that child. There's

nothing I'd like more than to keep her with me always. But she belongs with you. You're her family. Won't you stay? I'm sure everything will work out in the end."

Brandy wished she could believe that. If she thought for a moment—But, no. From the first, she'd recognized Adam's honor. He'd be torn when he learned the truth. He'd feel obligated to Brandy because of the love they'd shared. But he'd never be able to forget her father's past or to keep from associating it with what she did.

And even if he refused to ask her to leave because of what they'd shared, things would never be the same between them again. And seeing him, even hearing his voice, would be too painful after the beautiful dreams she'd allowed herself to have. Without Adam's love, she could never stay in Charming.

Brandy's anguish almost overcame her control. More than anything, she wanted to accept Carmel's assurances. Her heart pounded furiously, beseeching her to stay. But in her mind, she knew she'd only be inviting heartache. She stood to go.

"Just take care of Dani. Don't let the truth about Papa hurt her, if you can help it. Make her understand she's got a future here with you that I could never offer her. Tell her I love her."

Carmel's tears streamed down her lined cheeks. She dabbed her eyes with a lace-edged handkerchief, but it couldn't staunch the flow. Silently, she nodded.

Brandy went to her and knelt on the rug, hugging her fiercely. "Thank you, for everything."

"You're welcome, child. I'll miss you."

"I'll miss you, too. More than I thought possible."

"Send word. Let us know how you're faring."

Nodding briskly, Brandy swallowed her sorrow. "I will. I promise. Dry your tears or Dani will know something's wrong. I want to say good-bye to her." Her voice broke on the last word, and her throat worked back a mountain of emotion.

Mustering her strength, Brandy rose. "I better get this over with. I want to leave tonight."

Her words sent another flood of tears to Carmel's eyes, and Brandy smiled and took the handkerchief, dabbing them away. "Put on a smile. My sister's very smart for her age. She'll know if you're upset."

As Carmel collected herself, Brandy went to the kitchen to find her sister. She watched from the door as Dani and Jean rolled out creamy dough and pressed metal cutters into it. Flour dotted Dani's stylish clothes and dusted her dark braids. A smear of butter lined her jaw. Concentrating, she bent over her task, with her tongue stuck in one side of her lips.

Baking cookies. Such a small thing to be doing. But obviously important to Dani.

Now she'd have a chance, Brandy told herself. A chance to live a normal life, like other little girls. A chance to go to a real school, attend parties, and make friends. She'd grow up and find a man to love her. She'd be happy.

"Hiya," Brandy said, hiding her misery behind a smile. She went to the table and pinched a taste of the cookie dough.

"Brandy, I didn't know you were coming today. Maggie said she thought you needed to rest. Are you sick?"

Forcing a bright smile, Brandy shook her head. "No, just tired. I didn't sleep well last night."

"I could come back to the wagon," her sister offered, but Brandy saw the slight disappointment she couldn't completely hide. She reached out and touched her little sister's braid, fingering the dark strands.

"That's all right. I'm fine now. Besides, you look busy," Brandy added, changing the subject.

Her sister turned back to her task. "We're making cookies for Sunday. The church is having dinner after services. You're coming, aren't you?"

Unable to lie, but knowing she couldn't tell the truth, Brandy shrugged helplessly. "I might be too busy. But you go on. And have a good time."

"You sure you're okay? You look funny."

"I'm fine. Don't worry. Save me a cookie," she said, ruffling Dani's bangs. Her eyes met Jean's, and she knew the housekeeper suspected the truth. Her mouth turned down and her eyes grew bright.

"'Bye, Jean."

The girl twisted the dish towel she held and forced a smile. "Good-bye, Brandy." Silently she mouthed, "And thank you."

Brandy knew Jean and Hershall had been seeing a great deal of each other since the festival. Happiness for her friend momentarily dulled Brandy's hurt.

Lifting her head in silent acknowledgment, Brandy turned and left the warm, comfortable kitchen. She paused at the parlor door and lifted her fingers to Carmel in farewell. Then she opened the door and slipped out of the house. Her heart pounded, and her breath caught. She leaned against the doorframe, sucking the cold air into her burning lungs.

Down the street, she could see Bill Owens sweeping the walkway out in front of his store. Across the way, Hershall Putner came out of the harness shop, a worn leather saddle draped across his shoulder. Nell's Lemonade Parlor was just opening its doors for the day.

Oh, how she'd miss this place. These people had welcomed her, made her feel like a part of them from the first. She'd grown close to each and every one of them over the past weeks. No wonder her father had never stayed in one place too long. He must have known it would hurt too much when he had to go. She knew that now, but it couldn't stop her heart from breaking a little more.

Pulling her coat tightly around her, Brandy stepped off the porch. She would have liked to have said good-bye to everyone, but she feared the reception she'd get now that they knew about her father.

Opening the iron gate, she smiled in remembrance. Her mind sped back to the day Adam had lifted her over it. Had she known then that she loved him? Would things have turned out differently if she'd accepted his offer to give up selling her remedies and stay in Charming?

No matter. What was done was done. Suzanne made it clear how everyone would react to the news. And even if the other townsfolk were as kind as Maggie and Carmel had been, it was Adam's reaction she dreaded and feared.

Without looking back, Brandy headed for the wagon. Sal whinnied a welcome and pulled at the tether. The horse had been well enough to travel for some time, and she'd grown tired of standing in place all day.

"You're ready, aren't you, girl?" Brandy crooned.

She rubbed the mare's nose and collected the harness. After hitching up the wagon, Brandy went inside. She secured the bottles and jars of herbs, then put all the dishes into the small cupboard and fastened the latch. As she bent to close the trunk at the foot of her cot, her gaze caught on something yellow. Opening the lid, she saw Dani's doll, which their mother had sewn for the girl. Hugging it to her chest, Brandy wondered how Dani had forgotten about the doll. It was her sister's most precious possession.

Clutching the doll in her arms, she collected the shotgun and went back outside. Climbing onto the wagon seat, she slid the gun beneath her feet.

"Get up, Sal," she called. The reins felt foreign in her hands after so long, and she laid the doll in her lap as she turned the wagon back toward town. Brandy hoped that her sister would be in bed by now.

At the gate to Carmel's house, she pulled Sal to a stop. Hopping down, she eased the gate open and gained the porch steps. With one last glance at the button eyes and yarn hair, she laid the doll in the seat of the rocker where Dani would be sure to find it. Then Brandy hurried to the wagon without glancing back.

Darkness had settled fully over the town, except for scattered puddles of light spilling from windows. Brandy raised the collar of her coat against her neck and stared straight ahead as she headed south out of town.

To make matters worse, a light snow began to fall. Brandy considered stopping and going back. But she knew she couldn't. If she ever returned, she wouldn't have the strength to leave again. The pain in her chest grew with each step Sal took. Already Brandy missed her sister. Like pictures in a zoetrope, scenes from their lives moved before her eyes. A smile tipped her lips. They'd had some good times. But even as the thought crossed her mind, Brandy realized the time they'd spent in Charming had been the best by far.

Again she thought of Adam. Not even the snow could chill the fever that still burned in her for his touch and his kiss. She'd never regret a minute of their time together. Even knowing how it would turn out, she wouldn't have changed a thing they'd shared.

Adam gripped the reins between his chilled fingers. The snow had started about half an hour ago and already visibility was drastically limited.

He cursed and scanned the sky. Gray-black clouds all but obliterated the full moon overhead. Only the reflection of the light's glimmer on the white terrain kept total darkness at bay. His horse stumbled in a hole and whinnied. It would be foolhardy to go as far as town. He'd have to veer off and try to make it to his cabin, where he could wait out the worst of the storm.

Another hour and he could have spent the night with Brandy. But the snow had come up quickly and didn't show signs of letting up soon. He hoped Brandy would be all right in the wagon. She'd had plenty of wood for a fire when he'd left, and it wouldn't be the first time she'd braved the elements in the shabby dwelling. Still, he couldn't help being concerned about her.

And his restlessness grew. Now that he'd given in to the feelings he'd kept at bay for so long, they wouldn't be silenced. He needed to see her face, touch her cheek, and kiss her lips. He longed to hold her and love her.

And he meant to settle things between them before he did any of that. It wouldn't be easy. Her refusal to move to Carmel's hadn't seemed important earlier. But over the last few hours, a nagging thought had played at his mind. If Brandy couldn't give up living in the carnival wagon, how would she ever be able to renounce her Gypsy life?

He wanted marriage. He'd settle for nothing less. For the first time in his life, he wanted to commit to a woman. He pictured them together, waking side by side, growing old. Children, grandchildren. The whole ball of wax.

But in order for them to have any of that, she'd have to be willing to stay with him. She'd have to give up traveling from place to place. She'd have to give up a lot. He wasn't certain she could, or would, do that. Not even for him.

His body stirred to life and heat suffused him. Accustomed to going months at a time without release, it now seemed ablaze with insatiable need. But he knew not just any woman would do this time. He wanted Brandy. Forever.

In his mind he could hear her laugh and see her smile. Her joy brought him joy. Her love of life now colored his world. For the first time in a long time, he felt like lifting his face to the heavens and laughing aloud.

Everything would work out. He'd see to it. It would take time for her to accept his way of life, but now that he'd decided he wanted her to stay, time was one thing they had plenty of.

Chapter Twenty-one

Gone.

Adam sat still for a long minute, eyeing the empty space beneath the huge oak. A cold fist of apprehension gripped his heart. The snow had continued to fall all night, and about four inches now lay over any tracks Brandy's wagon might have made. That meant wherever she'd gone she'd left before the storm. Had she been upset? Could she be having doubts about their relationship as he'd feared?

He told himself he was being irrational. Just because the wagon was gone didn't mean Brandy had run away. In fact, a visit to Carmel's would have been his first guess, but it was within walking distance. Where else would she have gone in the wagon?

Maggie's. She must have ridden out to visit

Maggie and the boys. But why would she go with a storm on the way and her horse barely recovered? Something must be wrong. Only an emergency would have made Brandy hitch up the old mare so soon after her injury.

He spurred his horse away from town. That had to be it, he reasoned, trying to control his racing heart. Something must have happened with Davey, and Maggie had sent for Brandy. She'd go to Maggie and that little boy, no matter the weather.

Bitter wind lashed his cheeks as he galloped toward the little shack. He hoped it wasn't anything serious. He'd just spoken with Earl the day before yesterday, and the man had been walking on air. He'd asked Maggie to marry him, and although she hadn't said yes, he felt sure she was going to soon.

The snow, which had stopped only an hour earlier, began to fall once more. Fragile flakes settled on the brim of Adam's hat and against his lashes. He blinked them away, straining his eyes toward the horizon.

He didn't like the looks of the clouds gathering in the north. A blizzard could be on the way. He wanted to find Brandy and try to talk her into going to Carmel's before the weather got any worse. She'd fight him, but he considered all the sweet means of persuasion he'd use to convince her. The wind whipped up, ripping the few remaining leaves from the spindly tree branches and scattering them in Adam's path. But inside, he smoldered with passion like a summer storm.

As he topped the knoll overlooking Maggie's house, his desire cooled. The place looked empty, deserted. Even the cow and chickens were gone. And it didn't take more than a cursory glance to know Brandy's outrageous wagon was nowhere around. Frowning, Adam wondered if perhaps she'd changed her mind about staying with Carmel.

Yes, that had to be it. She'd probably taken the wagon and her mare to the stables and was, even now, warming herself before his aunt's fire. Feeling more than a little absurd for riding so far on a fool's errand, he turned his mount back toward town.

As he passed the stables an hour later, Adam stopped to glance through the open doorway. Not seeing Brandy's wagon, and knowing it couldn't very well be hidden from sight, he frowned.

"Adam."

He turned in the saddle at the sound of his name and narrowed his eyes in annoyance.

"Suzanne," he said, by way of a greeting.

"Adam McCullough, where have you been? I've been looking for you everywhere."

"I had business to tend to, Suzanne. And I'm kind of in a hurry."

She frowned darkly. "Well, you'd better make time for this. I've gone to a lot of trouble for you. And besides, I've waited two days to tell you and I can't wait another minute."

He imagined a long-winded diatribe about her latest coiffure and pushed his hat back farther on his head. "I don't have time right now. And frankly—"

"Make time," she snapped, her pretty face twisted in an ugly grimace.

Seeing she meant to harangue him until he listened, Adam decided to let her have her say so he could move on. He had to find Brandy. Dismounting, he motioned Suzanne toward the covered walkway in front of the harness shop and secured his horse to the post.

The snow had settled softly in her golden hair, and the sun caught the gemlike flakes and made them sparkle. Her soft, calf-length coat of beige cashmere with white trim made her look like a painting on the front of a Christmas card.

She really was a beautiful woman, Adam thought. But her beauty no longer affected him. He'd seen the spoiled child beneath the pretty packaging and considered himself lucky for having escaped her clutches relatively unscathed.

"I know how much you hated that peddler hanging around town, Adam," Suzanne began, not meeting his eyes. "And I'd have done anything to help you rid our Charming of the likes of her."

"Suzanne—"

"Let me speak," she interjected. "I saw the way her presence here upset you, and I just couldn't bear to see you suffer. So I took care

318

of it, darling. I've gotten rid of her for you."

A roaring began in his ears and spread a surge of alarm through him. Through the din he forced one word. "What?"

"Yes," Suzanne trilled, her laugh like sharp metal on slate.

Adam winced and lowered his face to look into hers. What he saw there chilled him worse than the air cutting beneath the overhanging roof.

"What are you talking about?"

"About that trashy little peddler, darling, aren't you listening? I got rid of her for you. She's gone. Didn't you pass the field on your way into town? It was empty, wasn't it?"

Adam grasped her shoulders roughly and drew her toward him. She gasped with pleasure and threw her head back dramatically, exposing her slender neck to him. He was sorely tempted to throttle her.

"What have you done?"

"Just what you said you wanted, darling. I found a way to expose that little cheap-jack for what she was. When I confronted her with the facts, she turned tail like a scared rabbit and left town under cover of darkness."

Adam's frantic gaze scanned the empty street. If what Suzanne said was true, he didn't want word of it getting around. Thankfully, the snow had kept most folks inside. He and Suzanne were virtually alone. Nevertheless, with a tight grip on her arm, he half dragged her across the boardwalk toward his office.

Opening the door, he thrust her inside. She stumbled slightly, but didn't seem to mind his rough treatment.

"Tell me," he demanded.

"I'll do better than that, darling. Here, see for yourself."

She withdrew a slip of paper from her pocket and handed it to him with a flourish. Adam clutched the page, dreading whatever it contained. If it brought Suzanne so much pleasure, it must be bad for Brandy.

It took only a moment for his mind to register the truth. Wade Ashton had been a criminal, a true charlatan. Was Brandy continuing her father's avocation in more ways than one? The thought that he might have been right all along brought him no pleasure, only pain.

Brandy's father had meant a lot to her, but Adam felt certain she hadn't known of Wade Ashton's previous occupation.

He didn't question the certainty of his conclusion. He just knew it to be true. Despite what he'd thought and said about Brandy, he realized now she was no fraud. Unlike the woman before him, Brandy didn't have a deceitful bone in her body. She must have been devastated by Suzanne's revelation. Would he ever get the chance to tell her how he felt, now that he was certain of his own feelings?

"You showed this to her?"

"Of course, darling. I wanted to give her a chance to explain, if she could. I guess the way she sneaked off in the night is all the answer we need."

Adam crushed the page in his hand with a vicious curse. "Have you shown it to anyone else?"

"Oh, yes. For all the good it did. These yokels don't even have the sense to recognize when they've been duped."

"I've been such a fool," he said, tossing the wadded ball of paper across the room.

"Don't blame yourself, darling. She fooled the whole town. Only you and I suspected she wasn't what she seemed to be."

He whirled to face her and caught the glimpse of satisfied triumph in her ice-blue eyes. She was enjoying every minute of this, he thought. She loved seeing Brandy humiliated. But more than that, she thrilled at the thought of him being in her debt.

"Well, I'm seeing things clearly now," he told her. "You deliberately hurt her because of me, didn't you? You knew I was falling in love with her, even before I knew it myself."

"Don't be absurd. And don't mistake lust for true feelings. You wanted her; any idiot could see that. It was disgusting the way you fawned over her." Suzanne's voice had grown shrill, but she took a deep breath and continued in softer tones. "I understand about men, Adam. You weren't ready for marriage, but she satisfied your baser needs. I won't hold that against you."

She reached for him, purposely rubbing her

breasts against his chest. He choked back the bile in his throat and pushed her away.

"Don't," Adam said. "The only thing I feel for you is disgust. And the only person I despise more than you at this moment is myself. I saw Brandy's true nature weeks ago, but I let my prejudice blind me to the truth. She's no fraud. She's a kind, caring person who only wanted to help others and be able to support her sister."

"Oh, spare me such drivel," Suzanne shrieked. "You know exactly what she is, but you don't want to admit it now because you know you'd have to get rid of your little whore. And don't think I don't know what you've been doing with her. She wore whisker marks on her face yesterday when I went to see her, and I could smell you all over her."

"You're disgusting," Adam said, taking a step around her. Suzanne reached out and grasped his elbow, spinning him to face her. She threw herself against him and let her hand wander down over his crotch.

"If I'd known all it would take to earn your undying love was a small sampling of my affections, I would have gladly spread my legs for you years ago. I just assumed you'd want your wife pure."

Once more, he shoved her away. "Pure? You're vile. If you're still pure it's because every other man in this county has already realized what I was too dumb to see. You're a conniving, spoiled little bitch, Suzanne."

She reached out and slapped him soundly

across the cheek. He was sorely tempted to return the favor, but he only smiled.

"I suppose I deserved that," Adam said. "But not from you. If my behavior has been inexcusable to anyone, it's Brandy. I just wish she were still here so I could tell her how wrong I was."

"Well, she isn't. She's gone for good. She'll never come back here now. And you'll come around, just as you always have. And I'll be waiting."

"God help me, I'd sooner bed down with a rattlesnake." Adam said, slamming out the door. He strode to his horse, loosened the reins, and started down the street.

He passed Nell, who was coming out of the swinging half doors of her establishment. She glanced behind him, saw Suzanne saunter out of his office, and cut him a black look. Knowing he deserved her censure, he couldn't meet her eyes.

Bill Owens stood by his plate-glass window, a frown marring his whiskered face. When Adam touched his hat in greeting, the man turned away and went back to work.

Apparently, everybody had heard about Brandy's father. And, like Suzanne, they thought he'd gotten what he wanted. If only they could feel the hole in his chest where it seemed as though his heart had been ripped out. If only they knew how sorry he was that it had taken him so long to see the truth.

They'd seen Brandy's goodness and concern.

And they'd welcomed her into their fold with open arms. Adam loved her, but he hadn't been able to put aside his doubts. He hadn't been able to give her the one thing she'd wanted most from him: his faith.

Adam ran into Earl coming out of the tobacco shop.

"Howdy, Sheriff. I'm headed to the stables. Be happy to take your mount over for you and save you the trip."

Adam eyed him warily and handed over his reins.

"I'll see he gets fed and rubbed down before I start home."

"Thank you, Earl," he said, a frown marring his brow.

"No trouble."

The man turned toward the two-story, rough-hewn building across the way. Adam called him back. "Earl?"

"Yeah, Sheriff?"

"You're not angry at me, too?"

Earl looked down the walkway and narrowed his eyes at Suzanne, who was still standing outside Adam's office. "I reckon you know what you've done to that little gal. And I figure you'll know how to fix it. Me, I'm right glad for what you did."

"You are?" Adam asked. He'd thought Earl liked Brandy the times they'd spent together. Finally finding an ally brought him no satisfaction. Instead, he narrowed his eyes, wondering why the man would be happy Brandy was gone.

"Yep. My Maggie went to see Brandy yesterday when Suzanne broke the news about her pa. Said the girl was terrible broke up. Wouldn't listen to reason a'tall. Maggie realized she'd been just as stubborn, refusin' to marry me because folks might talk if we didn't wait. She come to me last night when she found out Brandy had gone. Said love was too precious to throw away or waste. Well, you can imagine how glad I was to hear that. I fetched the preacher right then and there and married her before she could change her mind. Moved her out to my place first thing this mornin', bag and baggage. Not that she had much."

Earl's happiness couldn't dispel Adam's misery, but he held out his hand anyway. "Congratulations. I know you'll be very happy together."

"You bet. I've waited a long time for a woman like Maggie. I don't plan to let anythin' get in the way of our happiness."

Adam recognized the rebuke. With leaden steps, he continued toward Carmel's house. He dreaded facing it now, knowing Brandy and Dani wouldn't be there to liven it up any longer. They'd brought a special warmth to the place that it had lacked for a long time.

As he reached for the latch on the gate, he heard footsteps and whirled, hope leaping in his heart. But when he looked behind him, it was only Dorothy Walker. The man's boots she wore made large tracks in the shallow snow.

"Dorothy," he greeted.

"Humph," she snorted, throwing her nose into the air. She stomped past him and he shook his head in defeat. Not only had he lost the only woman he'd ever loved, but his whole town hated him now.

"Carmel," he called, his voice echoing in the entry hall. He removed his hat and hung it on the hall tree. In the mirror, he caught a glimpse of his haggard face. Only that morning, he'd been amazed to see a smile when he had faced his shaving mirror. Now it was gone. This time he feared it wouldn't return so easily.

Carmel wheeled out of the parlor, a dour look on her aged face. "So, you're back. You look terrible," she told him with her usual candor.

"Aren't you going to tell me what a fool I've been. I'm surprised you're still speaking to me. No one else is. Except Suzanne."

"Huh, I bet she had a mouthful to say. Nope, I figure you're suffering enough. No sense me rubbing salt in your wounds."

"I've lost her, Aunt Carmel. I didn't realize how much she meant to me until now." He plowed his hands through his hair, then dragged his fingers over his face. "What am I going to do without her?"

"I never figured you for a quitter."

"What are you talking about?"

"You sound beaten. Like you got no choice in the matter."

"She's gone. Whatever chance I had I ruined."

"You could go after her."

"She's got a full day's head start."

"In a broken-down wagon pulled by a half-lame nag. Your horse could catch up to her in no time."

Adam shook his head, thrusting one leg out in front of him as he propped his hands on his hips. "You're assuming she wants to come back. Why would she? Like everyone else in this town, she thinks I've gotten the proof I needed to expose her as a cheat. And that even if I allowed her to stay, I'd always be reminded of her father and consider her a fraud, too."

He tipped his head back and breathed deeply. "After the way I treated her, she'll never believe me if I say I love her now. Besides, Brandy considered herself reputable. If I know her, she's doubting her own abilities right now. And she knows the whole town is aware of her father's past. There's nothing that could make her come back."

From the kitchen he heard the sound of a child's voice, and his heart took flight once more. *Dani!*

"She's back," he whispered.

"No, Adam," Carmel called, but he didn't hear her. With long, eager strides, he raced to the kitchen. Jean sat at the table, peeling potatoes. Across from her he saw the back of Dani's head as she rested her face on her hands.

"Dani!" he cried, going to the girl and dropping to one knee.

She looked up, and Adam's heart slammed against his chest. Her little face was red and swollen, her eyes puffy and bloodshot. Her breath was coming in tiny hiccups as she fought to stifle her sobs.

"Dani?"

Sitting straight in the chair, she shot him a cold look. Her rosebud mouth hardened and thinned, and she narrowed her dark eyes.

"It's all your fault," she accused hotly, fresh tears filling her eyes. "She's gone for good. She left me here and she's never coming back. I hate you!" she screamed, jumping up so fast her chair toppled over backward. "I hate you!"

Dani turned and ran from the room, her cries reverberating through the big house. Adam slumped against the table, his own eyes suspiciously bright.

Chapter Twenty-two

"She's all alone."

Adam downed his second whiskey and refilled his glass. He stared out the window at the thick white blanket of snow. "She's all alone in the first damned blizzard of the season."

"There's nothing you can do now," Carmel told him for the hundredth time. "She'll take shelter in the wagon until it's over. She'll be fine."

Her words were meant to soothe him, but he could hear the slight tremor of uncertainty she couldn't completely hide.

Behind him, Dani's cries continued to echo through the house. Feeling betrayed by Carmel and Adam, she would only allow Jean to comfort her. And even then, the little girl would not be appeased. He was certain Brandy's departure had left her with a terrifying sense of loss. Brandy and Dani had been everything to each other. Without Dani, Brandy was truly alone in the world.

"Why would she go off alone like that? I know how upset she must be about her father. She shouldn't have to be by herself at a time like this."

"She wanted Dani to stay with us. She thought the child would be better off here, living a normal life."

"But Dani was all the family she had left. She loved her more than anything."

"Yes. And that's why she did it."

Another wail issued from upstairs, and Adam slammed his glass on the low table. He couldn't stand another minute of that girl's crying. It was tearing his heart out. He'd tried to assure Dani that her sister would be all right. Brandy knew how to survive the elements. But his own concern quickly eroded his faith in Brandy's abilities. He imagined all sorts of terrible things happening to her, from her being lost in the storm to her encountering a wild animal. He couldn't keep his glance from straying to the window once more. Damn, he'd almost swear the blizzard was worsening.

"I've got to go after her. There's no way she could have made it to the next town by now. And I don't know what she'll do in a storm like this."

He met Carmel's knowing glance and added

quickly, "Besides, she had no right to hurt that child like that." He moved toward the doorway.

"Adam."

Turning back, he faced his aunt. "Don't try to stop me. My mind is made up."

Carmel shook her head. "Oh, I don't intend to stop you. I know how foolish I would be to try. But you make sure you're doing this for the right reasons before you go. All those excuses won't be what Brandy will need to hear from you. Don't bring her back if nothing has changed. It'll only hurt her again."

"I'll never hurt her again, Aunt Carmel. I swear, if she'll just agree to come back, nothing will ever hurt her again." And Brandy just had to come back, he thought desperately. Otherwise, nothing would ever stop this pain burning inside him.

"Make sure you mean that before you go after her," Carmel warned him.

"Don't worry. I've never meant anything more." He kissed her cheek and took the steps two at a time. In his room, he donned another pair of socks, a flannel shirt, and his caped greatcoat.

Slamming his hat back on his head, he raced down the stairs. Pausing at the parlor door, he shot his aunt a broad smile. "Tell that one to stop her caterwauling," he told Carmel, motioning up the stairs. "I'll bring her sister back if I have to carry her over my shoulder trussed up like a Thanksgiving turkey."

Carmel gasped at Adam's bright grin and pressed a trembling hand to her chest. For so long, she had waited to see him happy. She prayed he was successful in bringing Brandy home. If not, this smile might have to last her a long time.

"Take care," she called. But Adam was already out the door. Carmel glanced out the front window and saw him jump the low fence as he hurried toward the stables.

Brandy shivered and tucked the heavy quilt closer around her legs. Shards of needlelike pain shot through her gloved fingers as she snapped the reins.

What an idiot she'd been to try leaving in the snow. The downfall had increased in the last hours and she feared stopping now. There was no telling how long the storm would last. If she took shelter in the wagon, she'd be trapped there until the snow melted. And Sal would have no shelter at all.

Cursing her foolishness, Brandy yelled to the old horse once more. But Sal didn't like the snow gathering on her head, and she shook her mane wildly.

Why hadn't she stayed in Charming? She didn't even know where the closest town was. She could travel for days without seeing another sign of life. She didn't know how much longer Sal could go on.

Tears filled Brandy's eyes, but the wind whipped them away before they could fall.

She missed Adam, Dani, and Carmel. She'd never faced life on her own, and she found all her confidence and self-assurance had stayed behind with those she loved.

"Come on, girl," Brandy called loudly.

Sal whinnied her displeasure as her feet sank into a snowdrift up to her shins. The horse reared, releasing her shod hooves. The wagon rolled to a stop and Brandy looked over the side. The snow was getting deeper. It had begun to cover the spokes of the wheels.

"I've made a big mistake, Sal," she said, pulling hard on the reins. She tugged to the right until Sal turned, following her lead.

"But maybe it's not too late to fix it."

With a hard slap, she brought the reins down on the mare's rump. Sal shot forward, heading the wagon back the way they'd come.

The snow collected on Adam's hat brim, weighing it down until it nearly covered his eyes. He removed it, shook off the moist flakes, and settled it back on his head.

Several times he'd wandered off the road, its rutted path long since covered with snow. Any tracks Brandy had made were likewise obscured. He knew he might very well be on a wild-goose chase. Common sense demanded he return to town. But the sounds of Dani's crying still rang in his ears. He couldn't go back without Brandy.

He loved Brandy. Why had it taken him so long to realize that? He had to find her. And not just for Dani's sake. He felt as if his own life depended on her continued presence in it.

Through the unrelenting downpour of fragile-looking flakes, he rode on. Even when his denims stiffened against his legs with damp and cold, he refused to turn back.

If only he could be sure Brandy had gone south, but that was only a hunch. If only this damned snow hadn't covered her trail. If only he'd told her how much he loved her.

It all came down to that now. He had to find her, had to let her know how much she meant to him. Nothing else mattered.

As the evening wore on, darkness settled around him. If he didn't turn back soon, he'd be lost in the blizzard. His pants were frozen to his saddle, his hands stiff on the reins. Twice he'd felt his mount quiver beneath him with cold.

He had to go back. Not wanting to even think about a life without Brandy, he assured himself it was only temporary. As soon as the snow stopped, he'd head out again. She couldn't get far in her wagon. He'd find her. And God help him, he'd never let her go again.

Before heading toward town, he decided he'd go just a little farther. His horse snorted and a heavy fog encircled his nose. Each step the animal took weighed heavily on Adam's heart. He didn't want to return without Brandy. He couldn't face Dani and Carmel. They were counting on him.

Feeling as though he'd disappointed everyone, he spied a shape up ahead, half covered in snow. Through the white blanket of snow falling around him, he recognized the bright orange and green of Brandy's wagon. A thrill rushed through his insides, and his heart began to pound.

But as he sped toward the wagon, his heart lurched to a shuddering halt before beating against his chest in fear.

The wagon looked deserted. Brandy's mare was nowhere in sight.

Adam kicked his mount into a stumbling run, but still the horse could only go a few feet more. The snow had blown against the north side of the wagon, piling up until it reached nearly to the top. The other side was still clear, though, and he slid from his saddle and staggered to the door, yanking it open.

"Brandy!" he shouted, pulling himself into the wagon so fast his head skimmed the frame of the door. He ducked and quickly scanned the interior. It looked just the same as it had the last time he'd been inside, except for one thing: Brandy was obviously not there.

Why would she have left the shelter of the wagon? Had something happened to Sal? Was Brandy wandering out there somewhere, lost in the blizzard?

Adam had no way of knowing how far he was from town, but at least he knew one thing. Her wagon was headed *toward* Charming. Whatever had happened, she'd been on her way back. He had a possible clue now, and it gave him the strength he needed to go on.

He'd return to town and organize a search. Everyone would help out; they all liked Brandy. Now that he had something to go on, he'd find her. He had to. The alternative was too painful to even consider.

With a new desperation, he scanned the clouds overhead. The snow had eased slightly, and he strained to see the half-moon through the precipitation. With barely a hint of illumination, he directed his mount north.

Sal shrieked and stumbled, and Brandy fell hard to one side. Without a saddle, she quickly lost her seat, and her booted foot slid over the horse's back. Sal staggered to a halt, and Brandy landed with a dull thud in a snowbank. Sinking up to her neck, she felt the bitter cold seep through her worn gloves and threadbare jacket.

"I should have taken the coat and gloves Carmel offered me," she said through clenched teeth, "instead of acting so prideful." Sal nickered a reply, and a halo of icy air encircled the mare's head.

Scrambling to her feet, Brandy brushed the snow from her clothes. At least the snow had broken her fall and kept her from being injured. But her boots were soaked through, and both pairs of stockings she'd donned couldn't ward off the frigid dampness.

Sal had given out almost as soon as Brandy had turned her back toward town. Favoring her injured leg, the horse cried out and stopped, refusing to go any farther. Brandy had decided to unhitch the mare from the wagon and ride her back to town. Now, Sal sidestepped and whinnied, her eyes darting wildly.

"You've hurt your leg again, haven't you, old gal? Let me have a look."

Stooping to inspect the favored leg, Brandy saw that the swelling had returned. The snow continued to fall, though it appeared to have slackened off slightly. Glancing around, Brandy realized she must have left the road somewhere along the way. And after her tumble, she felt disoriented. The barest hint of a glimmer could be seen from the moon. It was all she had now to direct her way.

Taking Sal's reins in her hand, Brandy murmured soothingly to the frightened animal. "Come on, girl. We've got a long walk ahead of us."

Holding the bridle in her stiff hands, Brandy started through the deep drifts. As she forced one foot in front of the other, she tried to ignore the sharp tingles emanating from her fingers and toes. Her expression clouded with uneasiness. Walking through the snow could cause frostbite or, even worse, hypothermia. Brandy had seen the effects of the cold before, and she knew there was a very real possibility she would never make it to town.

Within an hour, Adam could see faint lights in the distance. He no longer shivered because a numbness encompassed his body. He'd looked for Brandy along the road, but had seen no sign of her or Sal. He hated breaking the news to Carmel and Dani. Only his determination to find Brandy, safe and well, kept him going.

He knew he'd have to warm up before going back out again, or he'd risk severe frostbite. That wouldn't do him or Brandy any good. But he would only rest for a few minutes, he assured himself. His concern refused to allow him any more time than that.

Without stopping to stable his horse, he quickly made his way toward the light of Carmel's parlor window. He tied the gray behind the kitchen, under the shelter of the wash porch. Letting himself in the back door, he stomped the snow off his boots. He'd never been so cold in his life. He couldn't even remove his gloves. They'd frozen to his hands long ago.

He stepped into the hall and looked around. No one was in sight. Had Carmel gone to bed already? It wasn't like her to go off and leave the lamps burning.

He'd have to wake her and tell her about Brandy's wagon. Anxious to begin the search, he called out Carmel's name. Already planning his strategy, he counted off how many men he'd need and who would be the easiest to contact. Carmel's house would double as a headquarters, and the men could go out in groups and spread out. They'd cover more area that way, and their chances of finding Brandy would be better.

"Carmel," Adam called again.

Turning toward the parlor, his heart slammed to a stop. For a long moment, he thought he was hallucinating. Then slowly she turned toward him, as though she felt his eyes on her.

"Brandy?"

Happy tears sprang to her eyes, and she moved as though she'd rush into his arms. Then she stopped, her hands twisting nervously in front of her. She smiled hesitantly and nodded.

Still not believing his own eyes, Adam stepped into the warm room. Carmel wasn't there, but a fire blazed in the fireplace and two cups of hot cocoa sat on the oval table in the center of the room.

A cozy little scene, he thought, suddenly angry. While he'd been out freezing his tail off in a blizzard looking for her, Brandy had been sipping cocoa with his aunt in front of the hearth.

Chapter Twenty-three

"Adam?"

Seeming to sense his rapidly changing mood, Brandy took a tentative step toward him.

"Where the hell have you been?" he shouted. "I nearly froze to death looking for you. I found your wagon, but I couldn't imagine what had happened to you and Sal. I thought you were lost in the blizzard. And what do you mean going off like that in the first place, without a word to anyone? Your sister was devastated."

"I'm sorry for upsetting Dani. I thought it was the only way. Then the weather got bad, and Sal is old and not as strong as she used to be. I realized I couldn't leave Dani and all the people I'd come to care for in Charming. I turned around to come back, but Sal couldn't pull the wagon through the snow because it had gotten so deep. I unhitched her and rode for a while. Then she went lame again, and I had to walk the rest of the way. Thank goodness we weren't far by that time. She's at the stables now, and I think she's going to be fine. I'm sorry you were worried," she whispered, lowering her head.

"Sorry. Sorry?" Adam's anger topped out. He'd never been so frightened in his life, he realized, shuddering as a drop of melting snow ran down his neck.

With a muttered curse, he snatched off his hat before any more of the flakes could drip on him. But his pique made his movements more abrupt than he'd intended, and the hat snapped sharply, throwing the melting chips of ice all over Brandy.

Gasping, she threw her hands up to her chilled cheeks. Adam's anger died immediately as he saw what he'd done. He dropped the hat into the nearest chair and went to her.

"Damn, I'm sorry," he said, taking her hands in his. "I'm just so relieved you're all right. But I confess I had visions of me rescuing you from the blizzard and making up for the way I've behaved by earning your gratitude."

When Adam lowered her hands, he expected shock or even anger. But Brandy's expression made him step back.

She was *laughing*.

Brandy looked up, a giggle bursting through her tightened lips.

"What's so funny?" Adam demanded, refusing to release her hands. It felt so good to touch her again, and he had to fight the urge to clasp her in his arms.

Without warning, Brandy scooped a small pile of snow off his shoulder and patted it into a ball. "Gratitude, huh? And just how was I supposed to show my appreciation?" she asked, a wicked gleam in her eyes as she leveled them at his face.

"Oh, no—" he started, turning his face away.

But Brandy was quicker. The makeshift snowball hit him square in the nose.

"Why, you—" Adam pulled her against him, a threatening glint in his green eyes.

Brandy laughed and squirmed to free herself, but he held her close. He raised one hand and Brandy winced, chuckling and waiting for his retaliation. It came in the form of a long, slow kiss.

"Oh, Adam," she murmured, her despair quickly returning as he pulled back. "You were right to have your doubts. You heard about my father?"

"Yes, and it doesn't matter. I was wrong, so wrong. No matter how I felt about your healing abilities, I should have never doubted your goodness, your honesty. You are the most loving, caring woman I've ever known. And nothing," he said, drawing her back into his embrace, "will ever change the way I feel about you. I love you."

Brandy gasped and let her hands move slowly up to entwine his neck.

"I love you, too," she said, chuckling as the

drops of melting snow fell over them both. She laughed out loud with sheer joy, and Adam felt a smile tip his lips.

"I love you," he repeated, gently wiping the moisture from her face. He kissed her lips once more, lingeringly, then reached out with his tongue and tasted the melted snow on her lashes. Throwing back his head, he roared with laughter.

"Not that I didn't deserve the torment after the way I've acted, but don't ever leave me again. I was so damned scared I'd lost you."

"Adam," Brandy cried, touching his cheek. "You're laughing."

Her awe surprised him, and he hugged her and chortled loudly once more. "I'm happy. Aren't you supposed to laugh when you're happy?"

Pressing kisses along his jaw, she nodded her head. "Yes, oh, yes. Laugh all you want, darling. I'll never get tired of hearing it."

He drew back so he could look into her face, but his arms continued to hold her tightly, refusing to relinquish their hold.

"You're back for good? You're not going to leave again?"

"No, I can't. You, Dani, and Carmel—you all mean the world to me. I realized how much when I thought I might never see any of you again. Nothing else matters, except being with you all. I can stand the scandal my father's past will undoubtedly cause. If you'll be with me, I can stand anything."

"Just try to get away from me again," Adam warned, his lips coming down on hers with all the passion he'd fought so long.

As they parted, his smile lit the room, dispelling the last of the bitter cold and heating Brandy's blood. The fire behind her could not compare to the blaze burning between them.

"A while back, you mentioned something about finding me a reputable position," Brandy reminded Adam with a secretive smile. "Is the offer still open?"

He breathed raggedly and narrowed his eyes. "Yes, I have something in mind."

"Good. Because I've decided to retire the old wagon and put Sal out to pasture. I'll be needing to find work if I mean to support Dani and myself and live here in Charming. Forever."

"Do you mean it?" Adam asked, clutching her against him. He absorbed her warmth until his skin burned with the feel of her pressed against him. And still he couldn't seem to get close enough.

"I want Dani to live a normal life. I want her to have all the things she needs, all the things I never had growing up."

"And what about you, Brandy? What do you want?"

She snuggled closer and tipped her head back so she could stare into his jade eyes, which were dark with longing. "You, Adam. I want you."

Peeling off his gloves, his large hands took her face and held it gently. Reclaiming her lips, he crushed her to him desperately.

Brandy drank in the sweetness of his kiss. Blood pounded in her ears, sped through her heart, and weakened her knees. She wrapped her arms around his waist, and he bent her back over his arm. His mouth rained kisses over her neck and throat, then opened over the mound of her breast and nuzzled it through her clothing.

With a wild cry, she clutched his head and drew him back to her mouth. Their hands explored each other as their lips teased and pleasured. They couldn't get enough. They both knew, if they lived to be a hundred, they'd never get enough.

Their clothing was still wet, but instead of harboring the cold from the winter wind, it held the steam of their passion. They stood, half icy cold, half white-hot flame, neither wanting to end the precious moment.

Adam's hand trailed over her ribs and cupped her breast. Brandy arched against his palm, her nipple budding beneath his questing fingers.

Her body melted against his, and her world filled with pleasure, sweet and pure. She pressed her lips to his jaw, her kisses hot and light as a summer breeze.

"You're going to catch your death in those clothes," Brandy whispered, trying to rein in the careening emotions before they sped away with them both.

"You're as wet as I am," Adam reminded her.

"Carmel went to find me something dry to put on. She'll be back any minute."

With a final, lingering kiss he stepped back. His arms dropped to her waist and encircled her, holding their lower bodies firmly together.

"You're sure you want to stay here? You won't change your mind?" he asked.

"Never."

"Won't you miss traveling around?"

"Sometimes you have to journey a long way to find your heart's desire. But once you find it, you never have to roam again."

"Then I know just the position for you," he told her.

"A job?" she asked, her eyes bright with love and the sheer joy of being in his embrace.

"You might say that. There's a certain sheriff in town who desperately needs a wife to teach him how to enjoy life. She has to be beautiful and vivacious, and her smile has to warm his heart. She's got to be able to make him laugh and enjoy living."

"Me?" she gasped, not wanting to believe she could be so happy.

He gave her a serious look. "If you'll have me. It won't be easy. I can be grouchy and boorish at times. And I'm kind of rusty when it comes to having fun. You'll have to show me how to have a good time again. And I can be a damned fool sometimes," he said, his wonderful green eyes gazing into her dark ones. "You'll have to love me a lot and put up with me through it all."

"I'd love nothing better than to spend my life trying to do just that. If you can live with the fact that your wife brews remedies for everything from fever to gout and had a father with a shady past."

"I love the way you help people. I'm proud of you and your remedies. And didn't Carmel tell you? No one even cared about your father's crimes. In fact, you're going to have to marry me, or the whole town will probably throw me out on my ear and elect you mayor."

Brandy laughed and he stared down at her. "You've turned this town around, Brandy. And you have me head over boots. Let me out of my misery. Say you'll marry me."

"Oh, Adam, of course I'll marry you. Being your wife sounds like the perfect position for me. I can't wait to begin."

His mouth swooped down over hers, and all hint of tenderness was replaced with hot, driving need. Her lips parted and his tongue caressed every inch of her mouth. He drank deep of her sweet heat for several long moments.

"The sooner the better," he said, his eyes burning her flesh with their fiery glance.

Reaching up for another kiss, Brandy heard a noise in the doorway and pulled back. Her face drained of color and her gasp startled Adam. He whirled to see what had shocked her so and felt a curse wedge in his throat.

"My God!" he finally exclaimed, starting forward.

Brandy clasped his arm and held him back as they watched Carmel step into the parlor. She was leaning against the doorframe, the heavy curtain clutched in her hand. But she was *standing!*

Chapter Twenty-four

"Carmel, you're walking!"

"Bright boy," Adam's aunt said caustically to Brandy.

Brandy laughed and pressed trembling fingers to her lips. "Oh, this is wonderful," she cried.

Carmel's legs, still weak from years of disuse, began to shake. Adam stepped forward and grasped her elbow.

"Aunt Carmel, do you want to sit down?"

"I've been sittin' down for years, you knothead. I think I'll stand a bit longer."

Adam chuckled and Carmel touched his cheek to belie the harshness of her words. Her bright gaze met his and she smiled.

"What happened?" he asked, his voice breaking with emotion.

"I heard the most amazing sound, and I had to see for myself that it was true."

"What sound?"

"The sound of your laughter. I'd gone to my room to fetch Brandy something dry to put on, and I heard you laugh. I couldn't believe it. I've waited so long for you to be happy that I'd almost given up hoping. I was so excited I turned my chair too fast, and it dumped me right on the floor. Well, I couldn't get it set straight, so I pulled myself up using my dressing table for support. Once I saw I could stand, I decided it was time I tried out my new legs."

Her bright gaze lit on Brandy, and she smiled and winked. "Told you I was feeling better, didn't I?"

Brandy released a shaky breath and a watery giggle. "You sure did."

Once more Carmel's legs shook, and she tightened her hold on Adam's arm. "Maybe I will sit a spell, after all," she said, her knees buckling beneath her.

Adam swept her up and deposited her on the settee. He took Brandy's hand and sat beside his aunt, drawing Brandy down on his lap. She tried to protest, but he held her in place, his arms locked around her waist.

"I just can't believe this," Adam whispered, looking from his aunt to Brandy. "You've done it. You did everything you said you would and more."

"'Course she did. If you hadn't been so dull

witted, you'd have seen the girl has a real gift for healing. And not just body parts, either. Her kind of healing can salve the heart and soul, too."

Adam pressed a kiss to Brandy's cheek, and she snuggled against his chest.

"Carmel is right, Brandy. You really do have a gift for healing. But more than that, you have another powerful gift—the gift of love and laughter. And I'll thank God every day for sending you here to share those gifts with all of us."

"Hey, what's going on?"

Dani's sleepy voice reached them from the doorway, and they turned to see her standing wide-eyed as she took in the scene before her.

"Brandy!" she cried, running to her sister. Brandy leaped from Adam's lap and caught her sister in her arms.

"Hiya, Dani," she said through a new sheen of tears.

"Hiya, Brandy," Dani answered, her tiny voice shrill with happiness.

They hugged for a long minute; then Dani pulled away. "You came back."

"Yes. I'm sorry I upset you. I didn't get very far before I realized I couldn't stay away from you. Or Adam," she added, facing her husband-to-be.

"Look," Adam said. "Aunt Carmel walked in here all by herself. Isn't it great? Brandy made her all better, just as she said she would."

Dani narrowed her dark eyes at him and propped her tiny hands on her hips. "You ain't gotta tell me that. *I* wasn't the one who didn't believe her."

Adam chuckled and stood to enclose both sisters in his embrace. "You sure weren't," he admitted with a wide smile. "You knew all along she could do it."

"Yep. And she made you happy, too, just the way Aunt Carmel hoped she would."

Adam glanced at his aunt in time to see her cheeks pinken with embarrassment. "What is this all about?" he asked.

Carmel waved her hand, trying to shush Dani, but the little girl only waved back merrily and continued. "Aunt Carmel asked Brandy to make you happy again. Brandy didn't think she could do it. She said you were too sour. But I knew she could, if she tried hard enough."

"So you were working on my disposition, huh? All this was just to see me smile?"

"It worked," Brandy said, looking out from under her lashes flirtatiously.

Adam laughed again. "It sure did. You even got me to put on a pair of skates—something no one else has ever been able to do."

"I know what that old witch said about Papa, Brandy," Dani cut in. Her somber words cast an uncomfortable pall over the group. "But I knew all along you really had the gift. Just like Mama. I always wondered which one I took after, Mama or Papa," she said, her smile fading a bit. "Now I guess I know."

Looking confused, Adam knelt to face her. "What do you mean by that, sweetheart?" he asked.

Brandy and Carmel both guessed what her next words would be at the same time.

"Dani, don't—"

"Hush, child—"

Their words exploded into the room, drawing Adam's inquiring gaze toward them. "Go ahead, Dani," he coaxed, shooting the women a warning frown.

"It's okay if you know about me now, isn't it?" Dani asked, smiling reassuringly at Brandy and Carmel. Both women groaned and covered their faces. "'Cause I gave it up."

"Gave what up?"

"My hobby. That's what Aunt Carmel called it, but I know she was just being nice. You're gonna marry Brandy, aren't you?"

"Just as soon as I can," he assured her. "What does that have to do with what you wanted to tell me?"

"Well, I figure you'd never send Brandy to jail if you was married to her."

"Jail!"

"Now, Adam," Brandy started, holding her hand out pleadingly, "I can explain."

"I'm listening," he told her, his tone dark with suspicion.

"Carmel?" Brandy faced the older woman, a plea in her brown eyes.

"Dani was a pickpocket," Carmel announced without preamble.

Brandy cringed, but Dani grinned and nodded. Carmel faced her nephew staunchly.

"A what?" he said.

"Well, actually it was a little more than that. But she was a very troubled child and—"

"Carmel." Adam drew the name out threateningly.

"Oh, all right. For a time, not now, mind you, Dani was a—thief."

"Damn!" Adam exclaimed, going to the sideboard and pouring two fingers of whiskey. He downed it in a single gulp and set the glass aside. "All right, ladies, I'm ready. Let's hear the rest of this conspiracy everybody seems to have been aware of except me."

"I have a better idea," Carmel said, pushing to her feet. She motioned Dani over. The little girl wrapped her arm around Carmel's waist and helped her to stand. "Dani is going to help me, and the two of us are going to bed. Brandy will fill you in on all the details," she said, taking one slow, hesitant step forward.

She walked, with Dani's help, to the doorway and turned back. "That is if you can't think of anything better to do for the rest of the night."

She winked and let Dani lead her out of the parlor and to her room.

Adam laughed and took Brandy in his arms. "That old rascal. She knows just how to wrap me around her little finger."

"You're not angry about Dani?" Brandy asked, going into his outstretched arms. He kissed her soundly on the lips, and the banked embers of their smoldering passion blazed to life once more. "She really has quit taking things. And I owe it all to your aunt. Carmel's been very good for Dani."

"We'll talk about Carmel and Dani later," Adam said, nuzzling her neck, his arms tightening around her back. "Much, much later."

Epilogue

The snow stopped, the sun came out, and the temperature soared to a pleasant fifty-five degrees.

On the pavilion in the center of the town square, Brandy stood beside Adam, proudly reciting her wedding vows before the whole town.

To one side, Carmel and Dani stood up as witnesses. To the other side, Earl and Maggie looked on, their arms draped around one another, their hands each holding that of a twin.

Everybody had come out for the ceremony. Everybody, that is, except the doctor and his daughter. Suzanne refused to leave the house since Brandy's return, and Adam had heard from Dorothy Walker that her father's condition was quickly worsening. Most folks suspected it might be because of the ill-tempered and unfit nurse Suzanne reluctantly made.

But Suzanne's absence didn't detract from the beauty and joy of the wedding, and as the tufts of white powdery snow left from the blizzard melted on the ground, Adam proudly married the woman who'd finally made all his dreams come true.

"Congratulations," the minister announced loudly. "You may kiss your bride."

"You bet I will." Adam grinned, clasping Brandy to him. His head lowered, then paused inches from her lips. For a long moment, he studied her beautiful face and her dark eyes. His fingers brushed the waves of blue-black hair cascading over the bodice of her amethyst gown. Who but Brandy would look so lovely in a purple wedding dress?

He smiled and took her mouth in a long, slow kiss. As her arms wound around his neck, the group huddled closer, forming a circle around the happy couple.

The minister patted Dani on the top of her head, and she grinned up at him. Instantly her eyes landed on the polished silver cross hanging from a braided chain around his neck.

Her chubby little hand reached out to touch the shimmering object.

"That's a real pretty necklace you have there, sir," she said, her voice alive with interest.

Dreamweaver

Adam and Brandy spun apart, and their voices chimed with Carmel's as they all clutched the little girl at once.

"Dani, no!" they chorused.

Timeswept passion...timeless love.

Time's Healing Heart by Marti Jones. When a freak accident propels Madeline St. Thomas to the Old South, she is rescued by handsome Devon Crowe. Maddie drives Devon to distraction with her claims of coming from another era, but when she makes him a proposal no lady would make, Devon is tempted to lose himself in desires that promise to last forever.

_51954-2 $4.99 US/$5.99 CAN

A Love Beyond Time by Flora Speer. Accidentally thrust back to the eighth century by a computer time-travel program, Mike Bailey lands near Charlemagne's camp. There, a headstrong beauty discovers him, and soon they are both aroused by an all-consuming passion—and a desire that will conquer time itself.

_51948-8 $4.99 US/$5.99 CAN

LEISURE BOOKS
ATTN: Order Department
276 5th Avenue, New York, NY 10001

Please add $1.50 for shipping and handling for the first book and $.35 for each book thereafter. PA., N.Y.S. and N.Y.C. residents, please add appropriate sales tax. No cash, stamps, or C.O.D.s. All orders shipped within 6 weeks via postal service book rate. Canadian orders require $2.00 extra postage and must be paid in U.S. dollars through a U.S. banking facility.

Name _____

Address _____

City _____ State _____ Zip _____

I have enclosed $_____ in payment for the checked book(s).
Payment <u>must</u> accompany all orders.☐ Please send a free catalog.

WINDS ACROSS TEXAS

Susan Tanner

Bestselling Author of *Exiled Heart*

The Comanches name her Fierce Tongue; Texans call her a white squaw. Once the captive of a great warrior, Katherine Bellamy finds herself shunned by decent society, yet unable to return to the Indians who have accepted her as their own.

Slade is a hard-riding, hard-hitting lawman, out to avenge the deaths of his wife and son. Blinded by anger and bitterness, he will do anything, use anyone to have his revenge.

Both Katherine and Slade see in the other a means to escape misery, but they never expect to fall in love. Yet as the sultry desert breezes caress their yearning bodies, neither can deny the sweet, soaring ecstasy of their reckless desire.

__3582-0 $4.99 US/$5.99 CAN

Author Of More Than 4 Million Books In Print!

"Powerful, passionate, and action packed, Madeline Baker's historical romances will keep readers on the edge of their seats!"
—*Romantic Times*

Callie has the face of an angel and the body of a temptress. Her innocent kisses say she is still untouched, but her reputation says she is available to any man who has the price of a night's entertainment.

Callie's sweetness touches Caleb's heart, but he and the whole town of Cheyenne know she is no better than the woman who raised her—his own father's mistress. Torn by conflicting desires, the handsome half-breed doesn't know whether he wants her walking down the aisle in white satin, or warm and willing in his bed, clothed in nothing by ivory flesh.

_3581-2 $4.99 US/$5.99 CAN